BODYGUARDS, INC.

TABITHA GIBSON

BODYGUARDS, INC.

Guarding Madison:

Bodyguard Lucien Trace is hired to protect a Hollywood starlet from a stalker. Madison Jordan prefers her privacy until the Harley riding hottie first barges into her home, saves her life and captures her guarded heart in the process.

Under His Protection:

Security expert Lex Cameron takes on the task of finding out who wants to kill the pregnant woman he nearly ran over. Valentina Garrett will do anything to protect her unborn child. Even if it meant marrying the sexy biker with the heart of gold.

Watching Over Her:

Road warrior Jack Cameron rides back into town to find out who is stalking the woman he once, and still loves. Against her better judgement, songstress Arabella Carson agrees to let Jack watch over her until the stalker is found, then he's outta there. Her heart and body have different ideas.

Cover Art: Laideebug Digital

GUARDING MADISON

She'd be safe now that he was....

Guarding Madison

Tabitha Gibson

CHAPTER ONE

Fuckin' Hollywood. Miles of fence whizzed by before he came to the end of the driveway that would no doubt lead up to an entirely too big house. The Wide Glide Harley rumbled to a stop.

Ahh, the rich and famous. They never changed. No matter what the cost, they never changed. Was it any surprise that when his phone rang, it was for one of them? Not really. He had been expecting it actually. He just wondered what took so long.

With one last drag off his thin cigar, Lucien Trace flicked it to the ground and snuffed it out with his boot heel. Trace made a mental note on the height of the metal gate and frowned at the poor shape of the lock. Hardly protection if you asked him.

Keen eyes scanned the area and made mental notes of the other flawed areas: overgrown brush partially blocking one of the cameras, rusty bars and a large space between the last bar and the stone pillar. He was sure people thought the gate was impressive from far away, but up close it was pathetic.

His gloved hand reached out and pressed the call button. After a few moments, someone responded. Thankfully, the voice box was in working order.

"Yes?"

"Trace to see Jay Starler."

"Do you have an appointment?"

"Yes," Trace replied, hoping they would take the time to check. His hopes, however, were dashed when the gates creaked opened within seconds. He shook his head and climbed back onto his Harley.

Strike one.

Sliding dark RayBans over his eyes, he turned the key. The motorcycle roared to life and Trace traveled up the long drive.

A large pool house and Olympic style pool were off to the right but not too far from the main house. Mansion was more like it. He had seen some large houses in his life considering his line of work, but nothing prepared him for the size of this one.

A limousine was parked near the front entrance while its driver concentrated on buffing the already shiny chrome fenders. He gave Trace a glance but nothing more and went back to his work.

Strike two.

Trace shut the engine off and lifted tired limbs over the machine then stretched lightly. He never tired of the sensation riding his hog gave him. Some people might call it a cheap thrill and it might be, but it was a damn nice one. Only thing better was a good woman between his legs. Unfortunately, he hadn't found a good woman in a long time.

A very long time.

Maybe he was picky but Trace knew what he liked, and since Candice, he hadn't the desire for a female. Not that his level of need hadn't been raised a few times; Playboy bunnies, panty girls from Victoria's, a hard body from the gym. He wasn't dead; they just lacked that something special.

He strode to the door and out of curiosity, tested the door knob. It opened. He frowned.

Strike three. He's out.

Trace turned around to leave but stopped and took a deep breath. Usually after three mistakes he left. It had kept him sane and alive all these years. If he were smart, he'd stick to tradition. But Jay was family and Trace had made a promise.

He always kept his promises.

Trace turned back around, pulled the door shut and rang the bell. A moment later, an aging woman opened it. She looked up his chest to his face and quickly put her hand over her mouth in an attempted to cover her gasp at the sight of Trace. He could tell she thought about shutting the door so he cleared his throat and spoke.

"Ma'am. I'm here to see Jay Starler."

"Is... is he expecting you?"

"Yes."

The woman forced a smile, stepped back and motioned him in. "Please come in. I'll show you to him."

Trace kept his frown to himself. The woman was scared enough. Who could blame her though? It's not every day you see a large, leather-clad biker at your door.

Trace followed the small woman through a large foyer and inside a set of double doors. The living room he presumed. He noted three sets of French doors were open, letting the fresh air in. A curving staircase that disappeared into a darkened hallway cut off his surveillance. His guide then stopped at a large door in the corner of the house and knocked twice.

"Come in," a masculine voice called out.

She opened the door and motioned Trace in before silently retreating down the hall.

Trace peered inside before stepping into the office set up with yet another set of French doors leading out to a small patio. They too were open. He frowned briefly.

"Just set the coffee down Carol, I'll get it in a minute."

Trace watched the smaller man hunched over the filing cabinet then smiled hearing the familiar fussing over misplaced items. He allowed a small smirk before he spoke. "What? No thank you? Didn't your mother teach you any manners?"

Jay swung around from the filing cabinet and grinned widely. "Trace!"

Jay rushed over and hugged him tight. Trace returned the gesture then held Jay out at arm's length. "Look at you. Moving up in the world."

"Working for a superstar like Madison Jordan doesn't hurt," Jay replied with a laugh and motioned for Trace to sit in one of the leather chairs across from his own. Carol returned carrying a silver tray covered with dainty cups and saucers, a pot of coffee with all the trimmings and a single, large mug.

Trace looked up at Carol and gave her a nod. She set it on the desk and left without a backward glance.

"I think she likes you," Jay said with a chuckle.

Trace grunted. Jay poured the hot liquid into the dainty cup and filled the larger mug for Trace. Enjoying the fresh brew, they talked for a few minutes to catch up on each other's life.

"I was on my way to a long, overdue vacation when you called," Trace said.

"I really appreciate you coming."

"So you've said. About half a dozen times now. What's the deal?"

"Typical stalker. What else?"

"You wouldn't have called me if it was a typical stalker. I don't work that and you know it, Uncle Jay."

Jay was silent and lowered his gaze under Trace's intense stare. He ran his hand through graying hair and nodded. "You're right. It's more than just a typical stalker. There've been two murders."

Trace's expression didn't change. He senses kicked into gear and he was suddenly aware of everything in the room. The ticking of the clock behind Jay; the bee that buzzed around the open door; the steam that escaped from each of their cups. He returned his focus back to his uncle. "Why call me then? Sounds like a job for the locals to me."

"If it were that easy, trust me, I would have called them in. Unfortunately this guy is clever and appears unstoppable."

"No one is unstoppable," Trace said.

Jay pulled open a drawer and fished out a packet of papers bound together. He dropped them on the desk with a soft thud. "Perhaps this will help."

Trace picked up the packet and read the title.

The Circle of Friends End.

"What's this?"

"The current script that she's filming," Jay answered. "It's a story about five friends who form a bond in high school, treat outsiders like trash and mentally abuse a girl who wanted to be in. The girl kills each member of the circle one by one until the main character is left. Then she kills her before killing herself."

Trace gave Jay a look of disbelief. "Nice story."

"The sad thing is that this is a mirror image to her life. Two of her friends are dead."

Trace opened his mouth to speak but was cut off by a woman's scream. Trace dropped the script and pulled his nine millimeter from a holster hidden beneath his jacket. He yanked the door opened and raced across the hall. Finding the door locked he raised his booted foot to kick it in.

"Trace! Wait!" Jay called out.

MADISON JORDAN WAS STUNNED WHEN THE INCREDIBLY TALL AND handsome man burst into the room. She was even more stunned when he tackled her acting partner, Ethan James to the ground and put him in a headlock.

"What the hell?" Ethan managed to choke out.

The intruder was sexy, no doubt about that, but who the hell was he?

"Excuse me, but what do you think you are doing?" she asked, folding her arms.

Jay rushed into the room and tried to explain. "He's... he's the bodyguard. The one I was telling you about," Jay replied, somewhat breathless.

Madison frowned. "I told you it wasn't necessary."

"And I told you that it was." Jay crossed his arms and frowned back at her.

Jay had been her manager for a few years now. He was such a dear man, sneaking in her favorite snacks and off to private places for her cherished moments of solitude. She wasn't buying his theory that murders straight from her current film were being acted out in real life and that her time was coming.

Sure, she had lost two friends from high school but that was only coincidence. She hadn't seen them since graduation and they all lived in different states, different lives.

Jay had talked about hiring security for her but she nixed the idea. There were enough people in and around her life right now that adding a whole new entourage was unacceptable.

Jay had pleaded for just one person, for security purposes when she was out in public. She had promised to think about it. Jay apparently had other ideas.

"Really Madison, don't you care for your own safety?" Jay's voice snapped her back to the present.

"What...about...my safety?" said the man twisted like a pretzel between the well-muscled arms. Ethan's face was beat red, quickly heading for the next color in the rainbow.

"Oh, sorry." Jay waved his hand. "Trace, please let him go."

Trace frowned, but released the man who slumped to the floor and sucked wind hard.

"Ethan, perhaps we could practice our lines another time?" Madison gave a withering look to Trace, a trick she learned from her mother. Surprisingly, he was unaffected. Most men were. Secretly she was glad he didn't.

Instead, he crossed his arms and stared right back.

Ethan picked himself up and with a mock dusting, left the room.

Madison turned back to Jay and looked at him expectantly.

"Madison Jordan, this is Lucien Trace," he said, stepping backwards to allow the two to shake hands.

Madison slipped her hand in his. She wasn't a small woman by any means. Slightly above average in height and weight, she didn't expect to be dwarfed by anyone. But this man was different.

"Nice to meet you Mr. Trace," Madison said and gave him her best solid grip. She was rewarded with a strong grip from him. She held back her wince though, thanks in part to her training. *Never show emotion off camera. You don't get paid for that.*

Her mother had drilled that and several points other points of life into her.

"Just, Trace," he said, and turned to survey the damage to the door.

"I assume that you've come to terms with Jay on payment?" Madison knew she wasn't going to scare this one away. At least not today. She'd concede for now.

"Not yet, but I'll warn you, I'm not cheap," he said and raised a brow. "Think you can afford it?"

Madison looked around at the expensive furniture, art collection and rugs. "Maybe," she said with a shrug and headed towards the door. "Think you can afford to replace my door?"

"Maybe." She swore he smirked.

"Well I hope so, because you're on the payroll now. Or at least for as long as it takes to replace my door." Without a backward glance, she left the room.

~

SILENCE HUNG IN THE AIR. JAY STUDIED HIS FINGERNAILS, THEN A loose thread on his jacket.

Trace paced. That woman made him grind his teeth. She was haughty and insulting.

And sexy as hell.

It had been a long time since a woman had sparked his attention at first sight. Frankly he couldn't recall the last time and certainly not the spark that happened in his pants.

Damn, she was gorgeous. Red hair was turn on number one. He wondered if it was natural and almost smiled at the thought of investigating that. She had lovely skin too. Odd that someone who had such a nice pool wasn't more tan. It didn't matter though. He enjoyed the contrast of his sun darkened skin sliding against an ivory body in the heat of passion.

Trace took a deep breath and closed his eyes. He could still smell her perfume. He envisioned her fuller figure standing there challenging him, hands on rounded hips. And he swore her eyes flashed green fire at him.

"Trace?"

Trace shook his head trying to clear out very unprofessional thoughts and looked at Jay. "Sorry. What?"

"I asked if you were ready to discuss salary," Jay said and cleared his throat.

"Yeah. I'm ready."

Jay motioned back towards his office, stepping past the broken door. Trace followed Jay, taking a moment to look down the hall where she had just walked. He knew mixing with Hollywoodites was a mistake.

He also knew that he would protect her with his very life.

MADISON WAITED UNTIL SHE SHUT HER BEDROOM DOOR BEHIND her before releasing a deep breath. She put a hand over her racing heart.

She had been bored with rehearsing her lines and Ethan had been enjoying the kissing scene too much. She'd been ready for a break when her new employee broke through her door. Literally.

Though having Ethan put in his place by the tall stranger had been satisfying, she was annoyed when she found out who he was.

Was she such an invalid that she couldn't take care of herself? Who really could hurt her with the number of people that always surrounded her? So many sometimes that she wanted to scream.

Now, here was yet another person. One incredibly gorgeous person. Even now, her heart hammered thinking of him. Dark hair clipped short, full lips, sexy stubble and a strong jaw line that sported a thin scar curving up towards his left eye stopping just an inch short.

His body was clad in all black and she could feel heat radiate from him. A thick waist and thicker thighs brought a rush of heat between her own thighs. And lord was he tall. He had to be six and a half feet tall. She could almost imagine being lifted up by those strong arms to wrap her legs around his waist while going for the ride of a life time.

"Miss Jordan?"

Madison blushed deeply having been caught in such erotic thoughts. She sat at her vanity and began running a brush through her hair.

"Yes Carol, what is it?"

Carol carried in a small silver tray with a bottle of water and small cup of pills on top. "Your vitamins," she said and held out the tray.

"Thanks," Madison said and chased the foul tasting pills down with the cold liquid. She sat the bottle down and watched Carol tidy up her bedroom.

"It appears we have a new member of the household, at least for a short while," Madison commented. She was fishing for information and hoped Carol would bite.

"You mean the biker? He's going to stay with us?" She asked surprised.

Biker? So there was more than one ride to this man. Her face flamed again.

"Jay hired him."

"For what? To break down doors or stand around and look good?" Carol said with a wrinkled nose then she gave Madison an uncharacteristic saucy wink.

"Carol!" Madison said in a slightly normal than loud voice while covering a smile. "You don't miss a thing, do you?"

Carol hugged Madison and chuckled. "With age comes wisdom, my dear."

"Jay still thinks my life is in danger."

"Then you should listen to his advice. I'm not completely convinced he's wrong."

Madison sighed and flopped across her bed. "I used to be happy. Blissful even."

"You were alone then too," Carol commented.

"True, but it was then I truly enjoyed my job." Of course, how could you call being one of the most sought after actresses a job? It was a lifestyle. Not one that she particularly enjoyed but it was the price she paid for success.

They both turned to the sound of a door being opened and closed. Moments later, the door next to her vanity opened producing the muscular, luscious body of her newest employee.

"Do you ever knock?" Madison asked, startled when he just walked in then muttered under her breath, "I guess I should be glad you didn't break that door down too."

"Sorry. Just making sure I'm settling in the right room," he stated almost triumphantly.

Carol murmured something about checking on lunch and slipped quietly out of the room.

"The right room for what?"

"To stay in while I'm here," he answered with a slight shrug.

"Oh no you don't. I keep an empty room next to me for a purpose. It's called privacy. Need the definition?"

"Guarding your body. It's called doing my job. Need clarification?"

She bit her lip at his choice of words and warmed at the surge of flames that tickled her whole body, heating up all the right places. As much as she wanted him to check out those right places there was one place that she was going to make clear and that was where his was.

She watched while Trace wandered around her bedroom. He checked the window's lock, her closet and private bathroom.

"Let's get something straight here, Mr. Trace," Madison said and rose from the bed. "You work for me. Not the other way around."

Trace swung around and grabbed her suddenly, pulling her in his arms. She found herself enjoying his touch, but she knew it would lead to disaster.

He leaned down and took a deep breath, closing his eyes as he did. She froze, confused by the sudden urges her body screamed out for. How could any one man be so impossible and irresistible at the same time?

He leaned in further towards her neck. His whiskers brushed

lightly against her jaw. His warm lips moved closer to her ear. Chills raced through her straight to her nipples which she was sure he could sense through her silk blouse and his black, cotton tee shirt. She flushed but was it from how hot he was making her or embarrassment?

He said something then and she struggled to understand what he was saying. Forcing all thoughts of hot sex from her brain, she strained to hear what he was saying.

"And I *will* be staying next to you in the spare room whether you like it or not. So if you need me, I'll be there."

Slowly he released her. She lifted her gaze up and almost melted under his smoldering one. "Do we understand each other?"

She could only answer his question with a nod. He turned and left then, back to the room he claimed as his, through the connecting door.

She wiped the drool at the corner of her mouth with dignity and made a mental note to advise Levi's jeans that they should pay Trace for making their jeans look so damn good.

"By the way." His voice startled her straight into embarrassment. "This door stays open. Period."

His announcement sent her straight into a rage.

CHAPTER TWO

Trace eyed the driver curiously before approaching him. The driver nervously switched his cleaning rag from one hand to the other before setting his gaze on the driveway.

"Name?"

The man cleared his throat and stammered out, "Wil… William Williams, Sir."

Was he kidding? "You can call me Trace."

"Yes, Mr. Trace."

"No, just Trace."

"Certainly, Mr. Trace."

"What's with the whole mister thing around here," Trace wondered out loud.

"Well, protocol states—" William began but Trace cut him off.

"How long have you been working for Miss Jordan?"

"About two years. Mr. Starler got me this job."

Trace watched him stare around at everything but him. Trace had the sense this man was hiding something.

"You a con?"

William looked offended. "Most assuredly I am not a con artist. I have an excellent reputation—" he began but Trace cut him off.

"Ex-con. Does that clear it up for you, Willie?"

"It's William, not Willie," he stated with a tone of disdain. "And to answer your question," he began but was silent.

Trace watched several emotions play over his face before the driver hung his head. "I do have a record. I made a mistake and it has haunted me ever since."

Trace studied the man intently. He looked like a typical, stuffed shirt. What could the man have done that was so bad it cost him prison time?

"Hunger will make a person do things they wouldn't normally do, Mr. Trace," he began, then held up his hands in apology. "I beg your pardon, Trace."

"So you pocketed some grub. Is that it?"

William never lifted his head. "It was humiliating to say the least. My father disowned me. My mother died broken-hearted. I had tarnished the family name. I've floated from odd job to odd job ever since."

Trace made mental notes as he inspected the limousine. It was your typical *Here-I-Am-Look-At-Me* vehicle. He was glad to see at least the windows were tinted. He bet the glass wasn't bulletproof though.

"So am I dismissed from my employ here?"

Trace looked back to the driver and focused deep into his eyes. Trace had a way of reading people through their eyes. He could almost always tell if they were lying or worse. He could also tell if they were an honest soul and William was just that.

"No, you aren't fired. But from now on, you take orders directly from me. Understand?"

"Miss Jordan won't like that. She tends to just show up and we go." He began to wring his hands. Trace could see that he was afraid of the changes going on but they were necessary.

"I'll handle Miss Jordan. From this point on, all trips beyond these gates go through me. Savvy?"

"Yes, Sir. I mean, Trace."

"Good. Now, the doors are to be locked at all times, regardless of if the vehicle is behind the gates or not. No maintenance is to be done without me being present and under no circumstances is anyone other than a list of people I give you allowed inside the vehicle. Any questions?"

William shook his head no and let out a pent up breath when Trace stuck his hand out to shake. With a final look around, Trace headed back inside the house.

~

"I HAVE A QUESTION," MADISON SAID. HER ARMS WERE CROSSED and a scowl marred her features.

Jay looked up from his desk and sighed deeply.

"Don't sigh at me. Since when do you have the right to just hire people without asking me?"

"Since I became your manager," he said and stood, then gave her a fatherly kiss on the forehead. "And since I came to love you like a daughter."

Madison gave in to her softer side and hugged Jay. "I know you care, Jay, but a bodyguard? Really. The tabloids will have me at the top of the diva list in no time."

"No, they won't. Not unless they don't know you. And due to my brilliant skill in the PR department, they know just enough to keep them happy and your privacy intact." He went back to his chair and sat heavily.

"So, who is he?"

"Trace?" Madison nodded. "My nephew. I trust him completely and he's damn good at what he does. I might actually start sleeping better at nights."

"You're that worried?" Madison frowned. It wasn't like Jay to be so dramatic but his constant persistence now worried her where before it had been a minor annoyance.

Jay smiled. "Not anymore."

Madison smiled too and turned hearing Carol at the door. "Lunch is ready."

Jay rose and put his arm around Madison's shoulder and walked with her to the dining room.

She was surprised to see Trace already there. And in *her* chair. She walked over to where Trace sat and cleared her throat. "Ahem."

Trace looked up at her. She could've just drowned happily in his gorgeous velvet brown eyes. He had thick eyebrows but not overbearing. That belonged to his lashes; Long and lots of them, they were the type of lashes that most women would kill to have, and not just the women in her business. She wondered if he knew just how truly good looking he was?

"Yeah?" His voice warmed her still. The slightly gravelly tone held a commanding sound yet she was at ease. Still, he was sitting in her place at the table.

"That's my chair," she said, trying to sound full of authority.

"There are seven other chairs here."

"But I always sit here," she replied, raking her nails on her palms. Palms that itched to both slap his face and run the length of his muscular arms.

"Now you sit here," he said and motioned to the chair next to him.

"But then I can't see outside," she said and hated that she sounded almost whiny.

"And no one can see inside to where you are sitting."

She folded her arms; not to look mad but to cover the mad hard-on her nipples were taking once again. He was so damn infuriating and hot as hell, a lethal combination to be sure. Madison stood her ground and tapped her foot, waiting for him to move.

Trace sighed and stood, pulling out the chair next to the one he had vacated. Madison's smile was wide but cut short. She let out a yelp when he pushed her down into the very chair she didn't want. He sat back down in her chair and to her surprise, dropped a napkin in his lap.

Madison gave a very un-ladylike grunt and followed suit. She swore Carol chuckled as she set the grilled chicken salad on the table.

Madison peeked over at Trace who had a look of dismay on his face. She followed his gaze to the large bowl containing the green leafy lunch and allowed one corner of her mouth to rise. "Mmm, my favorite. Looks terrific, Carol."

"If you're a rabbit," Trace muttered.

"What's that, Trace?" Madison asked with all the innocence of a child hiding a marker while standing in front of a masterpiece on the newly painted wall.

"Nothing," he said and helped himself to an extra piece of the grilled chicken.

"Salad is good for you. Helps to keep your figure in fine shape."

"My figure is just fine," he groused then smiled as he saw the extra fixings of boiled eggs, bacon bits and croutons.

"Well the rest of us have to watch ours and it doesn't make sense to have Carol make two different meals," Madison said, a touch of defense shrouded her voice.

Madison had struggled with her weight all her life. Diets came and went as a child. As she got older, nutritionists became her guests instead of friends from school. Her mother had told her that she would become too fat and no more scripts would come her way and they would lose the life style they had become accustomed to. It was really the lifestyle that her *mother* had become accustomed to. Madison would have been just as happy with a one room cabin in the woods.

Her mother had scoffed at that thought and instructed Carol on the foods that Madison was to have daily. Thankfully she was gone on a vacation and wouldn't be back for a few more weeks. Still, Madison enjoyed chicken salad with ranch dressing. She just used the low-fat dressing when her mother was around. Today, it was full-fat with full-flavor.

"Your figure is just fine the way it is," Trace remarked without looking at Madison. He was busy enjoying one of Carol's homemade, flaky croissants.

Madison blinked at him speechless. No one had ever said her figure was fine. Well, no one that ever really meant it and somehow she knew in the back of her mind that he meant it. He didn't appear to have a hidden agenda like the other two did. The only two she had ever given herself to that is.

Her mother certainly had an issue with her figure and let her know about it as often as possible.

Madison's face flamed. She picked at her ranch covered lettuce and became very self-conscience of her weight. Memories of her mother's harsh comments, her former boyfriend's sadistic remarks and the tabloids constant haranguing of her larger size rushed to her, causing her to lose her appetite. She rose and without word, left the room leaving several stunned faces behind.

Once in her room, she closed the door behind her and moved quickly into her closet. She looked for then pulled out a specific shoe box and took off the lid. Inside was a secret stash of candy bars, chips and her weakness, Hershey kisses. She slid down on the floor and had three silver kiss wrappers opened and balled up empty before a knock interrupted her binge.

Assuming it was Jay or Carol she called out for them to come in and opened another kiss. Somehow, she wasn't surprised to see Trace's boots stop near her legs.

He didn't say anything, just sat down and held out his hand. Madison bit her lip and lost her fight with the tears. She hated herself for being so weak. She crushed the wrapper back around the candy, dropped it in the box and handed it to Trace.

Trace rooted around in the box and pulled out a Snickers bar then handed it back to Madison. He remained silent as he ripped open the wrapper and took a bite. The silence was broken by the smacking of his lips.

Madison dug back in the box and pulled out the same kiss, unwrapped it again and popped it in her mouth. She dared a look at Trace but he was too busy polishing off the candy. He finished by licking his fingertips, an act that brought a whole swarm of butterflies to Madison's stomach. She put the lid back on the box and pushed it to one side.

"Wanna tell me about it?"

Madison closed her eyes and turned her head away from Trace. What could she tell him? Oh, you know, the old battle of the bulge, nothing to worry about. She had never felt fatter than she did at this exact moment. And she was so damn embarrassed.

Here was a completely gorgeous guy who thought she looked fine, not heavy-set or chunky and what does she do? Run away and stuff her face. She sighed deeply.

"We don't have to talk about it if you don't want to."

Madison's heart hammered hard in her chest. An out was just what she needed, what she could count on to not face up to her problem and what she always depended on to push things out of her mind.

But she knew what she should do. Face the issue and not continue to run from it.

She turned towards him but continued to stare down at her hands in her lap. A bad habit she had acquired from the confrontations with her mother. At least she was trying.

"I've battled my weight all my life," she said, her voice shaky and filled with emotion. She dug her nails into her palms, raking them along their length.

Trace leaned over and took her hands in his. His warmth washed over her and she relaxed. How odd that this man who barreled into her life with the force of a freight train could be so gentle.

"Most of the time I lost," she said with a nervous laugh. "But with hard work, I could try to come out the winner."

"My comment was a compliment. Why the vanishing act?" Trace asked. He sounded confused and she didn't blame him.

"It's... It's hard to come face to face with it sometimes. Certainly not from a stranger like you."

"Stranger? I'm hurt," he said and sniffed dramatically. Madison peeked up and returned the smile she found on his handsome face.

"You know what I mean," Madison said and lowered her head again.

"Hey, none of that here," Trace said and lifted her chin with his roughened fingertips.

Madison was strangely comforted by this intimidating looking man. She looked up further to his eyes and stared for what seemed an eternity. She wasn't sure what she was looking for but something sparked in her then. An ally perhaps? A friend? Definitely a protector. Either way she should give trust a try with this man, and she would. At least, for now.

"Did you know that one of the sexiest actresses of all time, Marilyn Monroe, wore a size sixteen?"

"That's never been proven," Madison said with a laugh. Wait. Did he just put her in the same class as Marilyn Monroe? And did he just reference her as sexy?

An alarm sounded then, three short bursts, then a long one. Trace's hand went for his gun immediately before Madison could stop him. He rose and motioned for her to stay down.

"Trace, wait. It's not what you think."

He turned and looked down at Madison then offered her help as she began to stand. She hid the box of her secret treats and tried to move past Trace but he wouldn't let her.

"Not until I know what that alarm is for," he said. He looked fierce and sexy. Yet another lethal combination.

"I know what that alarm was for," Madison said and her stomach begin to churn. No amount of chocolate could make her feel better. No secret snack could help her face the impending doom that the alarm signaled was coming.

Her chest tightened while her palms became cold and clammy. She rushed out of the closet and to her mirror. A quick brushing of her hair and smoothing of her clothing didn't stop the panic that was quickly rising. Madison hurried to the door only to have Trace snake out an arm and hold it against the door to keep it shut.

"You aren't going out that door until I know what that alarm is for," he stated again.

She could see him gearing up for a fight but it was one she was sure he wouldn't win.

"I'm here to protect you Madison."

"You should worry about protecting yourself," she replied.

"What are you talking about?"

"My mother is home."

CHAPTER THREE

Trace couldn't believe what Madison just said. Her mother was home? An alarm sounds when her mother comes home? It was laughable. He almost did laugh, until he saw the intense worry and color draining from her face.

He followed her from the bedroom and down the stairs. Madison walked quickly into the living room and got into the line that had formed near the French doors. He frowned seeing the staff so uptight and what he could only pin down as scared. His uncle, who was in the line next to Madison, looked the worst out of the whole bunch.

He was curious to see this woman that placed such fear in the entire household. Except him, of course. He took up a position near the entrance to the living room but was slightly hidden by a tall plant.

Trace heard the front door open and the click of heels down the marbled hall heading in their direction. Adrenalin rushed through him hard and fast. He stood ready, itching for a fight with the figure that came through the doorway.

Once it did, he had to cover a grin.

A woman, barely five feet in height came into the room and

stopped before the line of people there to greet her. She looked fragile really. Steel grey hair was pulled back sharply into a bun at the nape of her neck. A black suit covered her rounding frame while Trace found the source of the clicking on the marble to be short, square heels.

Behind her was what Trace assumed to be her driver. He looked the same as the others, timid and afraid. He carried several bags and one medium sized basket with a white ball of fur inside. Great, just what he needed. An ankle-biter.

The dog seemed to be the only one to notice him. Trace gave the dog a stern look and was rewarded by its dark nose hiding further down in the basket.

It was eerily silent in the room. The whole pin dropping commercial came to mind. He opened his mouth to speak but stopped when the source of everyone's fear spoke first.

"The foyer is a mess."

The statement sent Carol running out of the room. Trace raised a brow.

"Apparently no one bothers to check messages around here. I asked for an update over an hour ago," she commented. Her voice was harsh and clipped.

Jay stepped forward. "Yes, Ma'am, the wifi has been spotty on and off today and—"

"Are you suggesting that I am incompetent?" Her voice raised an octave. It sliced through the air like a razor blade.

"No, Ma'am. Not at all, it's just—"

"I want a report in my hands in five minutes."

Jay rushed off, leaving Trace confused. The look on Madison's face made him angry. She looked like she was waiting for her turn at the guillotine. His gaze traveled down her body, noting how she shook inwardly while her nails dug into her palms over and over again.

The woman had made her way to Madison before he could speak. She began to berate Madison about her hair, her appearance and lack of structure.

"Ethan called and told me that you stopped rehearsal. You

should be focusing on learning your lines but instead, you rudely throw him out," she said bitterly.

"I didn't throw him out, Mother. I was ready for a break—"

"Now why is that Madison? Was it feeding time again?"

Trace had heard...

"Enough."

His voice filled the room, startling everyone including the dog, which barked but remained hidden in the basket.

Madison gave Trace a look that pleaded for his silence but he would have none of it. The woman at the center of the controversy turned around slowly and fixed her gaze on him.

On a bad day, she might have made him ill at ease but this wasn't one of those days.

Trace stepped forward, around the plush couch to stand in front of Madison and crossed his arms over his chest.

"Ah, you must be the piece of meat Ethan told me about."

Trace didn't say a word. He merely stared down at the offensive person before him. He took pride in having never hit a woman in his life but that record was sorely being tested.

"Everyone out." Trace's command was answered immediately by people tripping over each other to leave the area. A hand tugged at his arm but he never broke his gaze from Madison's mother.

"Trace, please. I can handle this." Madison's voice came across as soft and shaky, pleading.

"Madison, go to your room and wait for me," said the shrew.

"She does not need to go to her room. But she will step outside the living room and shut the door behind her," Trace said. There was no mistaking his authority.

Madison dropped her hand from Trace's arm and walked from the room, shutting the door behind her.

"How dare you—" she began but was cut off by Trace.

"Let's start with your name, or should I just refer to you as bitch?"

Trace enjoyed the stunned look on her face along with the moment of silence. He didn't let it show though. Years of training on holding back emotion came rushing back. He did step a few feet away though. He didn't want to intimidate her too much. He hoped that she would perhaps lighten up.

"You may call me Mrs. Jordan," she began but Trace didn't let her continue.

"Mrs. Jordan. Fine. Let's get a couple of things straight around here. If I'm right, your daughter is the breadwinner around here and you are merely the sponge."

"Sponge?"

"Yes, sponge. You know, sponging off your daughter's success. Sucking up her wealth and good will. Instead of insulting her, you should be on your knees thanking her for her generosity." Each word had Trace taking another step towards the bitter maternal figure.

"Well! I never—"

"And you never will. Ever again."

"By what right do you have to speak to me this way," she shrieked. Her voice was like nails down a chalkboard but Trace didn't let it bother him.

"You are Madison's mother and by that right, you deserve some respect."

She huffed and shook her head in agreement.

"But, your daughter deserves the same respect and by God you will show her respect or I will show you the door." He crossed his arms and stood, quietly staring down at the silent woman.

Trace watched several emotions cross her face. He wondered if anyone had ever put her in her place before. After today's events, he wondered if he would give her a place in the pool house or even the dog house.

"Maggie."

"What's that?"

"My name is Maggie."

"Nice to meet you, Maggie. My name is Trace."

Maggie sat down heavily on the sofa and took a deep breath. Trace joined her. "Hard being mean, isn't it?" he asked. He was surprised by her laugh.

"Hard being hard, Mr. Trace."

Trace half smiled. "Just Trace." He thought he would never get past explaining to people to drop the mister part.

"So why are you so hard, Maggie?"

"Why else? To keep things in order around here."

Trace could still detect a harsh tone to her voice but after years of taking that tone, it would be hard to let it go.

"You have a job, Maggie, and it's not to keep things in order around here. That's Jay's job."

She looked at him surprised. "What is my job then if not to keep things running smoothly?"

"Your job is to be a mother. Nothing more, nothing less."

Trace watched her bite the inside of her lip. Emotion ran deep in this cynical woman. He knew it and deep down, so did she.

"Then I guess I don't have a job. I'm not really much of a mother, am I?"

"Not from what I've seen."

"You don't hold back, do you Trace?"

"Why should I? You asked me a question and I gave you an answer."

"Fair enough," she replied. She sounded tired and somewhat sad.

"However," he continued, "I don't know you very well and there's always room for improvement."

Maggie gave Trace a smile, one that he suspected had been missing for a very long time.

"Improvement, eh? That'll take time."

"Well it's not going to happen overnight," he remarked. "But that doesn't mean it can't happen."

Maggie reached out and patted Trace's hand. "You're sharp. I smell education. Why the odd job here?"

"It's not so odd, but it is very lucrative," he gave her a grin, to which she cackled.

Trace heard a soft sound at the door and put his finger to his lips for Maggie to be silent. Stealthily, he made his way to the door and with a quick move, yanked it open.

Most of the staff almost fell inside the door. With red faces and mumbled apologies, they rushed from the room once again.

Maggie laughed louder than ever and stood. "I should go find Madison."

"I'll take care of that. Why don't you get with Carol and see if we can swing some pizza for dinner? The rabbit food just doesn't cut it for me."

"Pizza? Hmmm, good idea," she said and walked out past Trace heading for the kitchen.

Trace ran his fingers through his short hair and headed up the stairs to Madison's room. He knocked once and called out to her, but no response. Knowing her need for privacy, he knocked again but there was still no reply. Instinct took over then and he opened the door. A quick glance around told him that she wasn't in her room. He pushed away a tightening in his chest. She was fine, just upset.

Still, that was enough to cause him concern. He didn't like the thought of her upset or crying. It was then he noticed the French doors to the balcony were open. The curtains waved with the gentle breeze. A few short strides took him to the doorway where he peered out.

Madison was stretched out on a padded iron chaise with sunglasses on. He thought she was sleeping so he took the opportunity to study her even further.

She amazed him how strong she appeared both in the public eye and in her films. She never portrayed a fragile woman. Ironic how completely opposite she was from the characters she played. Still, he knew there was a great inner strength that kept her going. He hoped someday to find out what gave her that strength.

"Is she gone?"

Trace had to smile. She'd fooled him. Not so easy a feat to do. He took a seat opposite of her and stretched out his long, jeans covered legs frowning at the fray on the hem. "No, Maggie is checking with Carol on dinner."

Madison lifted the designer shades to rest on her head and raised a single brow. "Maggie?"

"That's her name isn't it?"

"Who told you that?"

"She did. Isn't it?"

Madison tilted her head in surprise. "Yes, that's her name," she finally answered and slid her shades back into place.

"You're surprised?" Trace asked.

"Perhaps," she said with a shrug of her shoulders. She picked up the book that was by her side and thumbed through it.

"Perhaps my ass," he said with a snort.

MADISON SMILED. IT HAD BEEN SO LONG SINCE SHE HAD TALKED to anyone other than her house staff. The entourage that accompanied her to rehearsals and filming never really spoke to her. She thought that had everything to do with her mother.

But something about Trace was different. He was raw and unrefined and oh so sexy. He oozed masculinity and probably knew it, though deep inside she knew he wouldn't really strut around like he was the cat's meow.

Still, he had to have some idea of how women react around him, how good looking he was. Madison sighed and set her book aside. Enough daydreaming. She would have to face her mother sooner or later. She started to dig her nails into her palms again but forced herself to stop. The sooner she did, the faster she could escape back to her secret stash and soften the blows with a kiss.

But what type of kiss? A chocolate one or hot one from Trace?

"Madison?"

Madison gazed over and was startled by her mother. She scrambled awkwardly up from the chair and stood at attention, head tilted down.

"At ease, solider," Maggie said with a laugh.

Madison bit her lower lip and tempted a glance up at her mother. She was surprised to find a half smile on her lightly withered face.

"Trace, would you give us some privacy?" Maggie asked.

"Sure. As far as the bedroom allows," he said and wandered inside the French doors leaving the two alone.

"Wow, he's bossy," Maggie muttered, then chuckled at the grunt from inside the door. Taking a seat, she motioned for Madison to join her.

Madison sat down tentatively and waited for her mother to snap out of this odd hallucination. Her nails began that familiar path on her palms. Surely this wasn't the woman who gave birth to her; the women who constantly reminded her that she was too heavy or not pretty enough and was damn lucky to have some type of talent to survive in the world today.

"How was your trip?" Madison's voice came out soft and weak. She cleared her throat and forced her chin up to look at her mother directly.

"Fine, fine. A bit humid though. I was ready to come home."

Madison began to dig her nails deeper into her palms. She was startled by her mother's hands covering hers. Afraid to see anger in her mother's eyes, she quickly lowered her head and kept her hands still.

"Madison, please look at me."

Tears gathered in her eyes before she raised her head to meet the stoic gaze of her mother. She fully expected the rage to begin lashing at her weakness and open display of emotion. Instead what Madison saw surprised her.

A sad look filled her mother's eyes. Creases of age crept silently across her face and reminded Madison that her mother was no spring chicken, having had Madison late in her life. Madison suspected that her mother hated her for making her become a mother, not before her time but at all.

Madison guessed that's why she worked so hard to be a success and provide her mother with all the things she missed out on because she had Madison. It hurt to think she was trying to buy her mother's love but that's exactly what she had been doing all her life.

Maggie reached up and brushed Madison's hair aside, tucking it behind her ear. Wrinkled hands cupped Madison's cheeks gently before dropping back down to hold her daughter's hands with care.

"I've not exactly been the model mother of late," Maggie began. She chuckled. "Hell, all your life."

"I'm sorry, Mother. I'll try harder—" Madison began but was cut off by her mother.

"You aren't the one that needs to try. You've gone above and beyond, Madison. It's high time that your mother stepped up to the plate."

Madison remained silent. She had dreamed of connecting with her mother her whole life. Now, that moment was here and it paralyzed Madison. Her arms ached to comfort the older woman but she just couldn't bring herself to do it. She wanted to tell her mother that it was ok but the words wouldn't come out. It dawned on her then why and shame washed over her.

For years, her mother had terrified everyone around her, including her own daughter. Madison wasn't ready to forgive her just yet but she still loved her. No matter what.

"I know that it's going to take some time, Madison. Time for your wounds to heal and for our relationship to mend. I hope that you'll grant me that time. But I understand if you don't. I certainly don't deserve it." This time, it was Maggie that lowered her head.

Madison bit at her lower lip again to keep it from trembling. She took several deep breaths and gripped her mother's hand tightly. Maggie looked up and Madison read shame in her mother's eyes. Maybe, just maybe they had a chance after all.

"We have all the time in the world, Mother," Madison said and gave her a slight smile.

Maggie returned it with a shuddering breath. She nodded to Madison in thanks and rose. "I'll go see where that pizza is."

Pizza?

On impulse, Maggie leaned down and gave Madison a quick peck on her forehead then turned to leave.

"Mother?" Madison called out before she walked away.

Maggie turned around to Madison. "Yes?"

"You're right," she began and gave her mother an uncustomary grin. "He is bossy."

Maggie winked at her daughter and disappeared inside the French doors.

Madison followed her and leaned against the door jam studying Trace who had taken up residence in her reading chair near the bathroom with his eyes shut. "Well, you are."

She was rewarded with another grunt and knew he heard everything. She wasn't embarrassed though. He was instrumental in getting her mother off the high horse she had been riding for years though she had no clue how he did it.

"Ready for dinner?" he asked, and stood, stretching like an exotic, wild cat.

"I can't believe you got her to allow pizza in the house," Madison commented and followed Trace out of the bedroom and down the stairs.

"What are you talking about? A pizza covers all the major food groups on one delicious pie."

They ran into the staff huddled around the dining room door, strangely silent.

Madison tapped Jay on the shoulder. "What? You all act like you've never seen a pizza in the house before." She laughed and elbowed him aside so she could get to the table then saw the reason for the silence and unsuccessfully covered her gasp.

The pizza boxes sat in the middle of the table stacked one on top of the other. A picture of Madison was lying on top of the pizza stack with a knife stuck through the middle of the picture. A red liquid oozed onto the picture from the wicked looking blade.

Madison didn't recognize her own voice as it cried out a now familiar name.

"Trace!"

CHAPTER FOUR

FROM THE STAIRWAY, MADISON WATCHED TRACE THANK THE police officer and lock the door behind him. She hadn't given much thought to the so-called stalker or as Jay put it, killer that was after her. Why should she? Now, she had never been so scared before in her life.

Detectives crawled all over her home while the staff and her mother had been questioned for hours before being allowed to retire to their rooms. Maggie had wanted to stay with her but Madison insisted she get some rest. Trace would be with her if she needed anything, so she wouldn't be alone. That itself wasn't much of a stretch though.

Madison was never alone, except in her bedroom of course which she insisted on. That was the only time she had to herself without someone fussing over her hair or make-up or wardrobe. Her mother had preached to them constantly not to let her out in public without looking like the millions of dollars she was worth. Maybe that's what this person wanted. Money. It was, after all, the root of all evil.

Madison flashed back to seeing the knife impaled through her photo. It was a recent one too, from a photo session for her last film that came out six months ago. It had been number one at the box office for five weeks and her best performance yet according to the critics.

Now the buzz was all about the current movie she was filming, *The Circle of Friends End*. Edgy. Moving. Surreal. Those had been the early quotes from the bigger critics. If only they knew. To Madison, it was more like life imitating art.

She had been so sure that the death of Amy Newton and Sherry Waters had been accidents. Car crashes were common enough weren't they? Her mind had to stretch about the electrocution but still, it wasn't the first time something like that had happened. She wasn't so sure now, and neither was Trace.

Seeing the knife had brought out the true guard in him, proving to Madison that he was indeed the right man for the job. Trace had taken Madison by the hand and led her to the corner of the room and placed himself in front of her, pulled out a cell phone she hadn't known he had and dialed 911. Within minutes, the cavalry arrived. Trace had been silent but strong until he was certain Madison was safe and had never taken his hand off his gun.

The shock was beginning to wear off now, leaving only confusion and fear behind. Trace's hand on her arm startled Madison, drawing her back into the present.

"Come on, I'm taking you to bed."

Madison blinked at his words, but was too numb to protest. She rose and slipped her hand in his. She reveled in his warmth and strength as she followed him up the stairs.

She watched as he checked her room once again then stood at her door and crossed his arms.

"I need to change," she said and picked up her cotton night shirt from the bed.

"Go ahead," Trace replied, but didn't move from his position.

Madison didn't bother to argue with him about leaving. She was sure it was useless. Instead, she retreated to the private bathroom and completed her nighttime ritual. She shut the light out and took a deep breath before she returned to her bed. He was still there.

Surprisingly, there was a cheeseburger and French fries arranged in picnic style on the bed. Madison's stomach rumbled in acceptance. She crawled across the king size mattress to sit near her food and began to eat.

"Aren't you hungry?" Madison asked as she finished off a handful of fries.

"Nope. I ate while you were changing."

"How did you get this so quickly?"

"I have my ways," he said. She could tell he was joking by his words but not by the look on his face or the tone in his voice. He was all business. Madison finished her late night meal in silence.

After she finished, she brushed her teeth again then returned to the bed. She pulled back the covers and climbed in, glancing at Trace.

"Trace?"

"Yeah?"

"Are you leaving?"

"Not a chance," Trace replied and moved over to the chair near the bath. He picked it up easily and sat it next to her bedside then pulled out his gun and set it on her night stand. It was an odd contrast next to her crystal lamp and delicate vase filled with lavender. She smiled though and curled up to her large pillow, laying on her right side so she could face him.

Madison turned the switch on the crystal lamp twice until the base was dimly lit by a tiny bulb inside. She had lived nearly thirty-three years and still couldn't go to sleep in the dark.

"Why do you do it?"

"Do what?"

"Put yourself in harm's way for virtual strangers."

Trace shrugged. "It's my job."

"I'm sure that there are other jobs that don't require guns and bullet proof vests."

"There are, they just don't interest me."

"Thrill junkie?" she questioned. His lack of concern for his own personal safety both interested and confused her.

"I don't bungee jump or sky dive, if that's what you're asking," he replied.

Madison was silent for a few moments. Her body was exhausted, but her mind was racing. It had been a long time since she had a man overnight in her bedroom. Granted he was in a chair but she was still conscience of the warmth his body radiated, his masculine scent, the cold steel of his gun nearby.

"Trace?"

"Yea?"

"Do you snore?"

"Go to sleep Madison."

She smiled in the semi darkness and closed her eyes.

Trace studied the starlet as she slept. Every fiber of his being screamed out to slip beneath the sheets and do more to her body than just guard it.

His mind drifted back to earlier when they had walked into the dining room and found the blade through her picture. It had been pizza sauce that covered a portion of the blade and Madison's picture. He figured it was supposed to represent blood, which made his boil.

He couldn't stop himself from looking into her face either. Hearing her call out his name in fear had really affected him so he looked. One of his own rules on what never to do while on the job and he broke it. Madison's look of pure terror would be fixed in his memory for a long, long time. Acting on a client's emotion could get him killed and he knew it.

He decided right then and there to treat Madison as nothing more than a client. Deep inside, he knew that was nothing but wishful thinking. Madison mattered more than what she should.

What was it about her that got under his skin? She was beautiful, no doubt about that. Had she not been a movie star, he doubted men would have given her the time of day because of her size. Trace thought she was perfect though. He guessed her to be about a size fourteen. Not exactly what social media had in mind for a Hollywood darling, yet she was.

So who wanted her dead? That thought brought him to his feet and he began to pace. He made mental lists of things to do tomorrow. It was back to business or he would lose his meal ticket. No, not just a meal ticket.

A special woman.

Trace stopped at the foot of Madison's bed and looked down at her. She had kicked the covers off her legs while her nightshirt and rode up affording him a view of her legs. He started at her perfectly pedicured toes and allowed his gaze to travel slowly upwards. Surprisingly trim ankles and calves led to nice looking thighs. Her ass was covered by white lace and silk that peeked out from underneath her nightshirt.

He held back a groan and paced again, trying unsuccessfully to ignore the tightening in his jeans. Visions of her silhouetted by the bathroom light reminded him of how luscious her fuller figure was. She was curved in all the right places. Just enough to remind him that he had manly needs that hadn't been satisfied in a long, damn time.

Trace needed a distraction. Swinging around, he headed for Madison's secret candy stash in the closet. A good Snickers bar ought to help. He took one step before the hairs on the back of his neck stood up on end.

A creak sounded outside of Madison's bedroom door. Tensing, he moved quickly to her bedside and picked up his gun then carefully stepped toward the door. The soft light of Madison's lamp allowed him a view of the brass handle. He waited for it to turn before making his move. Instead, he was surprised by a soft knock.

Trace holstered his weapon and cracked open the door to see Maggie. He stepped out into the hall and shut the door quietly.

"Is everything ok?" he asked, his voice softer than normal. Madison had a hard time falling asleep and he didn't want to wake her.

"Yes, I just wanted to see if my daughter was ok."

"She's fine and has finally fallen asleep. Isn't that where you should be as well?"

Maggie sighed and rubbed her eyes. "I wish I could sleep. I've never really thought about my daughter's safety much, Trace. I just assumed that she would never have this type of problem. I mean, she isn't some beauty queen—" Maggie began but was quickly interrupted by Trace.

"Let me tell you something about your daughter, Maggie. Madison is one of the most beautiful women I've ever seen. She's generous and kind and damn talented. You're lucky to have her as your daughter."

Maggie gave Trace a smile. "Well, I know of one fan," she began, then held up a hand before Trace could continue. "What I'm saying is, most stalker cases that I've read about deal with people who live for the limelight. Madison has never had this issue before. I've kept her sheltered from this type of lifestyle, regardless of what she has done. I'm really worried about this, Trace."

"Well, don't be. I've got her covered."

"Oh really?" Maggie gave him a sideways wink.

"She's just a job. Nothing more, nothing less."

Maggie patted him on the arm and turned around to leave. "If you say so," she tossed over her shoulder to him as she left.

Trace shook his head and returned to Madison's room. Shutting the door, he locked it as an extra precaution. She had turned on her other side, still sleeping.

The conversation with Maggie had managed to cool his adore. Still, he couldn't let himself get caught up in the emotion again. Not if he planned to keep her safe.

He sat back down in the chair, put his gun back on her nightstand and stretched out his legs. He wondered if taking this job had been a mistake. Perhaps it was, but then he never would have met Madison.

Madison Jordan. She was what fuller figure women called a *real* woman. Hell, he knew that just by looking at her. She was one *real* fine woman. A major distraction though. Again he wondered if taking this job had been a mistake.

Trace closed his eyes and drifted off to sleep, never seeing the tears that dotted Madison's pillow.

CHAPTER FIVE

THE NEXT FEW WEEKS MADISON KEPT BUSY LEARNING HER LINES. She remained silent and aloof towards Trace. After all, she was just a job wasn't she?

He was never far from her sight. A few times when she was inside with Jay or her mother, Trace would be outside checking the grounds. He had ordered a new staff of security guards while arranging to have several new additions to her front gate. A new alarm was installed for the house and windows.

Nothing had come of the knife found stabbed through her photograph so the police had nothing to go on. That meant Trace would stay longer. That also meant Madison would have double duty when it came to acting.

Since that first night, Madison insisted that Trace stay in his room. Trace tried to argue with her on the issue but Madison held firm, even threatening to fire him. She knew he was mad but it was all she could do to keep her emotions in tact until he gave in and walked away. A quick trip to the shower covered the rush of tears that blended with the hot water until she could no longer tell the difference between the two.

Late one afternoon, Stanley Stevens, the director for the film she was currently working on stopped by. Madison thought Stanley to be frog-like but brilliant. He was the most sought after director by stars all over, but was known for being picky about which script and who he would direct.

When the script for *The Circle of Friends End* came up, Madison had been surprised by Stanley insisting on her for the lead, but didn't question it. She knew of several other A-list actresses on a waiting list for Stanley Stevens. This film and its director would be the highlight of Madison's career.

"Hello Madison."

"Stanley, welcome to my home. Please sit down," Madison said and motioned to the sofa.

Stanley took a seat, pushed his glasses back up his nose and rolled the script he brought with him. Madison asked Carol to bring them some ice tea and turned back to the eccentric director.

"What brings you here today, Stanley?"

"I...I wanted to go...go over the script with you," he began.

Madison had studied him for a long time and had worked through his stuttering with no issues. Others on the set snickered behind his back but Madison ignored them.

"What about it?" Madison asked and leaned over to look at the script in his hands.

Stanley began to unroll it but it was knocked from his hands by Trace. Stanley stuttered a surprise when Trace stalked around the couch and pulled him up and began to pat him down.

"Trace! What are you doing?" Madison gasped out loud.

"My job," he said and turned Stanley around none too gently to continue his search.

"Stop it this instant!" Madison said and tugged at his muscular arms in effort to pull him away from Stanley.

"Wh...what is g...going on here?" Stanley's face was bright red and was either angry or embarrassed. Madison's face was red as well for both reasons. Who the hell did Trace think he was?

"Stanley, I apologize for Mr. Trace. Please sit down, I'll be right back."

Carol had entered with the ice tea and was startled by the scene.

Madison asked her to take care of Stanley while she stepped out for a moment then took Trace by the hand and dragged him out on the veranda.

"Are you insane?" Madison said loudly, then cleared her throat and lowered her voice. "That is one of the most premier directors not only in Hollywood, but all over the world! How dare you just come in and manhandle him like that?"

"Despite his too open invitation, he could be the perp."

"The perp? Do you listen to yourself? The man is in his fifties and in case you missed it, walks with a slight limp and stutters! Since the gates were locked and hadn't been tampered with, how do you suppose he got in? Scale the ten foot wall?"

Madison had put her hands on her hips and glared up at her fierce protector. She was surprised by the look of defeat she read in his eyes. Softening a bit, she took him by the hand and tried to give him a smile.

"I understand that you are just trying to do your job. I can't fault you for that. That's your line of work. But this is my line of work and feeling up the man who is going to make my career isn't a good thing."

"I wasn't feeling him up," Trace grunted.

"What do you call it then?"

"Patting him down. There is a big difference."

"You had me fooled," Madison said with a snort.

Trace stepped closer and leaned down to whisper in her ear. "I don't feel up men. I save that for my woman."

Chill bumps chased each other up and down Madison's body. She tried to keep her focus on the issue at hand, but was overwhelmed by visions of Trace feeling his way up her body. The titillating thoughts left a warm sensation within her.

"Yes, well," Madison said and cleared her throat. He was too close. She had to remember that she was just a job.

"Well what?"

"Well, now that we have that cleared up, I can continue with my meeting. Excuse me," she said and moved past him as fast as she could back into the house.

"Stanley," Madison began, "I'm so sorry about that. We've had a few... security issues here. Better safe than sorry." She gave Stanley a big smile and sat back down next to him. He didn't look happy, but accepted her explanation.

"Where...where was I?"

"The script. Was there some changes you wanted to make?"

"Well, not...not exactly. The f...final scene is the t...topic of discussion on the set," he stuttered out and fumbled through the script. Handing it to Madison, he pointed out a scene.

"This...this one. I th...think that instead of using a s...stunt person, perhaps you could do your own s...stunt."

"Like hell she will."

Madison had opened her mouth to speak but had been interrupted by Trace. God, this was a nightmare.

"Trace, please," she began but seeing the look in his eyes, knew it would be a cold day in hell before he would let her go through this. It was due to be shot in a few weeks and somehow she didn't think they would find this stalker by then.

Trace marched over and snatched the script from Stanley's hand and read the scene. Madison watched a red patch creep from under his shirt and move up his neck. He looked furious.

He took several deep breaths before he handed the script back to Stanley, surprising Madison, and said in a polite manner. "No."

"Now...now see here, I d...don't know who y... you are, but this is my film and I s...say what goes," Stanley sputtered out. Madison had never seen Stanley mad before. She was sure this was the end of her career.

"Then she doesn't finish the film," Trace said and took a seat across from them. He stretched out his legs casually and crossed his arms.

Madison and Stanley looked at each other then back to Trace. "Trace, please. This really is my decision."

"Not on my watch. Either a stunt person is used or it doesn't happen at all."

Stanley stood and rolled up the script. He gave Madison a nod before speaking. "W...we'll talk on set. Good day." Turning, he left.

Madison hung her head. She raised her hands to her head and rubbed her temples trying in vain to ward off the swift arriving migraine.

"You think I'm being unreasonable?"

Madison looked up at Trace's question. "Damn right I do." She surprised even herself with that reply.

"Then fire me."

His statement took her by surprise. Fire him? Was he kidding? She needed him.

That thought shocked her. When she really thought about it, did she really need him in particular or would any bodyguard do?

Without him, there would be less headaches and hassles, less drama in her life. She wouldn't be so frustrated at his crass comments and arrogance. She also wouldn't be longing for his never-to-be-felt touch at night. How many times had she crept to the door that connected his room to hers and listened? And when had it become his room? This whole situation was getting out of control.

Terminating him was best for everyone involved, wasn't it? She was just a job and she was sure that he could find another one with no problem. Yes, it was for the best.

"No, that won't be necessary," she said, going against what her mind told her was best, going with what her heart longed for.

"Good. Then no more nonsense of you doing your own stunts."

"We'll discuss it as that particular scene gets closer to being filmed."

"I'm not kidding, Madison. I don't want to take a chance on you getting hurt or worse."

"I'm sure there will be plenty of people there to ensure my safety."

"That's my job," Trace said. Madison thought he sounded a little possessive. It kind of thrilled her.

"I meant stunt wise. The pros. They know the contraptions inside and out. I'll be fine."

Trace scowled at her. Madison thought he was trying his best into scaring her into backing out. It wasn't working. Besides, the stunt was weeks away.

"I'll think about it," he said, sounding dejected and in charge all at the same time. Madison thought it cute, but didn't disclose that information. Instead she smiled up at him and held out her hand.

"Deal. Shake?"

Trace took her hand and shook it briefly before he pulled her close to him. Madison was too startled to speak. His other hand snaked up to bury in her hair and grip tightly, but not painfully before tilting her head backwards.

A slow throb began between Madison's legs. She knew Trace was rough and unrefined but that didn't deter her shameless reaction to his body. Madison leaned back with his pull, excited and anxious to see where this would go. He leaned over her and rubbed his whiskered chin against her neck while his lips touched her earlobe in the softest way.

Madison arched her back and pressed her breasts against his chest, not caring how wanton she must look. Trace turned her on and made her body hot like no other man had. Her breathing came fast, almost panting while her hands splayed his muscular, upper arms.

"See how easy it was to get to you?"

Huh?

Trace didn't want to prove this point. Madison thought just because he was around, that she was completely safe. The truth of it was if someone wanted her dead, no amount of security could stop them.

He couldn't make her understand that no matter all the precautions she took, it only takes one slip up and she could be dead.

That thought chilled him to the bone. Life without Madison didn't sound good at all. He knew this was just a job but even if he could see her from a distance, it would be worth it.

Her smile lit up any room she was in and he knew that because he watched her. Not just out of a business perspective but from a man's perspective. Perfect skin, luminous green eyes and lips meant for serious kissing. By him only, of course, he thought jealously.

And her body. He couldn't imagine anyone who had a more lovely body than hers. All he wanted to do was cover it with his own and show her how incredible she really was. Trace knew that she wasn't the wham, bam, thank you ma'am type of woman either. She was one to be carefully undressed and worshiped by his hands and his lips only before joining his body with hers. The visual left him hard as a rock.

Looking down at her now made the tightness in his pants worse. There was only one way to relieve it but he couldn't. His job of keeping her safe was his number one priority and Trace couldn't lose sight of that. It could cost Madison her life.

Perhaps he should take one taste of her lips. Maybe that would ease his need and sate the obvious desire that flowed between both of them.

His body thrilled the way her body reacted to his and he was very aware of the hardened center of her breasts pressing into his chest. Her soft panting and inviting lips drove him to distraction. It would be so easy.

Abruptly Trace released her. He took a few steps away to calm his racing heart and to get control over himself. A moment later, he turned back to Madison and winced at the look in her eyes.

"Point made," she whispered.

Trace could hear the hurt that was laced in her voice. God, he wanted to comfort her but he shouldn't. He had to make her face up to how easy it was to get close to her and slip a knife between her ribs. As much as it pained him, he would rather hurt her now than someone else hurt her later.

"Good," he said and cleared his throat.

"But we'll still discuss my doing the stunt closer to the filming date."

Trace wasn't surprised by her stubbornness. It was one of the many qualities that he appreciated about her. Still, he had to make her understand how vulnerable she was out in the open and what an easy mark she made attempting a stunt. He made a mental note to have a discussion with this Stanley person.

He watched her square her shoulders and with her head held high, leave the room. Damn, he hated this shit.

CHAPTER SIX

Madison didn't stop until she was safely in her room. She didn't bother to lock the door though. Trace would probably just kick it down if he wanted in and she didn't want to have to replace another door.

She thought about going out on the balcony to enjoy the warm weather but doubted her jailer would let her stay there. Instead she curled up on the chaise lounge and picked up the script to study.

Out of curiosity, she thumbed to the end of the script where the stunt was to occur and read it thoroughly to see what the big deal was. According to the script, her character is pushed off of the roof of a building but manages to survive. The killer falls with her but doesn't survive.

With special effects today, what really could go wrong?

She closed her eyes and tried to imagine the scene but visions of Trace kept invading instead.

His hand touched her hand and slid achingly slow up her bare arm. She bit her lower lip as he eased down next to her and leaned closer to her body.

She reveled in the warmth of his breath, the soft scrape of his chin whiskers tickling her neck.

She arched her back and pushed her breasts out against his hands while he cupped and tested their weight before his fingertips zeroed in. She smiled at his complaint of her bra and shirt in his way.

"Take it off then," she suggested and gave a sound between a gasp and laugh as he ripped open her expensive shirt open and made quick work of the bra clasp.

Flutters filled her stomach as he nipped and licked his way around the puckered flesh before settling center and drawing a long, shuddering sigh from her lips.

Her hands worked up his arm before her fingertips ran through his short hair trying in vain to tug and press him closer all at the same time. She smiled at his hand on her leg, moving slowly up under her skirt before resting on her hip. God she wanted more. She needed more.

"Please," she whispered and moved her hips towards his body.

And she was pleased when his hand continued its movement around to her back end and gripped one cheek firmly. She delighted in his strength and almost complained when his mouth left her bared breasts to kiss her neck.

Her leg lifted to curl around his thigh in an effort to experience the desire she knew he possessed when she noticed he had stopped kissing her. Something was wrong.

"I can't."

Madison opened her eyes to discover that this was not the hot dream she believed it was. It was very real, including the intense look in Trace's eyes. She was horrified to discover that her blouse had indeed been ripped open and her breasts were bare to his gaze while her skirt had been pushed up around her waist.

"Oh my God," she whispered and pushed at Trace to let her up then scrambled up herself to straighten her clothing. "Oh, God."

"Madison," he began but stopped.

Madison held her hands to her cheek, her hands warmed by slow burn left behind from embarrassment. She rushed to the bathroom and shut the door, locking it before he could stop her.

"Madison, please. Open the door."

"Trace, please just go away. Please," her voice shook as she struggled to keep her emotions in check. *Please go, Trace,* she thought.

"I'm sorry."

"No, please don't be sorry. Just go. I want to be alone."

She heard him sigh and after a minute, her bedroom door open and then close. Thankfully he had left. Now she could be properly mortified.

Madison turned on the shower and removed the rest of her clothing before stepping under the harsh, heated water. She had never been so embarrassed in her entire life. It's one thing to throw yourself at a guy, it's another to do it while half asleep and get turned down.

Why had he turned her on then turned her down? It had to be her body. Not the skin and bones he expected under her skirt. Never mind the fact that she was just a job. Her mind drifted back to seeing her slightly dimpled thighs when she stood up. He probably thought each one was the Grand Canyon. A visit to the closet was in order.

Leaving the shower, she dried off quickly and put on a robe before slipping quietly into her closet. She had devoured a half dozen kisses before putting the lid back on the box of hidden goodies.

This is not the way Madison, she chided herself.

Rising, she went back to the mirror and stared at herself closely. Coward. She just had to resign herself that she was destined to be the bridesmaid and never a bride.

A knock sounded on her door and startled her. God, what if it was Trace?

"Madison?"

It was Carol's voice. Relief swept over her. She tugged the door open and pulled her in.

"Are you okay?"

"Yes. Just exhausted."

"Well, dinner is ready. Then you can retire early for the night if you like," Carol suggested.

Madison's eyes lit up then. "Carol? I need a favor from you."

~

TRACE WATCHED MADISON ENTER THE DINING ROOM AND suppressed the now familiar tightening between his legs. His eyes never left her face, hoping to let her know silently that everything was ok but she never looked at him.

Dinner was awkwardly silent with the exception of light conversation between Jay and Maggie. Madison would comment on occasion but for the most part she remained silent. Trace brooded and grunted answers when questions were tossed his way. Damn, he wanted to talk to Madison. He wanted to apologize for his behavior in her bedroom but more importantly, make her understand that it wasn't her, it was him.

He was angry at himself for hurting her. He could see it in her eyes, her body language and could hear it in her voice. He should have known better than to get personally involved. Unfortunately, it was a little late for that.

"Excuse me. I'm a bit tired tonight so I'm going to bed early," Madison announced and interrupted his thoughts. He started to rise but she held out her hand for him to remain seated. "Carol can see me to my room. Good night."

Without a backward glance, she left the room with the housekeeper in tow.

Damn.

Trace rose with every intention of following her but stopped himself. *Keep it generic, Trace,* he thought to himself and made a turn for Jay's office instead. It's just a job.

Collapsing in his chair, Trace kicked his feet back on the desk and supported his head with his hands. He should have turned his hog around and rode off when they hit mistake number three. He made his uncle a promise though and had to at least give it a chance.

Now look at the mess he was in. Up to his leather chaps in

Hollywood horseshit and half in love with their number one darling.

Did he just think the word love? Oh hell.

Trace stood quickly and exited through one of the terrace doors. He had to get out of there for a while. Hell, forever if he knew what was good for him. But he knew he wouldn't leave her. Not as long as she needed his protection, he'd be back.

In one smooth movement, he straddled his vintage motorcycle and turned the key, loving how the engine purred under him. He closed his eyes and remembered Madison purring under him for a moment. He shuddered in hardened agony.

Trace glanced up at the house, focusing on Madison's bedroom balcony. He thought about going back in and letting her know that he was leaving. Instead, he cursed again and gave the throttle a hard twist before he roared off into the night.

THE SMALL BAR WAS MORE OF A DIVE BUT TRACE LIKED IT anyway. *Del's*, as it was called, mainly hosted bikers but with such a laid back atmosphere, it had a nice eclectic mix during the latter part of the week. There was the occasional fight, but what bar didn't have that problem?

Shaking hands with the bouncer at the door, a long-time friend, Trace made his way to the bar and ordered an overdue beer.

"Trace! Where ya been, man?"

The bartender greeted Trace with an enthusiastic handshake and a rarely seen smile.

"How's it hangin' Del?" Trace returned the cheerful greeting and sat at the end of the bar on a leather and wooden stool.

"Low and to the left," Del replied with a grin and loud laugh. His large belly shook with his glee and within a minute had a cold bottle of beer in his hand. "The usual?"

"You know it, my man." Trace reached in his pocket for the folded bills but stopped at Del's harsh glare. "You know your money's not good here." A smile replaced the glare. "As long as I live and breathe, which is mainly due to you, you drink for free here."

Trace clapped the burly man on the shoulder and thanked him before lifting the frosted bottle to his lips. A long drink later, he found the bottle drained and a fresh one waited for him. He wasn't surprised. Tossing the glass bottle in the recycle container, he slowed down on his drinking and merely enjoyed the momentary freedom while he could.

"Hey. You're in my seat."

Trace didn't flinch at the voice. In fact, he ignored it. Surely no intelligent man would pick a bar fight with someone his size. Unless he was bigger. He guessed they wanted to find out if the old cliché about being bigger and falling harder was true.

"I said you're in my seat," the voice said again, only this time with a tap on Trace's shoulder.

"Funny, I didn't see your name on it. Maybe you should just find another seat to take."

"Maybe you should just move your ass before I move it for you."

Trace let out a deep sigh and took another drink of his beer before rising and turning around. He sized up the man, noticing that he wasn't alone. He could take them both but was too damn tired to do it. On the other hand, maybe a good fight was just what he needed to work out his frustrations.

"Are you asking me to dance?" Trace asked before chuckling.

"Why I ought to –" he began but was interrupted by another man who had approached.

"Move along?"

The menacing man squirmed slightly before nodding. He swallowed hard and raising his hands in defeat, moved away from Trace.

"Aww damnit, Lex. I was just starting to have fun."

Alexander Cameron shook his head and closed the switchblade he had held discretely low. "Come on," he said and tugged Trace over toward his table.

"Trace! What's up, man?" A man sitting on one of the three

chairs surrounding a small table rose and clasped Trace's forearm with his hand. Trace gave the large man a crooked grin.

"Nate, good to see you." Trace returned his grip before joining the two men at the table.

Nathan Garrett took a big swig of his beverage and waved the empty mug at the bartender. "So where ya been, man?"

"On the job," Trace replied and leaned back in the chair's cushion to put his feet up on the short table.

Lex lit two thin cigars and passed one to Trace, the other to Nathan. The thin trail of smoke merely added to the already smoky atmosphere in the building. Trace took it eagerly and with a long drag, he blew several smoke rings before snapping his fingers. "I still got it."

"You alright, Trace?"

Trace turned to Lex and gave him the thumbs up before combining a drink with a drag from the cigar.

"It's a woman, isn't it?" Lex's question ended up sounding more like a statement. Nate nearly choked on his refreshed beverage from Del.

Trace didn't reply with a denial or confirmation. He merely kept drinking. Seeing he was near the end of the beer, he looked over to Del who was on his way with a small pail holding several bottles with ice to keep them cold. Saluting Del, Trace grabbed a fresh bottle and studied the fireball on the end of his cigar.

"Yep, it's a woman," Lex said in answer to his own question. "It's always a woman when they drive you to drink and smoke."

"We always drink and smoke," Nate said sounding confused. Lex reached out and smacked the back of his head. "Watch it baldy," Nate grumbled at Lex.

"Damn Hollywoodites," Trace muttered.

"Oh man. You back on the Walk-Of-Fame beat again?" Nate rubbed his hands together. "Who is it? Nicole? Julia? Oh, Beyonce?" Nate rose and gave a hip grind and belted out a line from her latest song.

Trace looked at Nate like he had lost his mind. "No. But it's profitable."

"I'll bet it is," Nate replied, collapsed in his chair and began rubbing his hands together again. "In more than one way too."

"Hey! Don't make me kick your ass."

Nate chuckled and took one of Trace's beers having found his glass empty again. "No need to get froggy, my man. Just havin' fun."

"Well don't. She not that kind of woman."

"You hit the big time my friend," Lex commented. Usually their clients were bitchy political or paranoid business moguls.

"He hit the bottle too," Nate said with a laugh then rose to head for the men's room.

"Damn Madison. Why did it have to be you?" Trace wondered out loud.

"Madison? As in Madison Jordan?" Lex questioned then whistled low at Trace's confirmation.

Trace grunted and motioned to Lex to give him another cigar. He lit the end with his other cigar and flicked it on the floor. Lex used his boot heel to snuff out the hot coals.

Trace waved the cigar back and forth slowly, watching the light from the burning embers dance in front of his eyes. Thoughts of Madison's flaming hair invaded Traces thoughts and he cursed. He stopped as Lex shook his head. "What?"

"You got personal, didn't you?"

"No."

"Dude, you can't get personal on the job. You know the code," Lex reminded him.

"I know the code. I didn't get personal."

"Yet. But you're damn close aren't you?"

Trace didn't reply. He took another drink and after a long drag from the cigar, he put it out inside the bottle. "I'm trying not to. It's just so hard. She's... incredible."

Lex cracked open one of Trace's beers from Del and took a swig. "I've seen her. Damn fine looking woman."

Trace squelched the sting of jealousy. Lex had been his best friend for years. He trusted him completely. They would give their lives for each other so Trace would certainly trust Lex to be alone with his woman.

With Madison.

A cheer rose from a small crowd gathered around the bar. Trace glanced over to see bottles being clinked in toast and looked away.

"So what's her story?"

"Jay called. He's her business manager."

"Jay? That old goat. How's he doing? I haven't seen him in years."

"Very well, considering he represents Madison."

"That lucky bastard."

"Not so lucky right now. He's convinced someone's trying to kill Madison by acting out the movie she's filming."

More cheers interrupted their conversation. Trace noticed Nate had joined in and returned his attention back to Lex.

"That's freaky. You sure about it?"

"I wasn't until a knife stabbed through her picture came with the pizza the other night."

"Was it familiar?"

"No, not at all. Just a standard knife that can be picked up at any local store."

"Cops any help?"

"Hell no. No one is, including her. Between her, her mother, Jay, the cook, the butler, the chauffeur, the gardener, the pool boy... I'm up to my pierced ear in babysitting."

Lex whistled low again. "You got your work cut out for you."

"Yeah, I guess."

They were both silent for a moment before Lex spoke. "She really has a pool boy?"

Trace shook his head no. "I was exaggerating. But there is a cleaning crew twice a week just for the damn pool. Did I mention the ankle bitter?"

Lex roared with laughter.

"Seriously, if you need any help, you know how to find me," Lex said with a familiar tone.

Trace gave Lex a short nod. They never had to say much when it came to watching each other's back.

Nate came running up with a big smile pasted on his face. "Oh man. You aren't going to believe who's here!"

"Beyonce?" Lex asked and rolled his eyes.

"Better!" Nate said with the squeal of a school boy.

"It's probably Madison Jordan," Trace said and rubbed his eyes.

Nate's grin faded. "How'd you know?"

CHAPTER SEVEN

Madison's heart pounded madly as she pressed her back against the wall. She hadn't expected to see Trace outside and wondered if he knew she had snuck out of the house. She watched as he stalked out to his motorcycle and raised one leg high to straddle it.

Wicked thoughts danced wildly through her mind on his ability to straddle so incredibly well that when the engine roared to life, she covered a gasp. He probably had super-hearing and would have dragged her back into the house.

She watched as he gazed up at the house. Madison followed his line of vision and almost teared up when she realized it was towards her room. She wanted to call out to him but embarrassment from earlier kept her silent. Though only a moment passed, it seemed forever before he rode off.

Madison tip-toed over to Carol's car and slid in before shutting the door with a quiet click. She took several deep breaths to calm her racing pulse, started the engine and drove towards the gate. The guard waved her through without stopping her. She had to remember to thank Carol later for the scarf to cover her hair. She returned the wave and set off for her adventure.

Madison drove around aimlessly studying the houses around her, the twinkling lights of the city and the solitude of a deserted road. This was just what she needed.

She always enjoyed being alone with her thoughts. She would close her eyes and imagine that she was someone else with a different career; a nurse; a secretary with a demanding boss who couldn't function without her; an astronaut.

A wife.

Madison gazed up at the stars and sighed deeply. Her life had never been more complicated than it was right now. Forget the crazy stalker apparently trying to kill her, she'd found herself drowning in her feelings for the most infuriating, incredible man. She imagined that life would be one adventure after another with Trace. And she loved a good adventure.

Madison heard a loud pop sound then the car began to shake. A tire on Carol's car had gone flat, ending her current adventure. She coasted as far as the bumpy ride would let her before ending up on the side of the road.

Great. Just great.

She snagged her purse and dug through it until she found her cell phone. She flipped open the top only to discover yet another bump in her road.

"No signal?" Madison groaned out loud and after yanking up the antenna and shifting around the car in attempt to get a signal, she got out.

Madison examined the tire and after checking out the trunk, she made a mental note to get lessons on how to change a flat.

Tucking her purse under her arm, she wandered down the dimly lit highway, keeping track of the bars on her phone in hopes of getting a signal for her phone. Faint music caught her attention and she noticed a small building up ahead. Hopefully they would have a phone she could use.

A few minutes later, she stood at the edge of the parking lot. A row of motorcycles stood in the back while various types of pick-up trucks and semi-trucks were parked haphazardly in the gravel lot. Could this get any worse?

Squaring her shoulders, she strode to the door and, giving it a hard yank, found herself on the doorstep of a small bar. It was smoky and very loud. Taking a linen handkerchief from her pocket, she covered her mouth and wandered up to the bar.

"Excuse me," Madison said in a loud voice. The bartender either ignored her or didn't hear her. Giving a good clearing of her throat, she spoke louder. "Excuse me."

The bartender glanced up from cleaning a glass and eyed her suspiciously. "What'll it be babe?"

Babe? "Yes, do you have a phone that I might use?"

"Pay phone is back by the john."

Madison wrinkled her nose. She hadn't heard the bathroom referred to as 'the john' in the longest time. She also noticed his finger pointed to the back of the bar. No way was she wandering through this place.

"Yes, well I was hoping you had a phone up here that I could borrow. Just for a minute or two."

"Lady, the phone in the back is for the public. The phone up here is for the staff. And I don't see you wearing my t-shirt so that means you don't work here and you can't use this phone."

Madison swallowed hard. She could do this. She wasn't helpless. She was an Academy Award nominee after all.

"I could pay you." She allowed her voice to sound husky and slightly seductive as she had in a film a few years ago. Of course, that was scripted to work.

The bartender's eyes lit up. "Really? How much?"

Madison discretely looked in her purse and pulled out a bill. "Twenty dollars?"

"Done."

Whew. That was easy enough. She handed him a fifty dollar bill. "Do you have change?"

The bartender grunted. "Let me check." He turned and wandered down the bar.

The sound of breaking glass and bottles being brought together in toast jolted her back to the reality she was facing at the moment. Please just let me get through this and I swear I'll be good, she thought and realized she was experiencing real fear. What if Trace found her here? She gave a nervous laugh at that thought.

A small shot glass slammed down in front of her filled with an amber colored liquid. Swallowing hard, Madison followed the length of a tattooed arm up to a large man. A very large man. Oh lord.

"How about a drink, honey?"

"No, thank you," Madison said and covered her face with her handkerchief.

"Why not? Are you too good to drink with me or are you just afraid?"

The latter was closer to the truth than he knew and she figured admitting to the first would only insult him.

"Of course not," she retorted, trying in vain to sound tough. "I'm just not thirsty, right now."

A small group gathered around Madison then. She wanted to rush screaming from the bar and for a moment thought about Trace. Where was he when she *really* needed him?

The crowd laughed. "Come on, toots, drink with us. House rules for new comers at *Del's*."

Madison wet her lips under her handkerchief then stuffed it down towards her pocket, not noticing that it fell to the floor. "Very well, then. Cheers." She lifted the shot glass and closing her eyes, downed the fiery drink.

Her scarf slipped from her head while she coughed. The drink blazed down her throat and set up a camp fire in the pit of her stomach while her eyes watered in protest. Carefully she set the glass down and gave a pained smile. Surprisingly, a cheer rose from the crowd. A moment later, her blood started to warm from the liquor. She grinned.

"Set 'em up barkeep! My treat!" Was that really her voice? She giggled and waved off the phone the bartender set down before her to make room for another glass of the liquid with kick. Another cheer rose from the crowd as several shot glasses were passed around then clinked together. Splashes of alcohol spilled out and decorated her scarf, now around her shoulders.

Madison watched people tipping their heads back with a jerk and slam their glasses on the bar top. When in Rome, she thought and with a toss back of her head, drank another shot. She joined the slamming of shot glasses on the bar top with a smile.

"This is way better than champagne," Madison said between wide grins and gales of laughter. She leaned into the arm that had quickly snaked around her shoulder and urged him to join her in a slow sway back and forth to an old '80s rock ballad playing in the background. This wasn't so bad after all.

Another round of drinks that she volunteered to pay for appeared, this time in the form of beer bottles and foamy topped mugs. Madison chose a bottle figuring somewhere in the back of her mind that it had to be cleaner than the glassware.

More cheers rose along with the frosty, beer filled mugs. She swore to use the phone once she finished this drink. Her taste buds were numb. That had to be the only way she could sip the golden liquid that didn't mix too well with the shots from before.

Oh God, she was seeing things. Is that what alcohol did to you? Because she swore she saw Trace's angry face standing right in front of her.

Oh God, she was going to be sick.

~

"Time to go," Trace said and held his hand out to Madison.

He had almost run Nate over trying to get across the room to the crowd that had gathered around the bar. There was no way that his Madison was here at *Del's*. She was safe and sound at home.

His protective instincts kicked in seeing her surrounded by bikers and truckers. Watching Madison tipping back the beer bottle scared him. Seeing the thug who had harassed him earlier put his arm around her made him see red. The few steps left between them could have been miles instead of the few feet it really was. His heart raced while his palms itched to curl up and bash the drunken biker wannabe until he didn't move.

Was she crazy? How the hell had she gotten here? He made mental notes to fire every single security person in a five mile radius when they got back.

This was so out of control. Trace stopped in front of Madison and took a long, deep breath and with all the strength he could muster, held his temper in check. He had to. Madison was in the middle of danger and without his wits, so was he.

He had to get her the hell out of here before something dangerous exploded. Like his rage.

Of course, it wasn't going to be easy. It never was where she was concerned. And he loved her for it.

Damn.

"Trace?" Madison's voice slurred further raising the bar on the trouble about to ensue.

"Let's go," Trace said and pulled her to her feet.

"Hold on there, buddy."

Trace sighed. Here we go.

Trace swung Madison around and pushed against the man who reached for her. He lowered his voice and spoke through clenched teeth in hopes the man would take his advice seriously.

"Trust me when I advise you to walk away."

The drunken man laughed and gave a short whistle. Several men rose from the bar and surrounding tables. Chains dangled from their fists and pockets while several suddenly sported short pipes in their hands.

"This is gonna hurt," Trace said with a shake of his head.

The man laughed and put his hands on his hips. "Which one? The chain? Or the pipe?"

Trace snaked out his fist and punched the man across the jaw then watched as his eyes crossed before he fell backward onto the floor.

"I'll take clueless at Del's for a thousand, Alex," Trace said, and jerked Madison with him to the floor. Covering her body with his, he lost count of the number of times pipes were laid across his back or ribs. He was just grateful when they stopped after a few seconds.

He looked up to see Lex holding out a hand to haul him up.

"Get her out of here," Lex said quietly and turned to step up on a chair, then a table before leaping onto a crowd of burly men heading their way. Always the mosher, Trace thought and leaned down for Madison.

His heart stopped seeing her pale face and closed eyes. No. God please let her be ok so he can strangle her himself. Thankfully, he was rewarded by a low groan.

He pulled her limp body up and bending, eased her body over his shoulder and walked cautiously towards the door. Del was holding it open and apologized to Trace several times.

"Don't worry about it Del."

Del held out the fifty dollar bill that Madison had handed him earlier. "Here, this is hers."

"Keep it. For damages."

"I can't. It's my fault this happened. I didn't know who she was or that she was with you."

Trace pressed it back to Del. "It's ok, Del. I'll be back later. I just want to get her home." With a final nod, he stepped out into the cool night air, heading for his Harley.

Damn. How did she get here? He was definitely losing his touch. Never had he had this problem happen during a job. Of course, he hadn't taken a job past three strikes.

And he hadn't ever taken a job and let it get personal.

He set her down on the leather seat and shook her shoulders several times. She groaned a protest, refusing to open her eyes.

"Come on, Madison. Wake up."

Madison cracked open one eye, then the other and gave Trace a bright smile. "Hey! Whatcha doin' here?" She hiccupped.

"I was drinking with my friends until you showed up. Which brings up the question of how you got here?"

Madison stuck her finger over Trace's lips and gave him the quiet noise. "Shh. I told Carol I wouldn't tell." Her eyes widened then and she slapped her hand over her mouth and laughed. "Oops."

Trace shook his head. It didn't take much for her to get drunk.

He removed her hand from her mouth and put it on the seat in front of her. "Steady yourself while I get on."

"I can't."

"Yes, you can."

"No, I can't."

"Why not?"

"I'm going to be sick," she said and covered her mouth.

Trace quickly hauled her off his bike and towards the edge of the parking lot before she retched long and hard. He felt bad for her. This was probably the first time she had ever had a drink. No, scratch that. All Hollywoodites drank champagne. This was her first real drink. And probably her last if she got the hangover he had when he first did shots.

The thought almost made him smile.

"Trace?"

"Yeah?"

"I don't feel so good," she whispered and turned to cling to his body for support.

With ease, Trace swung her up once again, this time cradling her close to his chest and walked back to his bike. He set her down again and quickly climbed on, instructing her to hang onto his waist. He should call for a car but the night air would do her good.

The low rumble of the engine broke the silence of the night as he shifted the gear and eased onto the road.

Madison had slipped closer to him and gripped his waist tightly. He tried to ignore the softness of her body against his and cursed the thick leather jacket that denied him the softness of her breasts against his back. *You can't have it both ways, Trace.*

He should leave this job. It was out of control and too personal. He couldn't concentrate on protecting her from whoever wanted to hurt her. All he could think about was burying himself so deeply inside her while tasting the sweet cries that came out of her mouth.

Realizing his speed, Trace slowed down. He took the upcoming curve in the road easy and forced his thoughts on getting her back home and safe again.

He would talk to Jay in the morning, make arrangements for another guard and be on his way by the afternoon. Simple as that.

Slowing to a stop at a red light, he turned to check on Madison. She glanced up with sleepy green eyes and gave him a smile before kissing him on the lips.

"I love you."

Simple my ass.

CHAPTER EIGHT

MADISON TUGGED THE BLANKET HIGHER TO COVER HER EYES when the drapes were pulled open. She groaned out loud when the blanket was yanked away from her head.

"Go away," she managed to croak out and turned on her side before raising a hand to grip her forehead.

"Hung over?"

Her eyes snapped open and she sat up quickly. "Mother?"

Too quickly. Scrambling, Madison stumbled past Maggie and into her bathroom, barely making it before emptying what was left in her stomach into the porcelain bowl.

Flicking the handle, she collapsed onto the floor, leaned against the wall and closed her eyes. A chuckle brought them back open again.

Her mother was laughing at her.

She almost wanted to make her laugh and cry at the same time, but she didn't have the strength for it. Madison couldn't remember the last time when she and her mother shared a funny moment.

"What's so funny?" Madison asked, lifting her hand to push her hair behind her ear.

"You, my dear. I haven't seen you drunk in a long time."

"I've never been drunk," Madison protested.

"Oh, but you have. Remember five years ago at the premier for your third film? You insisted on the fourth glass to celebrate fourth billing. I believe you said, four for four."

Madison squeezed her eyes shut and let out her own small chuckle.

"Of course, later that night you were trying to create some new tongue twister out of it and spit all over that reporter."

"Oh, God. I remember that," Madison said with a groan, then rubbed her temples in protest. "Still, I don't remember feeling this rotten the next day."

"Shots will do that to you."

Madison looked at her. "How did you know?"

"I helped Trace get you up the stairs," Maggie answered with a smile.

Madison hung her head. "I apologize for my behavior."

Maggie walked into the bathroom with Madison and, lowering the lid on the toilet, sat down. "Shit happens."

Madison looked at her in wonder. "You've changed."

All thanks to Trace.

Oh, God. How would she ever be able to face him again? Somewhere in the back of her mind, she recalled throwing up on the side of the road.

Worse, she recalled telling him she loved him. Please let that be just a bad dream and not reality.

"I suppose I have. Getting up there in years will do funny things to a person. Not to mention a bit of advice from a wise young man."

She had never thought of Trace as wise, but she supposed he was in his own way. Wasn't it his job a combination of both brains and brawn? Hopefully. He had to keep one step ahead of whomever this madman was that was out to get her.

Madison reached out slowly and slipped her hand in Maggie's. It was odd yet nice holding her mother's hand. She was like a little girl again for a moment. It was a good feeling.

"You aren't that old," Madison said awkwardly.

Maggie squeezed her hand and gave her a wink. "Only as old as I feel. Which if you don't mind me saying, right now I would almost give you a run for your money over that sexy bodyguard of yours."

Madison's eyes widened. "Mother!"

Maggie cackled and rose, helping Madison stand. "I said almost. Besides, I'm not his type." Maggie turned on the shower and tested the water before stepping towards the door.

"And with the way he looks at you, no one in the world has a shot. If you ask me, that is." With another wink, Maggie headed out.

Madison turned to look in the mirror and noted the red stain spreading over her cheeks. Was she his type? How did he look at her?

Who put her in her night clothes?

"THANKS LEX. I'LL BE IN TOUCH." TRACE SNAPPED THE PHONE shut and slid it into his pocket.

Dropping his exhausted frame on the couch, he closed his eyes and rubbed his temples before releasing a deep sigh.

"A handful, isn't she?"

Trace didn't open his eyes as Maggie sat down next to him. "You don't know the half of it."

"The hell I don't. Who do you think has been with her since birth?"

Trace grunted and opened his eyes to focus on the smiling older woman. "Ok, well, maybe you do know."

"What's that? You admitting I'm right about something?"

Maggie laughed heartily at Trace's frown and patted his hand. "They all have come to understand that. I knew it would only be a matter of time before you did, too."

"I'm bringing a friend on board. He can stay with Madison while I do the background on this stalker."

"Oh, really? You don't think I'm going to have Madison paying for another piece of meat do you?"

"Piece of meat?"

"On second thought, does he look like you?"

"What does that have to do with…" Trace began and frowned at the blush that threatened to creep up his neck. "You are bad, Maggie Jordan."

Maggie gave him a wink. "Old, not dead, honey."

"You sure aren't the same drill sergeant that marched into this house a few weeks ago, spewing venom with an ankle biter in tow."

"Yes, well, I've been shown the error of my ways by this bossy——"

"Piece of meat?"

Maggie gave him a final wink and left the room.

Trace rose and walked out onto the terrace. What was he doing here? This wasn't his lifestyle. There was more furniture in that living room than in his whole apartment. He never had a need for the soft things of life before. Hell, he didn't now. Except the soft touch of Madison.

God! What was wrong with him? He knew better than to get personal. He knew better than to fall in love. He had disciplined himself for years against this, yet here he was, lounging around on cushy patio furniture and enjoying the softness of that white rug near the fireplace under his bare feet. He needed to distance himself from this place. From her. It would be better when the job was over and he left.

Better for who? Her or himself?

"Trace?"

Damn. He was really slipping not hearing Jay come in. He stopped,mmm seeing the look on Jay's face. "What's wrong?"

"There's been another death."

Trace's gut tightened. "Where's Madison? Does she know?"

"Yeah, she does."

"Damn that bastard is bold," Trace began then gave Jay a confused look. "Why did you tell her before me?"

"I didn't. She got a call."

Trace sighed and headed out of the room but Jay's words

stopped him cold. "She got a call from the killer. He told her about Tina's death, then said she was next."

Trace's jaw tightened and his fist clenched tightly. "Like hell." Within the blink of an eye, he swung his fist against the wall and created a hole in the hard plaster. He didn't notice the pain or the blood that began to trickle down his bruising knuckles as he headed to find Madison.

He didn't see her when he opened her bedroom door. He stopped and listened and immediately picked up on her soft cries. Trace was torn on whether or not to invade her privacy. His heart tugged him to the closet door, however, and entered the darkness.

Trace left the door open a crack for light and dropping to his knees, crawled over to Madison. She had curled up in a fetal position, hugging a pillow she'd dragged in from her bed. She didn't fight him as he pulled her up to him and into his lap. Neither said a word but sat with each other, a jumbled mess of emotions.

Trace willed his strength to help her through this while Madison sobbed harder against his chest. Her hair was still wet from showering. He stroked her back in a slow motion, kissed her forehead and dug around for the snack box with his other hand.

"It's ok. I don't want any."

Her voice startled him. How did she know what he was doing? Was he really losing his touch that much? He hugged her tightly and continued to rub her back.

"I'm sorry about last night," Madison said quietly. "Things just got so crazy."

"You've got to be more careful Madison." He hadn't meant to sound like he was scolding her, but she scared the hell out of him.

They sat in silence again, her cheek rested against his chest. It felt so right.

"She was my best friend in high school."

"I won't let him get you, Madison."

She nodded wordlessly then yawned.

"You need some rest," Trace said and stood up, offering her his hand to help.

She took it and followed him to her vanity. Handing her a tissue, he went towards the bathroom then returned with a towel. Madison dried her eyes and discreetly blew her nose, discarding the tissue. He fished her hairbrush out of the drawer and began to towel-dry her hair.

Neither spoke while Trace rubbed her hair with the fluffy towel from her scalp to the tips. He watched her in the mirror before picking up the brush. She kept her eyes low but he could see how red they were from crying. His heart ached for her.

Trace began to brush her hair then. With long, slow strokes, he gently pulled the tangles from her hair. He loved the silky texture, the dark reddish color, the scent left behind by the shampoo. A short while later, her hair was dry.

"Come on, let's get you into bed."

With gentle tug at her elbow, he urged her to the bedside and tucked her in. He turned to leave, stopped only by her hand.

"Don't leave, Trace."

Trace took a deep breath but couldn't turn to look at her. It would be his undoing if he did.

"Please," she said with a shaky breath. "I don't want to be alone right now."

Compromise.

"I'm just going to sit in the chair, I won't leave."

"Alright." She said in a soft voice. Within moments he heard her even breathing and chanced a look.

Tear streaked cheeks were ashen in color while dark half-moons sat under her closed eyes. Even being an emotional mess she was still breathtaking.

Trace pulled the chair over to the bed and sat down to watch over her. Hours went by and though he thought of every reason to run away, he countered each one with only one reply.

He loved her.

He never saw it coming. Never thought he had to worry about it. No one had ever gotten under his skin like she did. Her flashing green eyes, her secret stash of candy in the closet, even the haughty way she tried to boss him around was endearing.

Trace's thoughts were interrupted by a soft knock at the door.

He found Maggie with a dinner tray for both her and Trace. He thanked her and sent her off to bed.

Trace locked the door and ate a good portion of the meal. He didn't think Madison would be waking up until the morning anyway. He was proven wrong hearing Madison begin to cry in her sleep.

Stay at arm's length, he told himself. *Yeah, right.*

MADISON'S SLEEP WAS FITFUL. VISIONS OF THE DEATHS OF HER friends plagued her dreams, while she stood at the edge of a cliff. A hand pushed her and she began to fall, screaming as the ground raced up to meet her. She cried out for Trace.

Madison sat up and stared wildly around the room. Trace's arms moved around her and she clung to him tightly.

"You're safe, Madison. I won't let anyone hurt you."

"Don't leave me," she said, drawing a shaky breath.

"I won't leave you. I told you I'd be sitting right there in that chair."

Madison looked up at Trace and her heart burst with love. She had to take the chance or she'd never know. "No, I mean stay the night with me. Here."

She heard him take in a deep breath. "Madison, you don't know what you're asking. You're highly emotional right now," he said before Madison cut him off.

"I know what I'm asking. I'm asking you to stay here with me, in this bed. I'm asking you to touch me like you've touched no other. I'm asking you to make my body scream out for more over and over again," Madison's voice took on a sultry tone but it wasn't a part she was playing. It was her, a woman who wanted to make love with the man she loved.

She shrugged the straps of her night gown down, baring her shoulders while she rose up on her knees. Farther the gown slipped down her arms until it pooled around her waist. She leaned closer to

Trace and pressed her lips against his, rewarded by his near devouring of her.

He groaned and pushed her back against the bed, quickly tugged off his black t-shirt and loomed over her. His hands dug in her hair as he dropped closer and closer to her.

Madison smiled up at him and raised her hand to caress his cheek. If he thought he would hold back, he had another thing coming. She wasn't going to let him. Not this time.

"I'm asking you to make love to me, Trace."

CHAPTER NINE

TRACE SWORE HIS HEART NEVER POUNDED SO HARD IN HIS LIFE. Not the time when he dangled from a cliff trying to avoid a car that almost ran him down; not the time when he had a gun held to his forehead by a nut job who wouldn't leave a client alone.

Never.

Yet here was this woman, this movie star, this Goddess, offering her body to him. He could barely breathe. This must be what cardiac arrest was like. Either that or he was dreaming.

And why was he having this discussion in his brain when he should be ravishing Madison?

Trace leaned down, pressed his face into her neck, inhaled her scent then with a slow stroke, drug his tongue up to her ear.

"Be sure, Madison. Be very sure. There's no going back once we start."

Madison responded with a turn of her head to capture his lips in a demanding kiss. That was all he needed.

He wanted to take his time with her, savor the softness of her skin, the taste of her lips. He had imagined this from the moment he saw her.

He quickly removed his jeans, then her nightgown. He didn't want anything between their bodies.

Madison almost growled then, scraping her nails along his arm and back, whispering demands in one breath, pleading;ps in the next. She was more than ready.

And Trace couldn't wait any longer either. Now, he would make their bodies' one. And he did just that.

MADISON HAD NEVER EXPERIENCED SEX LIKE THAT BEFORE. SHE had only dreamed of how amazing it was. Not just sex though. Pure, deep, lovemaking. It was a feeling she never wanted to end. She closed her eyes and remembered not only his touch but the sweet things he whispered to her. Words no one had ever spoken to her before.

Trace lay fully on her and buried his face in the nape of her neck. Madison could barely breathe but she didn't care. It was what she had always dreamed it should be. Not the sex.

Love.

Later, he curled his arm around her waist and pulled her closer to him. She was conscious of her body, of his hands moving across her stomach. The urge to run for her closet was squelched by a hard object pressing against the back of her thigh and a kiss on her shoulder.

Madison had a new secret craving.

TRACE SHUT OFF THE SHOWER FOR THE SECOND TIME. HE SMILED remembering the first shower. Water had never looked so good running down a body as it did Madison's.

Toweling off, he pulled on a fresh pair of jeans and walked barefoot to Madison's room. She was still asleep, curled around his pillow. Correction: her pillow that he had slept on. That is, when they slept.

When had he started thinking of things as his? Had he really forgotten that this was a job? He frowned and went back to his room to finish dressing, then down for some coffee.

Carol had been up for a while and handed him the mug he had come to think of as his own and frowned again. He was way too comfortable to do his job. He had to back off or it could cost Madison her life.

His mind drifted back to her bed and the way her hair fanned out across the pillow. The curve of her backside...

Damn! Trace stalked to the living room, slammed his mug on the table and sat heavily on the sofa. This had to stop. He couldn't protect her this way!

Madison's script caught his attention. He picked it up and thumbed through it. The first two deaths in the pages read like the *accidental* deaths of Madison's friends. But the third death just didn't fit.

Trace carried the script to Jay's office and easing down into the soft, leather chair, rooted around on Jay's desk until he found the information on the latest death. The young woman's name was Annette C. Charles. Didn't Jay say her name was Tina?

Tapping Jay's computer, Trace hit up Google for news articles on this latest mysterious information.

MADISON STRETCHED A LONG TIME BEFORE SHE OPENED HER eyes. Her first thought was of Trace, but he was gone. She bit her lower lip and fought the thought that he had abandoned her. He probably was checking the house, getting something to eat or taking a shower. She grinned at that thought but was cut short by her cell phone ringing.

She grabbed it from her bedside table and checked the caller ID. It was Stanley Stevens. Madison sat up quickly and fumbled to flip the phone open. A few minutes later, she dashed for the shower.

Madison headed for the garden after she dressed. Stanley had said that it was time for the final few scenes of the movie to be shot and he wanted to go over them with her. Of course, Trace wouldn't let her do the final scene herself. A stunt double would in her place. Thinking about it now, she was ok with it.

A sound caught her attention. She turned to see Stanley standing at the entrance. He looked more shaky than normal but Madison didn't think anything about it. She walked towards him in greeting.

"Stanley, thank you so much for coming. I'd love to talk about the end," she began with a smile but it faded as she watched Stanley sink to his knees before falling at her feet.

"Stanley?" Madison dropped next to him and tried to help him sit up. A warm liquid covered her hand and when she pulled it back, she found it coated in blood. She opened her mouth to scream but found it caught in her throat when a knife pressed against her throat.

"Don't make a sound."

CHAPTER TEN

Trace hung up the phone even more puzzled. He had to find Jay. As if on cue, Jay walked in.

"Jay. There's no body."

"Huh?"

"That last murder, Tina... what's her last name?"

"Tina Charles?"

"That's not what is listed on the report. It says Annette."

"Well, her name was Annette Christina Charles, but she always went by Tina. She didn't like her first name. It was too 60-ish. You know, Franki and Annette."

Trace frowned. "What about the body? You said there was a murder."

"No, the stalker said he murdered Tina. I'm waiting to hear back from the police to confirm."

Trace rose with a growl. "We let Madison think her friend was dead without confirming?" He paced, rolling the script hard in his hands.

Jay took the spot Trace vacated and began searching the internet for more information. He jumped when Trace slammed the script down on the desk.

"Who wrote this trash anyway?"

"Anita Carlos. It's one of those books that just quietly crept up on the public. She's also the one who turned it into a screenplay and submitted it to Stanley Stevens. Odd he's never met her." Jay shrugged. A cold chill race down Trace's spine. He rose, intending to check on Madison when a scream broke the quiet calm.

Trace raced out of Jay's office, heading for Madison's room when he nearly collided with Carol. She was white as a ghost.

"What's wrong?" he demanded and slipped easily back into his role as bodyguard instead of house guest.

"A body," she said, her voice shook faster than her hands. "In the garden."

"Madison," Trace breathed, his heart clenched tighter than his fist. God, not Madison.

"No, it's that director, Mr. Stevens."

Trace's head snapped towards the direction of the stairs and he was raced towards them, up two and three at a time. He pulled out his gun and kicked open Madison's door.

Silence filled the room. Keen eyes scanned her bed, then the opened closet door before landing on the bathroom door. She wasn't there. He moved quickly to his room through the adjoining door but found it empty, too. He didn't waste time searching the other rooms. He knew instinctively she was gone.

Trace headed back downstairs and barked out orders to Jay and Carol, then demanded to see the head of security.

"Mr. Steven's and his driver were the only ones. They came in by limousine about 15 minutes ago, then left a few minutes later."

Trace could have choked the man. "You're fired." He looked at the other two guards and his blood began to boil. "You're all fucking fired!" They left before he gave them more than just a verbal beating.

Trace went out to the garden and inspected the body, being careful not to disturb any evidence that might be around. They had to keep this quiet for Madison's safety.

He stared for a long time at the body, then his clothing before checking his pockets. Inside, he found a piece of paper with the name Anita written on it. He assumed that was the author of that script. Oddly, the first four letters were circled. He took it into Jay.

"I have no idea, Trace," Jay replied and handed it back to Trace.

Trace felt the breath leave his body as he looked at the back of the paper. He snatched it from Jay and held it up to the light, looking at the name from the back of the paper.

"A, Tina. Anita."

"I don't understand, Trace."

"We've been looking for a guy, but it's a woman. More specifically, Madison's supposedly dead friend, Tina."

Trace showed Jay the name on the paper the way he saw it. "And Carlos is Spanish for Charles."

Jay sat down stunned. "My God. Madison's friend?"

"Where is the final shoot supposed to be?"

"The roof top of a local high school."

Trace shook his head. "That's too easy," he began, then stood quickly. "Where did they graduate from high school?"

"Eastland High School in LA, why?"

Trace ran from Jay's office. Within moments, he was on his Harley and riding hard for the high school. For Madison.

"Tina, please. Let me go. We can work this out," Madison said, trying hard to not sound as scared as she was.

She couldn't believe Tina was alive. That voice had told her she was dead, yet here she was, waving a knife at her, backing her closer and closer to the edge of the roof. The script flashed in her mind. This was the end except there were no safety lines or large net to catch her if she fell. The stunt she fought Trace so hard to do.

Madison wished that Trace would stop this unscheduled stunt. This was no longer just practice or a movie. This was real.

"Shut up, Princess Jordan!" Tina looked around wildly before thrusting the knife toward Madison again. "Move!"

Madison backed up slowly, looking around for anything that might help stop this madness.

"The very least you could do is tell me why!" Madison demanded. What else did she have to lose?

"Why? You want to know why?" Tina screeched loudly and waved the knife in Madison's face. "I can't believe you have to ask why, considering what you did to me!"

Madison was confused. Tina was one of her best friends. They never had a misunderstanding throughout high school. "I'm sorry, Tina, I don't know what you're talking about. We've used to be friends."

"We used to be best friends!"

"That's right, best friends. So why are you doing this? What did I do to you?"

Tina went quiet and let her arm drop to her side. She looked up to Madison with tear filled eyes. "You left me behind."

Tina's statement shocked Madison. Tina had been the most popular one in high school. Head cheerleader. Class President. Class valedictorian. She had it all. So why was she this distraught over Madison?

"I don't understand. Is this about my career? It's been luck all the way."

"No, it's not that. It's you. Your life. You had a mother that loved you. People loved you!"

"Tina, you were the most popular person in school. How could you not think that people didn't care about you?"

"I bought it all, Maddie," Tina spit with contempt and used Madison's nick name from high school. "But I couldn't buy my parent's love. You had it naturally. You had it all. Remember our last lunch? We were still in our cap and gown. You said we'd be friends forever."

"I remember."

"Then where did you go? You became the famous Madison Jordan and didn't look back."

"I tried..." Madison began but Tina cut her off.

"Not hard enough!" Madison watched as Tina raised the knife

again and started toward her. "Not...hard...enough," Tina whispered and raised the knife for a downward swing. Madison screamed.

"Freeze!"

Both women turned towards the sound of the commanding, male voice. Madison took a step to run to Trace but he held out his hand for her to stay where she was.

She tried to look for him as he stalked towards them like prey, clinging to the shadows. The only evidence of him being there was the click of his boot heels, the sound of his voice and the flash of his gun in the light as he moved from shadow to shadow.

"I'll kill her," Tina said through clenched teeth.

"I'll kill you first," Trace replied.

Madison could hear his voice moving closer. She was at peace. Trace was here now. She would be alright.

A hand closed over her arm then, hard and cruel, but only for a moment. A shot rang out and the offending grip was removed. She heard Tina's screams mixed with Trace's voice telling her to get down.

Madison dropped to the ground and covered her head. Tina fell on her and grabbed a handful of her hair while her arm lifted high, gripping the knife before she screeched. "Die!"

Another shot rang out, and it was over. Madison kept her eyes squeezed shut and was startled when a hand touched her shoulder.

"Madison?"

Trace's voice washed over her like a warm, protective glove. Though she was drained of strength, she found enough to rise up into his waiting arms.

"I've got you. You're safe now."

Madison knew that, but that didn't stop the hot rush of tears that spilled down her cheeks. Trace's arms tightened around her. He lifted her up and carried her several feet away from Tina's body before sitting down with Madison on his lap.

Madison was soothed by the gentle rocking motion of Trace's strong body. She had never felt so protected, so loved. Now that this problem had been solved, how could she ever let him go?

"Thanks, we'll stay here on the roof and wait for you." Madison listened as Trace finished up his call and returned his other arm around her. She couldn't stop her eyes from straying to the other side of the roof where Tina's body was. Her stomach lurched and within moments, she was emptying its contents.

She couldn't be bothered to be embarrassed since she'd already had this scene with him. At the moment, she just wanted to stay in the safety of Trace's arms. Funny how she'd always found her safety within the walls of her closet next to her old friend, the secret stash of chocolate. Now her comfort came in the embrace of a surly biker with a bad habit of not using a door knob to enter a room. She almost laughed.

He dug into his pocket and fished out a peppermint candy. She took it but kept her head down for a few more minutes before she had the strength to face him. "All better?"

Madison nodded her head against Trace's chest and pulled back to look at him. "I was just thinking that surely this pays off the door you kicked in a few weeks ago," she began before finishing her comment quietly. "Guess you'll be on your way in the next day or so."

"Well, not exactly," he began, then told her about her bedroom door that contained one large boot print, along with a large crack suspiciously where the boot print was. She did laugh then.

"You don't have to keep breaking down my doors to stay."

"Yeah, well I also fired the whole security staff too."

"You did what?"

He shrugged. She laughed.

"I'll stay until you don't need me any longer."

"Guess you'll be staying around a long time then."

Trace looked surprised, and for once, speechless. Madison congratulated herself and continued.

"I was thinking that maybe you could head the security team."

He looked gloomy. "I'm not really long term bodyguard material."

"Are you long term husband material?"

Again with the speechless and surprised look. She had to remember to write this day down in her journal.

"I love you, Trace. I can't imagine my life without you."

"Madison," he began. "I don't know what to say."

Three times! She nearly cheered. Instead, she raised her hand up and placed it on his chest over his heart. "Why not tell me what's in here. It might help."

Madison gave him a smile.

"I'm not a feelings-sharing kinda guy either," he began. Madison's heart sank but she kept the smile pasted on her lips anyway. He cared for her, she was sure of that but he probably didn't love her. She squelched that familiar twinge of rejection and the need to console it with something chocolaty. She wouldn't though. It was time for her to grow up and deal with life's disappointments in a different way.

"However," he continued. Madison's spirits lifted and the smile became genuine. It also began to hurt to smile so wide.

"Aww, the hell with it. I love you too, Madison." Trace kissed her nose gently. "But," he said and paused. Madison looked at him confused.

"But what?" The sound of sirens began to fill the air. Red lights from arriving police cars flickered off the windows of the building across from them, casting a soft glow on his face. He was smiling.

"I'll be doing the marriage proposals around here."

"Boy, you're bossy."

He nodded at her. "Get used to it," he said with a wink, then kissed her once again.

UNDER HIS PROTECTION

Pregnant and running for her life, she's now...

Under His Protection

Tabitha Gibson

<hr>

CHAPTER ONE

<hr>

Alexander "Lex" Cameron's temper burned hotter than the rubber left on the pavement by his classic Harley. He'd never left a tire mark unless he had no choice. Tires cost too damn much to flex his masculinity against a bunch of cheese-heads.

In this case, he jammed on the breaks to stop from plowing into the woman who ran out in front of him. He hoped she smelled better than the rubber assaulting his senses right now.

And she better have a damn good reason for risking not only her life, but his.

Flicking the kickstand down with his booted heel, he pulled off the black helmet and wiped the sweat from his forehead. He hated wearing the damn thing but it made his mother feel better and since he was on his way to see her, why not score a few brownie points?

Lex stepped over the body of his chrome hog and shifted his head back and forth to work out a kink in his neck then stared down at the slip of a girl that didn't look more panicked about almost being run her over. He frowned.

"Are you crazy? I could have seriously hurt you."

She didn't answer him. Instead, she kept pushing up on her toes to look over his shoulder toward the tree line. Lex turned his head and followed her gaze but saw nothing. Still, he felt his heart beat a little bit faster and his blood begin to pump a little bit harder. Never a good sign for just a jaywalker.

"You need a lift or something?" He hoped she would say no and go about her business but she nodded wordlessly and held a small, dirty hand out to him. Again he frowned.

"Well, let's get going," he said and stepping easily over the chrome monster, hauled her up behind him. She shifted a backpack over her shoulder he hadn't noticed before.

He started to put the helmet on but handed it to her instead. "I think you should probably wear this."

She took one last look toward the tree line before putting the helmet on. She placed her hands on his shoulders, trying to hold her body away from his.

"Yeah that's not gonna work, honey," he said and taking her hands, slid them down to his waist. "Slide closer and hold tight. I gotta make one stop then I'll drop you off wherever you need to go."

He felt her nod against his back and shook his head. *This one's trouble.* He could just feel it. He'd be better off to drop her off first but he was already late. He'd make a quick stop at his parents then he'd get rid of the bad feeling in the shape of the female wrapped around his waist.

With the turn of the key, the engine once again roared to life. He gunned the motor causing his passenger to jolt at the sound. He grinned for a moment but didn't take further enjoyment at frightening her. Whatever she seemed to be running from had that covered.

Flicking the stand back up, he gunned the engine again and the cycle took off smoothly down the road.

～

"Well, where is she?"

"I'm sorry, sir. She got away."

"Three highly trained mercenaries like yourselves couldn't find one little girl? Do you know what she could do to me?"

The man's voice thundered across the room, followed by a crystal glass that shattered against the wall just a few feet from the messenger's head.

"We'll find her. We caught sight of her on a motorcycle leaving the area along with a partial plate. It shouldn't be too hard to track."

"Then why are you still here? Find her, now!"

LEX ROLLED UP TO THE FRONT DOOR OF A LARGE HOUSE. NOT quite the mansion his buddy Trace lived in now, but his family was quite comfortable with their life style. He shut off the motor and helped the girl down before setting the bike on its stand and dismounting himself.

He wondered all the way here what he would tell his mother about this bit of baggage. It didn't matter really. Within an hour she would be on her way to wherever it was she needed to be. Still, her body hugging tightly to his stirred something in him, things he shouldn't consider with a troubled stranger.

Her small frame held surprisingly large breasts and he felt them every mile from where he'd picked her up. Damn he needed one hot night and one hot woman to ease his rising adore. The sooner he got rid of this one, the sooner he could do just that.

"Come on," he said and walked toward the door before he realized she wasn't following. "This is my parent's home. You'll be fine here until we can get you on your way."

She tugged off the helmet, lowered her head with a nod and started to follow him when the door opened. Oddly, she ducked behind him and clutched her backpack in front of her.

"Lex! I was starting to worry."

The woman that came out with open arms hugged him tightly. He smiled and returned the affection. He loved his mother beyond all reasoning. Having nearly lost her a year ago to cancer, he came to realize how very precious life can be and to cherish it and those that were important to him.

"Sorry I'm late. I had an unplanned stop..." he began but his mother interrupted him.

"So I see," she said and gave him a withering look. He dropped his head.

Judith Cameron pushed Lex to the side and held her hand out to the tag-a-long trying to duck behind him again, but his mother was persistent.

"You poor thing! Having to ride on that dreadful bicycle. At least you had the good sense to wear a helmet," Judith said, taking it from the quiet woman and stuffing it in Lex's stomach with surprising force.

"Hey, wait a minute," Lex began but found himself talking to the retreating forms of the two women. He half chuckled and hooked the helmet onto his cycle before following them inside. "Pop, you here?"

"Lex, really, must you bellow? You scared our guest," Judith chided and steered her toward the stairs.

"She's not staying, Ma. I just wanted to stop here first because I was late. I'll be dropping her off at her final destination as soon as she tells me where she wants to go," Lex explained and snagged the newspaper lying on the foyer table.

"Well, your father is on his way home. I'll take," Judith began then frowned. "I'm sorry, where are my manners. My name is Judith Cameron. And you are?"

The woman kept her head lowered but spoke in a low tone to his mother.

"Lovely name, my dear. Come on, let's get you cleaned up before you have to get going. Perhaps some rest. Maybe you could join us for dinner?"

"Ma," Lex began, but was waved off dismissively as the two women walked upstairs.

"Well, what the hell is her name?" Lex asked out loud to an empty room before he shrugged and headed for his father's study.

~

VALENTINA GARRETT ALLOWED HERSELF A MOMENT OF relaxation, one tiny minute of freedom from the fear of the past few months of her life. Soon she would have to start looking over her shoulder and running for her life again.

She closed her eyes for a few seconds then opened them again to make sure her bag was still on the bench in front of the massive vanity. Her body screamed for more relaxation and rest but she couldn't. Not yet. Once she got downtown she could check into a motel under a false name and maybe, just maybe, get a long night of sleep before trying to figure out the rest of her life.

Tina glanced around the bathroom again. She swore it was bigger than her last studio apartment. How easy it would be to just soak up the luxury of this place she thought. Sighing, she stepped out of the claw-foot bathtub.

Taking the towel off of the curved holder, she found it warmed as if it were fresh out of a dryer. Hurriedly, she wrapped it around her body. It wrapped around her almost twice. She frowned, but inhaling the fresh linen scent deeply, she sighed. She hadn't been this pampered in a very long time.

Tina almost smiled at the memory that first brought her to California. Fresh out of college, she graduated at the top of her business class with honors but her passion was designing clothing. With her best friend, Carrie Callaghan, they spent all summer furiously sketching a collection they had long dreamed about. They giggled as they sent out samples to a few companies and some well-known designers hoping for an internship. That's when they met Marco Quinn.

Marco had invited them out to the west coast with whispers of success and promises of their dreams to come true. Within weeks, Marco had swept Tina off her feet and into his bed.

Cassie had voiced concerns to Tina about his failed promises but Tina had ignored them. Sooner or later their success would come. After all, Marco was a true gentleman in every sense of the word. Wasn't he?

Tina closed her eyes, fighting the burn of tears and hurriedly dried off. She pulled out her last clean pair of jeans and struggled with the button before it finally closed. She tugged on the threadbare tee shirt then covered it with a hooded sweat shirt.

She had to get out of here and some place safe. It wasn't just about her anymore and it wasn't fair to these innocent people to get caught up in her drama. Marco was a dangerous man. She was pretty sure the biker could handle himself but what if he wasn't around and his mother was hurt.

Tina couldn't bear the thought of that but it wouldn't surprise her if Marco did something so vile.

Tina tiptoed down the stairs, pausing at the raised voices behind the closed door. She closed her eyes and fought against begging them to stop. She wasn't worth it.

Clenching her jaw, she eased open the front door and took off toward the first car she saw. The convertible's top was down so she tossed her bag in and started looking for spare keys in the glove box, under the seat and above the visor.

Well, of course no one in their right mind would leave car keys in their car.

Tina opened the door wide and kneeled down, reaching under the dash near the gas petal for wires. *I can do this*, she thought. *Just cross two wires and poof, instant start right?*

A jingling set of keys sounded above her and she turned to see an older man, his brows raised dangling keys above her head.

"I'd rather just give you the keys so I don't have to pay for repairs in a failed hot-wiring attempt," he said with a kind smile.

Tina felt instantly horrible. She blushed madly and accepted his hand to help her stand.

"I think we should go on in and talk about this, eh?" He stepped back and motioned her forward. "After you."

LEX WAS SURPRISED WHEN HIS MOTHER PUSHED HIS FEET OFF OF his father's desk to the floor. "You know better."

"Sorry, Ma," he said, brushing off the bits of gravel left on the cherry's shiny finish.

"I'm not talking about that," she said dismissively and began to pace. Lex frowned.

"What's wrong?"

"What's wrong? Seriously? We've talked about this before, Alexander."

Lex stood quickly. His mother never addressed him with his full name unless he had really screwed the pooch. Oh God, did she hear about the naked surfing he did last weekend? His face began to warm and despite the good foot he had over his mother's height, he slunk down on the leather sofa across from the desk.

"I'm sorry, Ma, I didn't mean for you to find out about it."

"How did you expect to hide something like this? It's not like it won't be really obvious soon enough."

Lex's mind raced to who was with him and who ratted him out. There'd be an ass kicking to be dealt out later.

"It's no big deal. Just having fun."

Judith crossed the room and slapped him on the back of his shaved head.

"Ow! What did you do that for?"

"Fun? Do you have any idea what you've done? How could you be so irresponsible?"

"Ma, we didn't take pictures."

"Pictures! Oh Alexander, what is going on with you?"

"That's what I'd like to know," a strong male voice called out. Lex turned to see his father in the doorway, subtly urging his unexpected hitch hiker in with him. Lex stood quickly.

"Pop?"

"Caught this bit of baggage trying to hot-wire my convertible," he said, and nudged the sullen girl toward Lex.

"Hot-wiring?" Lex glared down at her. "Is this how you repay me?"

"Alexander Cameron! You mind your manners."

Lex snapped his mouth shut but continued to glare down at the girl, who surprisingly glared right back up at him. Then, he blinked.

The bath had done her good. She was freshly scrubbed and to his surprise, rather pretty. Still, hot-wiring? He shifted the glare to a frown.

Adam Cameron sat down in the chair behind the desk and lifted up the business section of the paper. It's what he always did when there was a situation he didn't want to deal with. Lex couldn't blame him though. It's not often you come home to find someone trying to steal your car.

"Well?"

Lex shifted his frown from the girl to his mother, softening at the look of concern on her face. "I'm sorry?" He was confused by what she wanted. "Well, what?"

"I said I hope you plan to do the right thing here, Lex."

"Of course I will, Ma," he promised and gave her a hug.

"I knew you would," she said and turned to her husband. "Adam, call Father Diebel. He can perform the ceremony tonight."

Lex quirked his brow. Damn, he was going to have confession right here at the house? He knew he should have made excuses and visited in a month or something.

Uncharacteristically, his father put the paper down and looked at Lex. "You sure about this, son?"

"If it will make Ma happy, yeah."

"What about her?" his father said and motioned to his hitch hiker who was trying to inch toward the door. Lex reached out and grabbed her arm, pulling her back into the room. He nudged her toward the couch.

"I'll drop her off at a women's shelter or wherever and be back in a flash," he began but was cut off by his mother's shriek.

"You will do no such thing. How are you supposed to marry her if she's not here?"

Lex's jaw dropped open while his equally surprised guest stood up, both their voices speaking out in shocked unison.

"Married?"

CHAPTER TWO

Tina clamped her mouth shut as the biker she caught a ride with, Lex was his name, argued with his mother. She felt the older man's eyes on her and reluctantly looked his way. They were kind eyes and he motioned with his head for her to follow him. She didn't hesitate.

He led Tina to the kitchen and started pulling out items to make a sandwich.

"Ham or turkey?"

"Turkey, please," she said and her stomach growled. Tina blushed in embarrassment. She supposed it was the fear that had been squelching her hunger before. She set her bag down on the counter and took a seat on the cushioned stool.

"My name is Adam Cameron," the older gentleman said, easing around the kitchen to get plates for the sandwiches. "Mayo?"

Tina nodded silently.

Adam passed her a plate with a large turkey sandwich on it and smiled. "Here you go..." he stopped, his eyebrows rising in wait for her to tell him her name.

"Tina." It was a common enough name wasn't it? She could have kicked herself for telling his mom her full name but nothing could be done about it now. She would eat, then try to get the hell out of this house before that surly biker came back.

And before his mother tried to marry her off to him.

"Thanks," she said and took a huge bite of the delicious concoction Adam had put together. Onion, a white cheese, crisp lettuce and fresh tomato accompanied the thick turkey slices between a hardy wheat bread. It was heaven.

Adam took a bite of his own sandwich and turned to get out a pitcher of lemonade. Returning to the cabinet that held the plates, he got out two glasses and poured a glass for her. Smiling, he slid it across the countertop.

"So, when are you due?"

Tina nearly choked on the bite she had been chewing. Wildly, her eyes darted up to his and she swore he had a twinkle in his own. Struggling to swallow the now, seemingly dry bread, she took a long drink of the lemonade and knew that he had planned that just right.

"Due?" Her voice squeaked and she took another drink.

"Yeah, you are pregnant with my grandchild, aren't you?"

This time, she choked on the lemonade. "This is not his child," she began but snapped her mouth shut. Too late. She had just confirmed his query. Could this day get any worse?

"Ah, I didn't think so. But you are pregnant and are in some kind of trouble. All the signs are there."

He was very nonchalant as he spoke and ate his oversized sandwich. He also was right. Tina was in trouble. Very serious trouble.

"I'm sorry. I don't mean to bring my problems to your doorstep," Tina said and pushed the half eaten sandwich away. Adam pushed it back.

"The other half is for the baby," he said with a gentle smile. Tina nodded and kept eating.

"Don't you worry about whatever is bothering you. My son will fix it. That's his job."

"I don't think there's a fix for this," she said, and finished off her lemonade.

She was startled when Adam patted her hand. "You don't know my son very well... yet."

Yet? That sounded ominous.

Adam hummed as he cleaned up the dishes and sandwich fixings. Everything was so normal. Calm. Nothing compared to the raging argument she had last night with Marco. It had taken her hours to calm her racing heart and the knotting in her stomach. She feared she would miscarry at this rate. It was what prompted her to take the first chance she could to run.

Being let out for a shower gave her that chance, sooner rather than later, to try to escape. As to not draw suspicion, she could only take in her backpack that carried a change of clothing. That is what she escaped with, along with her sketch pad she stuffed in at the last second. This sketch pad had drawings that Marco hadn't seen yet. These were not only drawings of a new line of gowns but her old drawings that would prove that she, not Marco, had created the last three collections of evening wear that he claimed publicly were his.

Tina knew that doing so would humiliate him, labeling him as a fraud. It was this very thing that cost Carrie her life.

But there was more on the line than just Tina's desire to become a famous designer, or even her own life, but that of her child.

Marco's child.

She was terrified of him finding out about the baby. He would surely keep her locked up until it was born then take the baby away. After that, she dreaded what he would do to her.

Tina couldn't think of that right now. She had to make sure that she was safe so her baby would be safe. She would do anything to make that happen.

"Tina?"

"Huh? Sorry. Just lost in my thoughts."

"So I see. Come on, let's see what's left of my study," Adam winked and helped her off the stool.

They wandered quietly back and stood just outside the door and listened.

"Lex, you have to do the right thing."

"I said I would, but that baby isn't mine."

"How do you know?"

"Ma! For one, I use protection. For two, I've never," he began covering his face with his hands. "God, I am not having this conversation with my mother."

"Don't blasphemy! And the right thing would be to make sure she was protected and despite your job, there are other kinds of security you could offer. Like a stable home and husband."

"What makes you think she would even marry me?"

Tina's heart hammered hard again and without thinking, she walked right into the conversation. "I will."

Lex turned and looked at her. "You will what?"

"I will marry you."

LEX PUT HIS FOOT DOWN AND REFUSED, BUT DID AGREE TO TRY TO help her. Not that he wouldn't have. That's what he did. Helped people. But she wasn't the only one to consider. There was also her baby. Until then, she would stay with his parents.

His mother fussed over her the first day and Lex, sensing her unease, talked his father into taking a long weekend up the coast. Lex had brought a few things with him from home and stored them in the bedroom his parents still kept for him.

The scent of oregano and tomato sauce drew his attention. He headed downstairs and found his fiancée in the kitchen cooking. He watched her quietly for a while.

Fiancée? How the hell did he get himself into this situation? *Soft-hearted sucker.* You'd never know it though, his looks were very deceiving.

Her soft humming drew his attention back to her. She was stirring the sauce while he heard the distinct sounds of water boiling. Setting the spoon on the counter top, she turned and picked up the box of pasta. Seeing him standing there Tina gave a gasp and dropped it.

Lex's reflexes were good and he caught the box, handing it back to her.

"Sorry." They both said at the same time, then both gave a short, nervous laugh.

"I didn't mean to startle you," Lex offered, then motioned to the stove. "Smells good."

"Thanks," she murmured and turned her attention back to the stove.

Within thirty minutes, they were eating. He enjoyed the Italian meal thoroughly in spite of the silence.

Surreptitiously, he watched her while she ate. It had taken a few days for her to relax around him when they ate or was even in the same room together, which wasn't often. She had kept to herself for the most part which made getting information out of her hard.

She also stopped wolfing down her meals like he was going to take the food away from her. He frowned. Is that what had happened to her? How could anyone deny a pregnant woman food?

"Is something wrong with your dinner?"

Lex lifted his eyes to meet hers. She almost looked scared. He softened his features and shook his head. "Sorry, I was just thinking how you have finally stopped inhaling your dinner like I would take it away."

He smiled in jest but instantly regretted his choice of words. Tina was biting her lower lip and set her fork down.

"Oh, I didn't mean anything by that," Lex said, his voice gentle. "Please, finish your dinner."

She hesitated before retrieving the fork and resumed eating. Lex noticed that her speed had increased and he fumed inwardly, but was careful to keep his expression calm.

She had looked thin when he first saw her. Too thin for someone expecting a baby in his opinion. Of course, he was basing his knowledge off of his sister's current pregnancy. Jennifer was happily married and expecting a baby and looked like it, too.

Tina, however, was way too thin and looked like she could use several more hours of sleep every day. Even when she had gotten up late in the mornings, she still looked tired. He made a mental note to ask Jennifer specifics about the whole pregnancy thing.

In the meantime, he had some other things to catch up on work wise. He had let them slip while trying to find out what he could about Tina Garrett, but it was like the preverbal needle in a haystack. No missing person reports. No family that he could define, unless you counted the thousands of Garretts that came up on just a generic search.

Maybe he had a wrong spelling of her name? Christina or maybe it was without the H or maybe her name started with a K. Time to put his skills to work.

Lex helped her clear the table and as she was stacking the dishwasher, he struck up a conversation.

"So, will it be a boy or a girl?"

Tina stopped mid rinse of her plate. He swore she almost tensed so he grabbed the dish cloth and moved to clean up the stove from the few dots of sauce that had popped out when it began to bubble.

"Not sure."

Lex sighed to himself. This was what teeth pulling must be like, having heard the phrase throughout his whole life. Lex never had problems getting information before. Then again, the type of people he dealt with usually were too intimidated by his very appearance and didn't want to anger him by dancing around questions he asked.

"Oh, so I guess you wouldn't have names picked out then," he continued, trying to keep the conversation light.

"Not yet," she agreed and swirled water around their glasses before putting them in the top rack.

"I suppose it's tradition to name boys after fathers and add on Junior or "the third" or something like that," Lex said, having tossed the towel to the side and leaned against the counter. He made quotes with his fingers when he said the third. "Kind of a stuffy tradition if you ask me. Our family has the tradition of boy's names that start with A, which isn't so bad."

Tina nodded, squeezing soap into the little compartment and closing it before lifting the door and locking it into place.

"Girls aren't normally named after their mothers, are they?"

Tina pressed the wash button and turned the water back on to wash her hands. "Not normally. Perhaps in other countries it's more of a tradition."

She shook the excess water from her hands and picked up the towel Lex had discarded, drying them.

"So I suppose Christina is out then? I mean, we could hardly call her Junior, could we?" He smiled and gave a little laugh.

"Actually, we could get away with calling her Christina. We just couldn't shorten it to Tina. If someone called out Tina, then we would both might answer," she replied with a small smile.

It didn't escape Lex that she hadn't really answered his unspoken question. Time for a more stealthy verbal approach.

"I suppose so. Still, it would be odd to have two Christina's, you and the baby if it is indeed a girl. Maybe two different spellings?"

Tina tilted her head and looked confused. "My name isn't Christina."

"Oh, I'm sorry. I just assumed Tina was short for Christina," he said and when she said nothing else, he went for the direct approach.

"What is your full, first name then?"

"Valentina," she said and excused herself for the evening.

Valentina?

Tina paced the bedroom that evening. Things were getting too complicated. She was sure the conversation with Lex earlier was him fishing for information yet again. Now he had her full first name. It wouldn't be hard to track down her family and she didn't want that. They were safer not knowing what was going on and coming to her rescue.

What if they did and confronted Marco? What would he do to them? It scared her more than she wanted to admit. She should have called them immediately when she had come here but she didn't. It had been her impulsive decisions that had gotten her into this mess to start with. Now that she had escaped Marco and was safe, she swore that she would stop and think from now on. She had to consider all decisions before acting in the future and bringing her parents into this mess. They were safer that way.

Safe. That was the key word to her sanity at the moment. Despite that her leather-wearing, Harley-riding savior looked like a Hells Angel, he was more like an angel from Heaven.

Of course, he was good-looking but he was also a gentleman. No, she hadn't shared her story with him yet but not out of not trusting him. He could have betrayed her at any time over the past week and hadn't. He and his family had done more for her than anyone in her situation could have dreamed of without making any demands on her. Maybe she should go that extra step and tell him what was going on.

Tina felt more tense than ever and decided on a late night bath. Checking to make sure her door was locked, she kicked off the sandals that Judith had bought for her and padded barefoot into the private bathroom.

Several minutes later, she lowered into the hot water, leaned her head back against the tub pillow and closed her eyes. Having sprinkled lavender bath salts in the steaming bath, the scent went a long way in helping her to relax.

Her thoughts drifted back to Lex. Now that he had her name, would he do a full investigation and draw out her parents? She cursed her stupidity at revealing such important information. She should just come clean and beg him to leave them out of it. Maybe he would help her forge a new identity and smuggle her to another state or better yet, another country.

The water began to cool and though she didn't want to, she rose out of the water and toweled dry. She slipped on the silk pajamas, another loan from Judith, bless her and climbed into bed.

When she closed her eyes, visions of Marco sneering at her and raising his fist haunted her, causing her eyes to snap open and her breath to come out harsh and fast.

This nightmarish ritual seemed to happen every night. She hated to think would be a permanent part of her life. She started forcing herself to stay awake until she fell into an exhausted, dreamless sleep.

Lex invaded her thoughts once again. He and his family were in just as much danger as her own family. It was just best to not say anything and encourage him to get her as far away from California as she possibly could.

Yawning, she was grateful when sleep finally claimed her. Blissful, dreamless sleep.

∾

LEX FINISHED THE PAPERWORK NEEDED TO COMPLETE THE JOB. HE hadn't taken any other jobs in the past week since Tina had come into his life. Not that he needed the money; it was the sense of accomplishment that fueled him. He prided himself on keeping both buildings and computer systems safe from petty criminals and hackers.

He loaded the paperwork into his briefcase and opted for his jeep instead of the Harley. It looked like rain and he didn't want to chance either the paperwork or his baby getting drenched.

Baby. His thoughts drifted back to a few days ago when Tina had finally divulged her full first name.

Valentina. It really was a beautiful name and fit its beautiful owner. He hadn't run a check on her with the updated information yet. He hadn't really had the time.

His parents had returned earlier than he thought they would. Lex stuck around the house to make sure his sweet mother didn't drive Tina crazy with questions about what had brought her to their door.

Today was different, however, and Lex had to leave for a few hours. Just two more stops and he would head back.

He spent a few minutes with this client. He could finish up the security system the following week when the part he ordered came in. Shaking hands, he headed back to his jeep, stopping to fish out his cell phone and check message when the paper stapled to the wooden light pole caught his eye.

He frowned, feeling his heart tighten in his chest while he focused on the photo-copied photograph.

He recognized Tina immediately, despite the age of the photograph. She had longer hair, fuller cheeks and a smile. The words above made his blood run cold.

Missing:
Please contact if you've seen this woman.
Dead or Alive.

There was a number below but Lex couldn't chance calling it with his personal cell phone. He ripped the paper down and folding it up, stuffed it in his pocket.

Lex never made it to his second stop. He gunned the gas pedal and made a beeline straight for his parents' home.

TINA SMILED AT JUDITH WHO HAD OFFERED TO TAKE HER shopping the following day.

"Not that I mind loaning you clothing but I'm betting you'll be more comfortable with your own things," she had said.

"I'll pay you back as soon as I can," Tina promised.

"Don't be silly!" Judith had chided her. "My girls are grown up and I have no one to shop for anymore. Not that you are a child, mind you. I like to consider it a blank canvass that we can fill with many beautiful things."

Tina sipped tea from the delicate cup, setting it back on the matching saucer. She loved this time with Judith. It reminded her of monthly visits with her own mother. They would have tea and splurge on icing topped cupcakes and sigh about their dream vacations, gowns at the latest award event and purses. Her mother had a fetish for purses.

"On my dime," Adam said from behind a raised newspaper, his voice filled with dry humor.

"Your dime? Try your dollar," Judith said and both she and Tina giggled.

The front door banged, startling them and within seconds, Lex strode in right up to Tina and stopped. He looked fierce, angry to the point she nearly dropped her tea cup and saucer.

"For heaven's sake, Alexander," Judith had begun but he held up his hand to silence her.

Adam lowered his paper, folded it and rose, a slight frown on his lips. "What's wrong, Son?"

"It's time."

Tina was confused. What was time? She set her cup and saucer on the table next to her and began to pick at her nails. Oh god. He had done the investigation and wanted answers about Marco.

"Lex, I…" Tina began, glad she had set her tea down. Her hands were shaking badly.

Judith rose but again, Lex held up his hand for her to not speak. This brought Adam to his feet.

"Alexander, you really need to start explaining yourself."

Tina recognized a strict but fatherly tone and leaving the two women speechless. Lex took a piece of paper from his pocket, unfolded it and showed it to Adam.

Tina watched his expression carefully, wincing as the frown deepened. Adam then nodded and motioned Judith to him and showed her the paper. Judith's eyes widened and her hand rose to her open mouth to cover the gasp.

Tina's heart began to beat wildly. What had Lex found out about her? She couldn't bear the looks on the faces of Adam and Judith. They had been so kind to her and now, she was disappointing them but how?

Lex took the paper from his father and walked up to Tina. It took her a full minute to tear her eyes away from his parents and focus on him.

"It's time," he repeated, the paper trembled in his hand before he crushed it.

"Time for what?" Her voice cracked. Time for her to go? What about her baby. She had to protect her baby. She had to make sure her baby was safe.

"Time to get married," Lex said and handed her the paper.

Tina took one look at the paper and collapsed in his arms.

CHAPTER THREE

Lex stood staring out the window of the courthouse. What the hell had just happened these past few weeks? All he wanted was to have dinner with his folks when suddenly he picks up a hitchhiker and is about to marry her?

And why was he doing this? Marrying a complete stranger wasn't his idea of a good plan. Hell, getting married wasn't really in his plans for, well, ever. He had too much fun being single, playing the field, and being able to walk away. So why didn't he walk away from this, what was sure to be the biggest mistake he had ever made in his life?

Lex turned to the woman who would soon become his wife. Short in height, tiny in size, you could barely tell she was even pregnant. With the exception of her slight baby bump and more than generous breast size, she looked like any other woman.

Scratch that. She had a soft face that seemed to glow. Pregnancy glow, wasn't that the term for that? Large, blue eyes that were so expressive he could almost read her thoughts. A small pert nose sat just above a set of very full and very kissable lips. Even without make up, she was very pretty. But did all this make him want to marry her? No, only one thing was making him step up to the plate to take this particular plunge.

He had to keep her and her baby safe.

Lex himself had been adopted by Adam and Judith Cameron. His biological mother had been in and out of trouble with the law, a borderline crack addict and took less than better care of herself throughout her pregnancy. When she gave birth, she had no problem signing over her parental rights to the Cameron's.

He had known most of his life but to him, Adam and Judith were his parents in every way that mattered and counted. Their love was unconditional for a child that needed safety and security and he would do the same for Valentina's.

Lex half smiled at her name. Such a big name for a woman so small. He watched her take another step forward to the clerk who would be issuing them a marriage license. Lex couldn't believe his ears when Tina had said she would marry him. Was she crazy?

His first thought was money. The Cameron's were pretty well to do. Not as rich or even famous as his buddy, Trace's wife-to-be, Madison Jordan. Of course, she was a movie star so there was a big difference there. But there was something different about Tina.

He had found her running away from something, but what? She had tried to hotwire his dad's car when she had gotten to the house then suddenly announces that she would marry a man she had just met an hour earlier? What would possess someone to do that?

The baby.

He also noticed that when she agreed to marry him, her hand was on her stomach in a protective way. That memory stood out to him and was very telling. He had made up his mind after finding the veiled threat in the form of a missing person's flyer. No child would ever be left in danger on his watch.

Lex saw they were next and moved to stand next to her. He watched her nervously tap her fingers against the form they had filled out. Her license was almost expired and beat up pretty bad. He'd have to get her a new one soon which would be a good idea anyway once she had his last name.

How did that thought come out so comfortable?

An hour later, they were on their way back to his parents. His mother had ushered them out of the house to get the needed documents while she took care of everything else. And take care of that she did.

Lex and Tina walked back into a house bustling with activity. Three large vases of flowers on tall pedestals decorated and brightened the normally darker study. Since the living room was being remodeled, his father's sanctuary would just have to do.

"Ready son?" His father's hand slapped on his back.

Lex took in a deep breath and released it with a nod.

"Pop? I, uh, would appreciate it if you stood up with me. Trace and Maddie are out of town at a charity event this evening and considering this is rather last minute, I find myself without my best friend for my best man."

Adam smiled and put his arm around Lex. "I'd be honored to. Let me go get a fresh shirt and tie on that's more appropriate."

"Thanks, Pop," Lex said. His stomach felt strange, as if he actually had butterflies. Maybe food would help, he thought, and spied what he was looking for instantly.

Two platters of vegetables and finger sandwiches sat on the desk, beckoning Lex to taste and he did, only to be rewarded with a hand slap from Judith.

"You, upstairs and shower and change. I refuse to see my son get married wearing jeans and leather. I'll take care of Tina. See you in an hour," she said and escorted his bride to be out of the room.

Lex raised a brow at his mother's change in attitude but said nothing. He shook his head and taking a look around, grabbed another sandwich and ran upstairs.

❧

"You know, you don't have to do this."

Judith's words shocked Tina. Wasn't this her idea?

"I want to," Tina replied and chanced a glance in the mirror at her future mother-in-law. She was eyeing her critically.

"Why?"

That was a very good question. Why the hell was she doing this? This man and his whole family were complete strangers to her and she was putting them in danger by even being in their house.

Tina should just turn, walk right out of the door without looking back. Every nerve ending in her body agreed with that assessment but her brain told her differently and smoothing the dress down over her stomach sealed her decision. Marco was searching for her and she would do anything to keep her baby safe.

"It's best for my child," was all she could manage without breaking down into an emotional wreck. But it was, after all, the truth.

"You know if you just need some money," Judith began but stopped as Tina turned around and half glared at her.

"I don't want your money," Tina huffed before lowering her gaze. "I'm sorry. I don't mean to be rude."

Judith's silence was an uncomfortable break for Tina. She had done nothing but let her fear envelop her to the point she wasn't taking proper care of herself or her unborn child.

A moment later, Judith put her hand on Tina's. She half smiled at her. "We all do what what's best for our children," Judith said and turned for the door.

"I'll see you downstairs."

Tina inhaled deeply and followed her a few minutes later.

Several people introduced themselves to her before the ceremony.

Donald Blackthorn, the family attorney, insisted she sign a prenuptial agreement before their vows were spoken. Lex glanced at her but said nothing.

"Yes," Tina agreed before anyone else spoke and stepped up to take the pen from the lawyer. She signed her name and frowned at how terrible her penmanship was and handing the pen back, noticed how bad her hands were shaking. She would have signed anything as long as it kept her child was safe.

An arm hugged around her waist, drawing her attention. Judith planted a kiss on her cheek and whispered in her ear. "Welcome to the family."

Tina gave Judith a smile and relaxed a little bit. Trust was earned both ways. She had earned quite a bit by signing that legal document but she didn't do it to earn any ones trust. It had been the right thing to do. She'd meant it when she told Judith earlier she didn't want their money.

Judith stood at her side in the role of matron of honor. Tina's heart ached for who should have had been standing next to her on the most important day of her life. But Carrie was gone, murdered by Marco and God only knows how or where her body was.

Hadn't they dreamed and whispered about this as young women? They'd design each other's wedding gown, pick out the most beautiful flowers for their bouquet and taste test every cake they could until they were sick to their stomachs. But that fantasy just wasn't to be.

Within the hour, Tina had said the two words she thought she would never say in her life; two words that would bind her to a complete stranger for the rest of her life, or as long as he would have her.

"I do."

Her voice shook when she spoke. She thought she might have fainted had Lex not been holding her hands in front of the priest. His voice cracked when he spoke his vows, too. She almost laughed that a man his size seemed just as scared as she was. But he had done it and they were husband and wife.

"You may kiss your bride."

Her knees began to knock and she swore she was going to pass out for sure this time but he had put his arms around her and placed a surprisingly gentle kiss on her lips. Tina stared into his eyes and felt a calm flow through her. She was safe. She was finally safe.

Julie Cameron, Lex's younger sister hugged Tina tightly. She had been at work and couldn't get away for the event considering it had been planned within two hours. She arrived in the middle of the ceremony. Still, Julie did the best she could and welcomed Tina into the family.

Lex's older sister, Jennifer, offered her hand in congratulations to Tina as well, rubbing her own stomach. Being a mother of two, she went on and on about her own pregnancies and offered her number should Tina need any advice.

"We never thought this playboy brother of ours would settle down," Jennifer joked while Julie nodded in agreement.

"But considering the circumstances," Julie said, motioning to Tina's slightly rounded stomach. "We understand the need for haste."

"Julie!" Jennifer scolded and Julie smiled sheepishly.

Tina opened her mouth to correct Lex's two sisters but Lex appeared and chastised the two for not calling him in such a long time. She noticed he didn't correct them about him not being the father of her child and wondered why. Maybe it was best that the less people knew the better. She turned away while Lex chatted with his sisters.

Tina watched Adam shaking hands with the priest while passing a wad of cash with the other hand. God, they were all going to hell. A quickie wedding and bribing a priest; this was all her fault. She said a very long prayer and promise to change her ways if her child stayed safe and healthy.

Tina spied the trays of food and made her way over. Several small sandwiches later, she smiled contently and looked at her reflection in the mirror.

The dark circles were still there, just not as prominent. Judith had a silk, off-white summer dress delivered from a local store and though it was a size too big, it fit her just perfect around the waist. Judith had added white roses to her hair which was swept upward into a loose ponytail. Curls escaped and had framed her face.

Who would have thought a year ago when she had come out to California that she would be pregnant, running for her life and suddenly married to a biker?

Lex appeared in the mirror, standing behind her. He put his hand on her shoulder and gave her a gentle massage. "You ok?"

Tina almost cringed at his touch but forced herself to remember that she was safe now. This man was her husband. He had his rights, too.

Oh god, the wedding night.

Tina nodded wordlessly and forced a smile while a whole new set of worries plagued her.

"Good, because it's time for cake," he said with a grin.

They went through the regular wedding rituals of cutting the cake, feeding each other a bite and Adam's best man toast. Thankfully, Adam kept it short and generic but the love for his son was obvious.

Since Julie was the only single female, Tina just handed her the fresh picked roses with a smile. Julie giggled and blushed. "First time I got the bouquet," she admitted.

After a few more pictures, it was time to go. Tina picked at her nails and clutched her worn backpack to her. How would she ride that motorcycle in this dress? But Lex had steered her to the car she had attempted to hot-wire earlier in the day. She flushed furiously and turned to his parents.

"Thank you, so very much for…" she began but didn't know how to finish her statement. Thank you for not turning me out? For not having me arrested for trying to steal your car? For convincing your son to marry me, a total stranger?

Judith squeezed her tightly. "You're family now. Remember that."

Tina nodded wordlessly and turned to Adam. He said nothing, but gave her a gentle hug and kissed her forehead before giving his son a handshake.

Lex opened the car door for her then got in himself. They were spared dragging cans and condoms from the bumper for obvious reasons. Lex started the car and turned to Tina.

"Time to go home," he said.

Yeah, wedding night time.

CHAPTER FOUR

Lex drove home the long way. He needed more time to think. What the hell was he going to do now? This morning he had taken a swim in the ocean and ate cold pizza as a late breakfast. Twelve hours later he was a married man with a baby on the way.

Talk about your extreme lifestyle changes.

But he knew he had done the right thing. Tina and her child were safe as far as he was concerned. He just had to convince her of that now.

Lex had watched her throughout the evening, seeing her eyes dart toward the door every time it opened or closed and flinch at each hand that had touched her arm or shoulder including his own. What the hell had she been through?

He glanced over at his new wife but found her sleeping, still clutching her ratty backpack. Maybe the answer to his questions would find answers within that bag. There were things he had to know if he were to protect her and their child.

Their child?

He frowned at how quickly he began to think of her unborn child as his. But hadn't he agreed to that when he said, I do?

Regardless of the biology of her unborn child, he had made his vows, to protect her and their family, and he planned to follow through with them, no matter what.

A short time later, they arrived at his beach front condo. He nudged her gently and though she stretched slowly at first, her eyes snapped open and she gripped her backpack with white knuckles.

"We're home," he said quietly, not commenting on her sudden fear. They would be addressing that soon enough.

Tina seemed to relax a little and got out of the car. She followed him mutely to the door and inside.

Lex was glad that he had cleaned up. He didn't want Tina to think he was a total slob. Still, his style shined through in the black leather furniture, glass and chrome tables and dark shelves painted black displaying his beloved collection of Harley Davidson memorabilia.

"Welcome home, Tina."

~

WELCOME HOME, INDEED. WHAT A BEAUTIFUL LITTLE HOUSE ON the beach he had. She was surprised at how clean it was. Most single men kind of let themselves go, which included their homes. She was glad to see her husband wasn't one of them.

Her husband.

It was so surreal to her that just a few weeks ago, she had been fighting for her life and now she was a married woman. Thankfully it wasn't to Marco. She couldn't imagine having to spend one more day, let alone the rest of her life with that man.

Tina walked over to the sliding glass door and looked out. She could see the waves rolling gently up the sand then trickling back into the ocean, as if beckoning her to come play with them. But she couldn't. Despite living so near the water, she was terrified of it.

She turned away to find Lex watching her. She bit her lower lip and moved to sit down on the couch. The leather was surprisingly cool and comfortable. She stashed her bag on the floor beside the couch and took a deep breath.

"You have a nice place here," she said, and wrinkled her nose up at her lame attempt in making small talk.

Lex collapsed next to her and pulled off his boots, tossing them over by the door. He leaned back and propped his chin on his fist.

"It's our place now," he reminded her.

"Right," she said and half smiled, trying to cover her nervousness.

"Hey," he said quietly, and reached out to hold her hand.

Tina forced herself to let him and found it not to be as hard as she thought it would be.

"You're safe now, ok? I won't let anyone hurt you again."

A flood of tears rushed down her cheeks, fast and hot. Her whole body shook as she began to sob into her hands. Weeks and months of fear trapped within her seeped from every pour. She felt Lex pull her to him, holding her close to him while his hands rubbed her back gently. She really did feel safe.

It was several moments before she composed herself and with several hiccups, pulled away from him. He rose and walked away from her for a moment only to appear with a bottle of water. She took a few sips and sat back again.

"Do you want to talk about it?"

His question didn't surprise her. But she shook her head no anyway. The pain of losing Carrie, learning she was pregnant and the viciousness of Marco's threat still too fresh in her mind.

"I'll accept that for now, Tina. But at some point you are going to have to trust me."

Tina looked over at him. He was staring intently at her but she didn't see the coldness behind his eyes. Instead, she found compassion and determination within the velvet brown depths, which were framed by strangely long lashes and thick, arched brows.

She studied him further, really seeing him and how attractive he was. His head was shaved and looked very smooth. She was sure that a strong chin was hidden behind a neatly trimmed goatee. His nose was slightly crooked, probably due to being broken a few times but that didn't distract from his looks.

She nodded wordlessly before looking away. He had a right to know. He had a right to keep himself safe too, not just her and her child. She should tell him. She would tell him.

Tomorrow.

They sat in silence for a while. Lex had opened the patio door letting the fresh air and quiet sounds of the waves over her. Hesitantly, she kicked off the soft flat shoes given to her by Judith and propped her feet on the cushion between her and Lex. Within moments, she was asleep.

LEX STUDIED THE SLEEPING FORM OF HIS NEW WIFE. SHE MIGHT have been small in stature but she was strong in spirit. He knew she was something special.

And beautiful.

Her long dark hair, once swept up with flowers at their quickie wedding was now loose and framed her pale face.

Lex frowned at the dark circles that were still prominent under her now closed eyes, despite having been with him and his family for a few weeks. He should have made sure she had been resting more.

Full lips parted as she took a deep breath and her head lolled to the left. She had pierced ears, he could tell but she wasn't wearing any jewelry except the wedding band he put on hours before.

He rose slowly and with great care, lifted Tina in his arms, frowning again at how light she felt. His eyes drifted to her slightly rounding stomach. Tina wasn't the only fighter, he thought and only then did he allow himself a smile.

He carried her to the guest bedroom and laid her down on the bed and covered her with the quilt that was folded neatly at the end of the bed. She curled up in the fetal position, her hand drifting down to rest against her stomach. Lex felt an odd sense of pride swell in his chest.

Taking the time to check the locks on the window, he drew the blinds closed and moved quietly out of the room, pulling the door almost all the way closed. He didn't want her to be in the dark totally if she needed a bathroom break.

Or him.

Lex went back out to the living room, his mind occupied with Tina and whatever has her in the mess she seemed to be in.

Going through his evening ritual, he removed the gun he had hidden behind his back, checked the safety and taking a metal lock box from the closet near the door, stored the weapon out of sight. Kneeling, he lifted his pants leg and pulled out a wicked looking knife that was strapped to his leg, then the holder and once again, stored the weapon but this time, on top of the refrigerator.

Stretching, he rounded the couch to get the water bottle and tripped over Tina's backpack. He glanced toward the bedroom where she lay sleeping and hearing no movement, picked up the bag and sat down.

Lex looked at it for several minutes, noting the slight rips and tears, worn places and how dirty it was. A dark spot near the zipper caught his eye. Was that blood?

Rage flared in him. Who would treat a woman in such a way that they drew blood, let alone one that was pregnant? He wanted to rip open this bag and demand that answers present themselves to him.

But another part of him said to respect her privacy. He had to trust in the fact that Tina would talk to him when she was ready and until then, he would keep her safe.

With a soft grunt, he stood and took the bag to the room Tina slept in, leaving it where she could see it when she woke up and headed to his room.

Stripping down to his boxers, he threw back the covers and lay down, crossing his arms behind his head. It was a long time before sleep came.

~

TINA WOKE UP LATE THE NEXT MORNING. VERY LATE. SHE stretched and for once felt like she had really slept the whole night through.

She looked around the room and when her eyes landed on her

bag, she scrambled out of the bed. A quick look through it showed her that nothing was out of place or gone. Not that she thought Lex would steal from her or that she had anything worth stealing but she had to check. Her whole life was in that bag.

But she had a new life now. She had to accept it for her child's sake. Glancing at the clock she gasped. It was nearly noon. Tiptoeing to the door, she listened intently and hearing nothing, opened it.

Tina wandered out into the living room. She was alone. It was fairly dark so she opened the blinds. Sunlight streamed in, bathing the room with its brightness. Her skin warmed under its glow. It had been a long time since she was able to stand at a window and enjoy the sun, have the freedom of doing what she wanted. She felt like she could stand here forever.

But her stomach had other ideas.

A slow blush crept over her face as the growl was loud. She would blame it on the baby! With a smile, she headed toward the kitchen. A note was waiting for her on the kitchen counter. It was from Lex and said that he was out for a little bit but there were some muffins in the bag and fresh fruit in the refrigerator.

Tina smiled. Taking the muffins she put them on a plate and got the fruit from the refrigerator. Another note was inside, taped to the carton of orange juice.

Drink this.

She smiled again and did as commanded.

After a full plate of good food and a tall glass of orange juice, she curled up on the couch to watch the ocean from inside. She felt sleepy even after sleeping so long the night before. Maybe she would just close her eyes for a few minutes.

Tina woke with a start, having dozed on the couch. A quick glance at the clock showed her it was almost two in the afternoon. She called out for Lex but only silence greeted her. Biting her lower lip, she got up and peered out the window. No car or motorcycle was parked near the house but she didn't know if that was comforting or not.

She began to pace, worried that perhaps Marco had found out

about Lex marrying her and had done something horrible to him and would come for her.

Panic gripped her and without really thinking it through, she ran to the bedroom and grabbed her knapsack. Shoving her feet into the soft flats she had worn at her wedding she dashed to the kitchen. Stuffing a few apples in her bag, she raced toward the door and screamed when it swung open revealing a large figure blocking her escape.

CHAPTER FIVE

LEX DROPPED THE BAGS THAT HAD FILLED HIS ARMS AND CAUGHT Tina as she fell forward, almost as if she had thrown herself at him to knock him down. Her scream filled him with a tense fear but only for a moment.

Her arms were flailing but he caught them easily and held her to him calling her name several times.

"Tina! Tina it's me, Lex!"

It was a few moments before she had calmed down enough to catch her breath. She clung to him, shaking still but at least coherent enough to realize it was indeed him and not someone else.

He helped her up and to the couch. While she sat there, he drug in the bags then grabbed a bottle of water out of the refrigerator. He handed it to her and stood over her until she took several drinks and sat back. Lex sat down next to her.

"Better?"

Tina nodded wordlessly but refused to meet his eyes though. Lex felt a deep sigh aching to release itself but instead clapped his hands together once.

"Good, because I have presents for you."

Tina glanced up at him shyly and gave a hiccup. "For me?"

"Well, sort of," Lex replied and dragged the bags over to her.

One by one, Tina looked through the bags; a wide smile seemed to be permanently plastered to her lips. Lex puffed out his chest at his choice of baby items from bibs to baby blankets to little pajamas with rocking horses embroidered on them. Though some of the items were in colors of yellow and green, there were several items in blue.

"So I'm having a boy, am I?"

Lex grunted at Tina's laugh.

She reached out and took his hand and smiled up at him. "Thank you."

Lex's heart beat a bit faster at her beautiful smile. He returned her smile with one of his own and gave her hand a gentle squeeze.

"If you are feeling up to it, I thought we could go out to dinner. There's a nice little steakhouse down the road," he offered.

"I'd love to, if we can make it an early one. I'm afraid I slept late and haven't had any lunch," she replied.

"You didn't eat at all?" Lex almost roared causing her to wince slightly. He cleared his throat. "I cut up the fruit myself," he said, his voice held a ton of pride.

Tina grinned. "Of course I ate that but that was hours ago. I'd be fine waiting but someone else here is impatient," she said and gave her lightly rounding stomach a pat.

Hesitantly, Lex reached out and with a look at Tina who nodded, put his hand on her stomach. He swore he felt a flutter.

Their eyes met then and Lex wanted to kiss her. The dark circles that had been fixed under her eyes since he had met her had finally started to fade. For the first time, he noticed the true color of her eyes.

He thought he had never seen a more lovely shade of blue. He bet the ocean would voice jealousy at how clear and deep the color of her eyes were, if it were able. Long, dark lashes framed those gorgeous eyes too, leaving no doubt that she didn't need make up to get them to stand out like most women used.

Her nose was small but thin but who would really notice it when those kissable lips nearly pouted for just that: A long, deep kiss filled with promises of more to come.

Not being able to resist, he brought his hand up and brushed her cheek with his fingertips to confirm how soft it was. Lex saw her lip quiver sending his gaze back to hers. He searched for something, but what? An approval to kiss her or was she sending him a signal that it was too soon.

Tina swallowed and with a clearing of her throat, rose. His hands dropped to his lap.

"So, about that steak?"

Lex smiled and rose. "Oh wait a second," he said and ran out the door. A minute later he returned with a large box. Tina looked at him confused.

"It's a bassinet. I'll put it together while you're out tomorrow," he announced and steered her toward the door.

"Where am I going tomorrow?"

"The doctor."

TINA FRETTED THROUGH DINNER, DESPITE HOW TASTY THE FILET mignon had been. What would the doctor say knowing how far along she was and hadn't been to see any doctors or started prenatal care? She had picked through her salad before the main course had arrived. Abandoning the healthy greens and fears of the doctor scolding her, she dug into the meal with gusto.

Lex had laughed when she cut a bite and ate it and did it again instead of cutting up several bites then taking one.

"It's been a long time since I've had steak. Well, good meat of any kind to be honest," she said and stabbed another piece hurriedly.

"Slow down, Tina, no one is going to take it away from you," Lex said with half a laugh.

Tina felt her face flush in embarrassment. The truth was Marco *had* taken food away from her many times. Either she wasn't eating fast enough so she could get back to sketching or her lack of inspiration to draw a new gown; he used food as both a weapon and reward.

A short while later, she pushed her plate back and sighed happily and rubbed her stomach. "He approves."

Lex snorted and waved to the server. "I have something else for him to approve," he said and a tray of plated deserts was laid on a tray stand.

Tina's eyes widened. She didn't think she had room for one more bite until she smelled the decadent delights placed next to her.

Chocolate cake, three layers tall called to her but the fresh key lime pie won out... until she saw the large slice of cheesecake topped with fresh strawberries and glaze.

He ordered two and within moments they were delivered. Tina ate the dessert so slow, savoring each and every bite. It was another thirty minutes before Lex paid the bill and they were on their way back home.

"So, tomorrow, do I have to hot-wire this car or you going to leave out the keys," she said with a sideways grin at him.

Lex chuckled. "Neither. My mother is coming over to take you to your appointment then she mentioned something about shopping. Do you know she actually yelled at me for your lack of wardrobe?"

Tina was quiet. She really didn't have much anyway when she had packed the few things she did before running away from Marco.

Lex's hand over hers startled her but she didn't pull away. "I'm sorry. I didn't mean to make you feel bad."

"No, you didn't. I'll make sure she knows that you are totally innocent," Tina replied and smiled.

"Oh I wouldn't say I'm totally innocent," Lex said with a wicked grin.

Tina laughed out loud and laying her hand on her stomach, enjoyed the rest of the ride home.

It wasn't too late but Tina decided to head to bed anyway. Lex walked her to her room and gave her a swift kiss on her cheek. "Sweet dreams, Tina."

She blushed and nodded and closed her door behind her. Lex

had loaned her a few tee shirts to sleep in so she changed into one and climbed into bed. It had been a good day. And her dreams for once in a very long time, were indeed sweet.

~

THE NEXT DAY, JUDITH ARRIVED AT EXACTLY TEN. HER appointment was at eleven but they had to get there early to fill out paperwork. With a wave to Lex who was already digging parts out of the bassinet they set out for the doctor.

An hour later it was over. With only a light scolding, Tina learned she was almost five months pregnant and would indeed be having a boy. She almost hated the thought of telling Lex they would be having a son. She was certain he would gloat.

They?

She had come so easily to think of Lex as her sons' father that it frightened her. She should have learned her lesson with Marco. He, too, had started out nice and generous before he changed and became a total nightmare.

No. Lex wasn't that type of man. She had to learn to trust him at some point, didn't she? For her son's sake.

They had stopped for lunch after her appointment. Judith chattered away non-stop about her unborn grandson and if she picked out any names yet. Tina smiled at how Lex's family had taken her in and considered her one of their own without question. In the back of her mind she worried for their safety but being such a prominent family, she couldn't imagine Marco would take such a chance.

Or would he?

"Tina?"

"Oh, I'm sorry, Judith. Just lost in my thoughts," Tina said with a sheepish smile. "What did you say?"

"I asked if you were ready to go," Judith replied. Tina could see worry in her mother-in-law's gaze.

"Oh, yes. Lex might need help with that bassinet," Tina began but stopped at Judith's laugh.

"Oh, my dear, you have a lot to learn about your husband. He's very handy and I think that he will be just fine. You and I have some shopping to do," Judith announced and rose.

Hours later, Tina and Judith burst through the door of the beach house loaded down with bags. Lex immediately took the bags from Tina and pointed her to the couch. Tina smiled and sat down appreciatively.

"Ma, did you wipe out the store and dad's credit card with one fell swoop?"

"Don't be silly, Son. I spread the wealth over several stores," Judith replied dismissively with a wave of her hand and started to dig through a bag.

Lex retrieved a cold bottle of water and knelt down next to Tina. She gave him a grateful smile.

"She tends to overdo," Lex said in a half whisper and craned his neck to see if she overheard then turning back to Tina, gave her a wink.

"I heard that," Judith said with a mock frown before giving a delighted squeal.

She pulled out a tiny leather jacket and held it up for his inspection.

Lex roared with laughter and hugged his mother tightly. "You're the best," he said and gave her cheek a big kiss.

"I know," she smiled and winked. "Ok, time for me to go. Tina dear, get some rest. We'll talk soon."

"Thank you so much, Judith," Tina said with a wave and Judith left.

"Wow, that lady is a whirlwind!"

Lex nodded looking around at the amount of shopping bags strewn all over the floor, table and chairs. "Babies need all this stuff?"

Tina chuckled. "This and more, but the majority of these bags are clothes for me."

Lex turned quickly to Tina and looked stricken. Tina held up her hand before he could speak.

"Don't beat yourself up. It's not like I've been very forthcoming with information and maybe you thought I had clothing in my bag."

"Honestly, I didn't know," Lex said.

"Well, your mother picked up on it since I'm not exactly a fashion plate plus there's that whole same clothing day after day." Tina rose and patted Lex on the hand. "It's a girl thing."

"'Nuff said," Lex snorted.

Tina gave a laugh and looked around. "So, where's the bassinet?"

Lex gave Tina a huge smile and held out his hand. She took it without hesitation and followed him to her room.

"Close your eyes," Lex requested when they reached the door, which was closed.

Tina hesitated. Marco had asked her to close her eyes once. The end result had left her bruised and bloody.

But this was Lex. Not Marco. So she closed her eyes. She heard the door open and Lex urged her to step forward. He moved behind her and whispered in her ear. "Open your eyes."

Tina took a deep breath and opened her eyes. A tiny baby's cradle covered in a soft, white sheet and coverlet set and sat next to her bed, under a canopy of white gauze that billowed lightly in the breeze from the open window. Lex had moved the bedroom around to accommodate the cradle which surprisingly matched the wood color of her bed and dresser, while a fully stocked changing table stood near the closet. A large rocking chair sat in the corner.

"Oh, Lex," Tina gasped, her mouth still open in wonder. She walked slowly over to the cradle and touched it lightly, smiling as it rocked.

"You like it?"

Tina turned to him, tears streaming down her face. Lex looked stricken once again. "Oh, well if you prefer one that doesn't rock, I can –"

She cut him off by crossing the room and throwing her arms around his neck, which required a little jump. He caught her and lifted her off her feet and returned her embrace.

Tina covered a cry of surprise. The room was gorgeous. Not

only had he bought and built a place for her newborn, but tastefully decorated the walls, curtains for the window and new bedding for her. He was unbelievable.

As he lowered her back on her feet, she kissed him on the lips. "Thank you, thank you, thank you so very much," she said through a very large smile.

CHAPTER SIX

Tina sat down in the rocking chair, closed her eyes and rocked slowly with her hands on her stomach. Lex thought no other woman he had ever seen looked more beautiful.

She *did* glow.

He wished she would tell him what brought her to him though. No matter how safe she felt or the smiles that passed those kissable lips, he knew she was still in danger from something. But what?

Tina began to hum softly, a lullaby Lex assumed. It was actually soothing to his ears and calmed his fears for her, for now.

Quietly he backed out of the room and started gathering up the bags and bringing them to her room. She opened her eyes to smile at him as he began depositing them on her bed. After three trips, he had both the bags for her and the baby items all in her room.

"I can help, if you need," he offered but she declined.

"I'll have to wash everything before it gets put away," she explained.

"Doesn't it come clean from the stores?"

Tina giggled. "Yes, of course. I'm just funny about things like that."

"Ok. You'll find the washer and dryer in the closet in the

bathroom. I have to do some things for work. I'll be gone a few hours."

Tina tilted her head inquisitively at him. "Oh, I had no idea. I mean, what do you do for a living?"

"I am a security consultant for businesses and homes but mainly, I'm a bodyguard."

She looked stunned. Lex grinned and motioned for her to follow him. Going to the closet, he took out the metal box and set it on the counter. Opening the lid, Tina stifled a gasp through her hands and backed away.

Lex moved to her side quickly. "Hey, it's ok. It's not loaded right now."

"I don't like guns," Tina said, her voice trembled.

"I understand. But I have to carry one for my job on occasion," he said.

Tina nodded and with urging from Lex, moved back over to the counter. Lex pulled the gun out and loaded it with a loud click. Checking the safety, he put it in the holster at his back.

"I thought you should know it was here and that I kept it stored in this box," Lex said and put the box away.

Tina nodded again and looked a little pale. He steered her back to her room and the rocking chair. After a few minutes, she looked more relaxed. He knelt down next to her.

"Firearm safety is number one with me when it comes to my job and my weapons. And I know that you said you don't like guns, but I want you to learn about them," he said and felt her tense up.

Lex took her hand and squeezed it, drawing her eyes to his. "It's very important that you know, too. How to handle them, load them and shoot them. Not that I think you will ever have to do this, but you never know." His voice trailed off and she gave a stiff nod. Lex was pretty sure that she understood that he was referencing whatever drove her to him.

"I'll teach you myself," he said and gave her a smile. She tried to smile too but it came across as a grimace.

"Oh," Lex said, hoping a subject change would lighten the

mood. "We have a lunch invitation on Friday. I'd like for you to meet a few friends of mine, Trace and Maddie."

Her eyes lit up. "That's two days away. I need to get ready," she said and pushed up from the rocking chair.

"You get ready for lunch two days in advance?"

Tina waved him off, reminding him about all the washing she had to do and began to dig into her bags. He stopped her long enough to kiss her forehead.

"Don't forget to take it easy," he said in a gentle reminder and headed for the door.

"You were right, you know."

Lex turned back to her. "About?"

"It's a boy."

"Told you so."

He ducked the socks she threw in his direction and left.

Friday came faster than what Tina would have liked. She fussed over first her hair, then her makeup and started on her clothing before Lex ushered her out of the beach house.

"You look beautiful," he said and really meant it. Blue was definitely her color. She had bought a combination of maternity clothing and regular clothing just a few sizes larger than she normally wore. She wasn't as large as his sister, Jennifer, was currently but she was sure to get there as the pregnancy progressed.

Today, the top she wore fell off one shoulder while the hem hung down past her waist over a crisp, white, flowy skirt that tickled her calves. Strappy, flat, open sandals covered her small feet but a toe ring glinted in the sunlight.

The drive was beautiful and the weather couldn't have been better. Lex had a different car, one he had stored in a garage down the beach from the house, and they put the top down. Though she had tied her hair back with a long scarf, several strands escaped and danced around her face in the breeze.

An hour later, they pulled up to a large gate. Lex pushed the button on the intercom and a moment later, a woman's voice answered.

"Yes?"

"Carol, love. Can you spare a poor man entrance and perhaps some of that delicious apple ice tea you make?"

Tina felt a pang of jealousy but dismissed it.

The woman giggled over the intercom. "Oh, Mr. Cameron. Please come right in."

The gate slowly opened and they drove up to the door. A man stood by a long limousine and straightened up as they pulled to a stop. When Lex got out, he seemed to relax his stance a little.

"Big Willie, how's it going?"

The man grimaced but smiled. "Very well, Sir. I trust you are having a good day, too?"

"Exceedingly well," Lex said and went to open the door for Tina.

The man bowed low to Tina. She looked confused for a moment and stuck out her hand. "Nice to meet you."

He hesitated for a moment, shook her outstretched hand briefly and motioned to the door. "Carol said to go right in. The living room I believe."

Lex held his hand up high for a *high five* but was only rewarded with a blank stare by the man. "Ok, we'll work on that. Later, Willie," Lex said and escorted Tina in the house.

"I don't think he likes being called that," Tina remarked.

"I know. William is too stiff for his own good. I'm just helping him out."

Tina made a sound that resembled a snort and a cough which made Lex laugh.

"Who lives here?"

"I told you, Trace and Maddie. Oh, shh. I like to make an entrance."

Lex tip-toed up to a double door and twisted the handle and before Tina knew what was going on, he rushed into the room with a roar and tackled a man inside.

They rolled on the floor for a few second before knocking into the door that lead to the veranda and nearly broke one of the window panes. The man Lex had tackled ended up on top and smirked down at Lex before saying in a loud voice: "Winner!"

~

"HONESTLY, DO YOU TWO HAVE ANY MANNERS? YOU ARE WELL past your teenage years."

Tina hadn't seen her when Lex went barreling through the door. Still, her voice was familiar and when she came into view, Tina gasped out loud.

The woman turned to Tina and looked surprised. "Oh, Lex. You brought a guest."

Lex and the other man rose from the floor laughing and slapping each other on the back while the woman approached Tina.

"You're… you're Madison Jordan," Tina whispered, her mouth still open. She dropped her large purse to the floor.

Madison smiled. "That's what they tell me. And you are?"

Tina didn't answer. She was still gaping at Madison, then realized how dumb she must look and snapped her mouth shut. Thankfully, Lex came to her rescue.

"Maddie, Trace, this is Valentina Cameron. My wife."

"Your what?" Both Madison and Trace had nearly shouted this question.

"Is that a rhetorical question?" Lex asked and retrieved Tina's bag from the floor. He pushed it into her shaking hands.

Tina blushed hotly, gripping the bag.

"Did you just say, your *wife*?" the man that Lex had tackled asked. He stared hard enough at Tina that she took a step back and behind Lex. She peered back around Lex at the fierce looking man.

"Stop scaring her, Trace. Pregnant women don't need that kind of stress."

"Pregnant?" Again with the loud question from both the man Lex had called Trace and the Hollywood starlet, Madison Jordan.

"Is there an echo in here?" Lex asked, muttering something about an entirely too large room before turning to pull Tina from behind him. "Here, sit down." Lex steered her to one of the cream colored sofas and sat down next to her.

Madison waved Lex out of the way and sat down next to her. "Valentina, you say?"

"Tina is fine," she replied with a squeak in her voice.

"Tina, it is. Well, Tina, I'm Madison and this beast," she motioned to the frowning man sitting across from them, "is my husband to be, Lucien Trace."

"Trace," he corrected with a frown.

Madison looked at him and frowned back. "Don't you and Lex have some motorcycle stuff to talk about elsewhere?"

Lex punched Trace lightly in the shoulder. "Yeah, I wanted to see those new tires you told me about."

Trace rose and gave Madison a long, lingering kiss before giving Tina a final curious stare and followed Lex from the living room.

Tina couldn't have been more uncomfortable. Boy, was Lex going to hear about this. Dropping her in the middle of the living room of Madison Jordan?

Before Madison could say anything further, an older woman entered carrying a tray with a large pitcher of ice tea and several glasses.

"Thank you, Carol," Madison said and turned to Tina. "She makes the best apple ice tea. Would you care for some?"

Tina nodded and wrung her hands for a moment before taking the outstretched glass from the movie star.

How crazy had her life become? From sketching in near dungeon like conditions one week to being married and served tea by Hollywood's biggest star the next week. She didn't want to wake up from this dream back to the nightmare she had just left.

"Mmm, this is delicious!" Tina exclaimed having taken several drinks. Carol seemed to beam and after Madison introduced her, she clapped.

"Finally that boy has settled down," Carol said with a chuckle and went to see about getting lunch ready.

Madison drank deeply before setting the glass down and turning to Tina. "So, how did you and Lex meet?"

Well Madison, I'm on the run from a maniac killer who has kept me prisoner for the last six months, Tina thought but just shrugged instead. "He nearly ran me over with his motorcycle."

Madison let out a loud laugh. "That sounds like him."

Tina smiled. Though you hear that movie stars are real people, too, it's hard to believe with all the media coverage telling other tales. Seeing a mansion like this up close made her wonder, too. But as Madison started talking about how she met Trace and their life together, Tina instantly knew different.

"That night I rode home on the back of his motorcycle drunk. I barely remember it but Trace assures me that I was the epitome of grace," Madison said then leaned in to whisper to Tina. "I think he's fibbing about that but I'll let him believe he's got one over on me."

Madison gave Tina a wink, who laughed in return.

The doorbell chimed and a moment later, Carol appeared at the living room door. "It's that designer, Madison. He claims you asked him to stop by and show you some ideas for your wedding gown," Carol informed her, an obvious tone of distain in her voice.

Madison patted Tina's hand and scolded Carol lightly. "I don't know why you don't like Marco. He's put out several gorgeous items over the past year. Tina, I'll be right back," Madison said and exited the room to head to the front door.

Tina froze. Marco? Here? No, it couldn't be him. Her hands shook violently as she stood, snatching up her bag and listened for his voice.

"Ah, Madison. You look fabulous."

Tina nearly retched. His voice carried down the hallway and washed over her like an evil shroud.

No. God, please no!

She whirled around in panic nearly knocking over the tea glasses sitting on the table. There was no place to hide. She had to get out.

Her heart hammered hard in her chest and her stomach started to hurt a little. She could hear them coming closer as she put a hand to her stomach trying to force herself to calm down. She had to protect her baby.

Footsteps outside the living room grew louder but they didn't drown out the blood rushing to thunder in her ears. Surely he wouldn't attack her here in Madison Jordan's living room.

Lex! Where was he? He would keep her safe. Oh god. Marco was coming in here. He would see her and know she was still in California and try harder to find her. He would see her stomach and know she was pregnant and that he was the father. She had to get out. Now!

Tina dashed through the veranda door and to one side just as the living room door opened. She was trapped between the open door and window behind a large, brick wall. He would see her if she tried to run past the window, so she remained frozen in place.

She clutched her bag in front of her stomach and turned her head to one side, frightened of who might come out and find her.

"Marco, I'm glad you could stop by. I'd love to look at your ideas if you have them with you," Madison said. Her words slowed and Tina knew she was wondering where she had gone.

"I'm actually putting the finishing touches on something that I'm sure will take your breath away," Marco replied. "I had a few ideas I wanted to run by you first."

While they chatted, Tina stood frozen in agony. *Please go away. Please don't see me.*

Madison answered his questions, but Tina could tell she was looking around the room. A moment later, footsteps came to the veranda door and Madison was there.

Tina shoved her finger up to her mouth, silently pleading for Madison to not say anything about her being here. Madison looked thoroughly confused but to Tina's great relief said nothing. Marco's next words gripped her in total fear, causing her to shed hot tears, to shake her head violently and slide down the wall to a crumpled heap.

"It's to die for."

"I'm sorry Marco, I'm going to have to ask you to leave now. I'm suddenly feeling sick."

Carol, who had brought in fresh ice tea, looked quickly at Madison.

"Oh, well, of course. I'll be in touch."

"Thank you, Marco. Carol, please show him out and come back here right away."

When Marco had left the room, Madison knelt next to Tina and tried to sit her up but Tina was too paralyzed. She gripped her bag tightly and murmured Lex's name.

Carol rushed back in the room and to Madison's side. She gasped out loud seeing Tina on the ground. Madison turned to her.

"Get me water, a cold wash cloth and hit the panic button," she ordered.

Seconds later, a loud wailing and beeping sounded.

"Hang on, Tina. He's coming. Lex is coming."

CHAPTER SEVEN

TRACE GRUNTED AS THE CAR THAT DROVE PAST AND UP TO THE main door. Lex looked up questioningly.

"I don't like that man," Trace shrugged.

"Who is it?"

"Some designer. He's been hounding Madison to buy his designs exclusively from him. Greedy bastard."

Lex shrugged. He didn't get Trace's new world. Trace had gone from a small clientele to strictly one client who was soon to be his wife.

He had teased him about it once but seeing what Madison had to go through to do her job, Lex knew that Trace had made the right call in stepping back from the business of having other clients. His second stepped up so Trace had some flexibility but could focus on being in charge of Madison's security only.

Lex himself had helped out on a few security consulting details before turning all information over to Trace. He, of course, would keep Trace and Madison updated with the latest and greatest when it came to keeping her safe.

"So, married and expecting. I'm shocked. What is she, some old girlfriend that you forget to use protection with? Gonna take a DNA test later?" Trace asked a hint of a smile at his lips.

"The baby isn't mine."

Trace couldn't contain his surprise. "You know this child isn't yours but you married her anyway? How did she talk you into that?"

Lex felt a slight bit of annoyance. "She didn't talk me into anything and she didn't hesitate to sign a pre-nuptial," Lex said defensively. "She needed me." He explained briefly how they met.

Trace flexed his shoulders a bit and Lex knew that he felt the surge of the need to beat someone's ass for hurting a pregnant woman.

"Why don't you make her tell you what's going on?"

"Like that piece of shit that has her on the run to start with? Making her do God knows what? No. She'll tell me when she's ready," Lex spat then noticed the car that had arrived was leaving.

Lex felt the hair on the back of his neck stand on end. Without thinking, he pulled out his gun from behind him causing Trace to draw out his.

"What the hell, Lex?"

Seconds later, the panic alarm sounded and both men barely spent a second looking at each other before dashing out of the garage and toward the house.

Within a minute, they had made it to the house and burst in, scaring Carol as she stood at the living room door. She motioned for them to come there and pointed inside.

Trace barreled in first followed very closely by Lex. Madison shouted for Lex and before the sound of her voice died, they were both out on the patio.

A vice like grip squeezed in his chest at seeing Tina lying on the ground. Tucking his gun away, he knelt on her other side and lifted her up in his arms. Carefully, he walked back inside with her and to the couch. Though he tried to lay her down, she shook her head violently and clung to him.

Instead, he sat with her on his lap and held her tightly to him, his heart hammering in his chest. With the exception of hearing his mother had cancer, he could never recall when he had been more scared. Tina was alive and breathing and had a death grip on his hand.

As his own breathing returned to normal, he could hear the sounds around him; Trace punching in the code for the all clear; the phone ringing and him telling the person on the other end that everything was ok; Madison shouting for Carol to hurry up with some water. All these were signs that he could focus solely on Tina and he did.

"Tina? Are you ok? Is it the baby?"

Tina gulped in several mouthfuls of air, deep shuddering breaths before answering him. "Baby is ok."

Her hands shook… hell, her whole body shook. What the hell had happened?

"What the hell happened in here?" Traces voice boomed, mirroring Lex's thoughts.

Madison shook her head confused. "I'm not sure. One minute we were laughing then Marco showed up…" Madison began, eliciting a strangled sob from Tina.

Lex rubbed his hand up and down her back, speaking soft, soothing words to her. "Tina, it's ok. I won't let anyone hurt you."

She shivered again.

"Maybe we should call an ambulance," Lex suggested but Tina shook her head no and tried in vain to pull herself together by pushing off of Lex and wiping her face. Lex wasn't convinced but waved off the call for now.

So what had caused this episode and why had the name of Madison's fashion designer caused such panic in his wife?

Trace took a seat on the coffee table across from Tina and fixed her with a hard stare. "I'm going to need some questions answered, Tina."

"Back off, Trace," Lex said in a low tone.

"Lex, it's time that she told you what's going on and if it involves that piece of shit, Marco, I need to know."

"Trace, I'm not kidding, back off," Lex growled.

"No," Tina said in a quiet voice looking first from Lex to Trace. "He's right. It's time I came clean."

Lex frowned at his friend. This wasn't how he wanted to find this out. He wanted Tina to feel like she could totally trust him with her past and come to *him*. If what he suspected was right, she had been forced enough.

Carol came in with Madison's requested items then disappeared. Trace looked impatient but said nothing. Lex made Tina take several sips of the water and take just as many deep breaths before she began.

"My best friend, Carrie, and I came here about nine months ago. We were fresh from college and hoped to make it big in the world of fashion," she began.

"You're a fashion designer?" Madison asked.

Tina nodded. It hurt to think of the past few months but she had to tell someone what happened. She had to tell Lex.

"After a few weeks, we met Marco Quinn at a party and one thing led to another and we were living the high life in his house and sketching designs. He promised to introduce us to the right people and help make our dreams come true."

"I'll just bet he did," sneered Trace. Lex silently agreed and motioned for Tina to continue.

"After a few months, we became, involved," Tina said quietly refusing to look at Lex. He could tell she was embarrassed at what he might think of her. She'd be surprised at what he thought of her and to put her mind at ease, he brought her hand to his lips and kissed it gently.

"Go on," he said in his own quiet tone. Inside he was raging. Jealousy? Maybe, but knowing now that this was the father of her child, he was more concerned with how she got pregnant; willingly or unwillingly.

"After months of our sketching we began to question him about how soon we would be meeting with people to show them our designs and ideas. He had taken them after we completed them to test the waters he said, but he always told us they had shown no interest and to keep trying."

Madison sat on the table now, next to Trace and put her hand in his. Lex noticed it was shaking just a little. She had been through her own hell a few months ago so this was sure to bring back bad memories. Tina's voice interrupted his memory of that dark time for Trace and Madison as she continued.

"One day, while upstairs for lunch, Carrie found a newspaper with a photo section on an awards show from the night before. There, bold in color, were several of our designs but they were labeled as Exclusive Designs by Marco Quinn. She brought me the paper. We were stunned."

Madison had let out a gasp. Lex frowned. This Marco person had taken designs by Tina and her friend and paraded them around as his own? What a fuckin' fraud.

"So we confronted him. To our surprise, he didn't deny it. We headed back downstairs to pack and leave. We told him that we were going to take our lives and designs back and he would be labeled a fraud. That's when…" her voice croaked a little. "He killed her."

"What?" Lex roared scaring both women. "What the hell? Right in front of you?"

Tina nodded, struggling to continue as tears raced down her cheeks. Madison snatched tissues out of a box on the table near her and motioned for Lex to move. He did so only so he could pace out his anger.

"We had turned to leave when he shoved me aside and hit her with one of his precious vases," she sobbed. Her hands trembled violently as she wrung them and continued her tale.

"He was angry. So, very angry. I couldn't believe what I was seeing. It was like I was watching it from someone else's body. He ripped off the cord from the patio blinds and wrapped it around her neck until she didn't move anymore." Tina's voice was barely a whisper, her eyes nearly vacant.

"It wouldn't have mattered if I tried to help. My head was spinning from having hit the table when I fell. His main bodyguard, Richard, stood over me with his knee pressed onto my head, twisting my arm behind my back and forced me to watch."

Lex fumed but said nothing. He watched as Tina tried to stifle the urge to vomit. His stomach burned, too.

"I've dealt with some really bad people in my time but this is really bad," Trace said, his voice filled with disgust.

"You also should know that I didn't tell him about..."

Lex stopped pacing to look at her in surprise. "He doesn't know you are pregnant with his child?"

Tina shook her head no and mopped her eyes while Madison put an arm around her and rubbed her back.

"I didn't know until couple of month ago that I was pregnant. I thought I was just sick, tired and weak from lack of food, water and sunlight."

Lex fumed inwardly. Marco just made the top of his list of people who didn't just need an ass kicking, but were going to receive one.

"He had his men take Carrie's body away and locked me in the room downstairs for two days with no food or water before he came back. He told me that I was to keep sketching for him and if they were good enough, he would reward me with food and water. If they weren't, I got nothing."

Lex began to pace again. He was ready to track this son of a bitch down and forget the ass beating; he was just going to kill him.

"How did you get away?" Madison asked. Her own voice quivered.

"I was allowed showers once a week. During my allotted shower times, the guard left the bathroom door to smoke outside. I had my bag ready at all times with what I could carry. On the way out, I grabbed a few of the old sketches Marco had left on his desk along with the pad I had been working out of and ran out the back door."

Tina stopped to take several more sips of water. Lex was torn between telling her to stop talking about it all to demanding to hear it all. He could see that it was hard on her but another part of him didn't want her to stop so he had all the details and knew what he was up against.

"I hid in bushes, behind trees and behind dumpsters. I considered hiding in the ocean because I know they wouldn't look for me there."

"Why not?" Trace asked.

"I can't swim," she whispered. "But I didn't want to chance drowning since I had my child to think about. So I kept running. That's when I found Lex."

That's why she kept looking back behind her when he nearly hit her with his motorcycle. Lex frowned. He should have waited it out to see if anyone came around that group of trees. At least then she might not have had to keep this secret to herself for so long.

"So you have proof that he stole your designs?" Trace asked, and motioned to her bag.

Tina nodded and pulled the bag up from the floor, unzipped it and pulled out a large sketch pad. As she flipped the front cover over, several loose papers fell out. Madison picked them up and thumbed through them before stopping on one and gasping out loud. She looked up at Trace.

"I wore this two months ago at a charity benefit for the policeman's association," she whispered.

Lex thought Madison was going to be sick. He took the paper from her and looked at the pencil sketching on a well-worn piece of paper. The gown had wide straps at the shoulders and a skirt that hung loose from the hips down.

Lex remembered the gown on Madison. He had stopped by to update their intercom system and got a smack in the back of his head by Trace for wolf-whistling at Madison. Peering at the corner of the paper was a date and Tina's name: Valentina Designs.

He almost crushed the sketch but held back. Someone was going to pay. And that someone was Marco Quinn.

Tina felt relief wash over her body. She had held this secret inside her for so long, it hurt. A huge weight had been lifted off of her shoulders and she could finally breathe normal again.

But could she?

Hearing Marco's voice had impaled Tina with ferocious fear. She thought she had gotten lost enough in this city, in this state that she would never have to worry about Marco until she was ready to claim what was rightfully hers.

She looked first at Trace, who sat in front of her. Though he was staring at her in disbelief, he *did* believe her. She just knew it and as her eyes traveled down to his hands watching them flex open and closed in a fist and shake with rage.

Tina shifted her gaze to Madison who was looking through her designs, stopping every once in a while to study the sketch and mummer to Trace that she had either seen it on a colleague or friend or had looked at it herself. Madison brushed away a stray tear that had slipped from the corner of her eye.

Finally, Tina looked at Lex. He was pacing and looked angry. Maybe a few days ago, she might have worried the anger was directed her way but as she got to know him more, she knew that he truly was one of the good guys.

She took a few sips of the water and let her hand drift down to her stomach and felt a fierce protectiveness for her child. Marco was a monster. She would die before she let him get his hands on her baby.

Right now, she had to say something, anything to break the silence. It was more deafening than a jackhammer. She turned to Madison.

"Miss Jordan, I'm so very sorry."

Madison looked from Trace to her in surprise. "For what?"

"For bringing this craziness to your doorstep. I didn't mean…" she began but Madison held up a hand.

"First, you must call me Madison. You are Lex's wife and Lex is family here. Which means you are now family, too. Second, this is *not* your fault," Madison said.

"Madison is right," Trace said, surprising Tina. She didn't think that he liked her very well. After all, here was a complete stranger in his home, married to his best friend carrying a child that wasn't Lex's. He probably had thought she conned Lex into marrying him but to Trace's credit, he said nothing.

Instead, he was offering support, and she would take it for her child. But she would find some way to make it up to Madison and make Trace believe that she really did care about Lex.

Because she really did.

Lex motioned to Trace and they wandered over to a corner and began whispering. They almost looked like they were arguing but she couldn't tell. Madison startled her by taking her hand and patting it gently.

"You know you are safe now, right?"

Tina let out a deep breath and nodded.

"These two don't play around when it comes to safety and security. It's their job."

Tina nodded. She knew that Lex seemed capable enough but what could stop a bullet?

"You know, Tina, you are very good," Madison said, surprising Tina.

"I'm sorry?"

"Designing. You have a definite talent and you should be proud of yourself."

"Yeah, I guess so." How could Tina be proud when her dream got Carrie killed. She should have known better. Hadn't her mother always said if it's too good to be real, it wasn't? Of course, her mother was cynical about everything life had to offer. But not Tina. She had dreams and she planned to follow them no matter where they led.

Maybe she should have listened to her mother. Her dreams got Carrie killed.

"Tina?"

Lex's voice brought her out of her reverie. He still looked a combination of angry and concerned.

"I'm taking you home now," he said.

Madison stood with them and hugged her tightly. Tina was touched by her immediate welcome and concern for her welfare. But Tina was concerned, too. Marco was treacherous and movie star status or not, Tina knew that if someone stood in Marco's way, he'd do whatever it took to remove them.

"Madison," Tina began and stared at her new friend. "Please be careful. Marco is dangerous."

"You are kind to worry, Tina, but I promise you, nothing is going to happen to Madison while I'm around," Trace said, a hard glint in his eyes.

Tina nodded and smiled as Madison promised to see her soon. Lex and Tina left to head home.

CHAPTER EIGHT

Lex was quiet as they drove home. So was Tina, he noticed. He hadn't expected that bombshell but he wasn't surprised. In his line of work, he's seen it all, heard it all. More and more, he was glad that Tina hadn't told Marco about her pregnancy. God only knows what he would have done to her, pregnant with his child or not.

Once home, he had her put her feet up on the couch and made her a cup of tea. A good cup of tea solves everything, he told her. "That's what my mother says," he said with a shrug.

So did a big gun and a clip full of bullets, he had replied to her with a grin. Judith had frowned at him and denied him a piece of apple pie that day.

Taking the cup out to Tina, she thanked him and sipped at the steaming liquid. He sat down at the end of the couch, then on impulse, lifted her feet up and scooted over so her feet rested in his lap.

"I'm so sorry," he said.

"Why are you sorry? You probably have saved my life," Tina said, then put her hand on her stomach. "Our lives."

Lex watched her carefully noting her nose starting to redden as she struggled to keep the tears from falling.

"I'm sorry that you had to go through that only to have to relive it like you did. But I promise you one thing. He will never hurt you again."

She nodded at him wordlessly and sipped the tea.

Lex absently began to massage her feet. He was inwardly fuming still after hearing her story. She was so small, yet so damn brave.

"Thank you, Lex." Her voice startled him. He gazed over at her.

So damn brave and beautiful.

"For what?"

"Believing in me."

He merely nodded then suggested that she head to bed and get some sleep. She agreed and with a surprising hug from her, she turned and went to her room.

Lex opened the patio door and headed out on the small wooden deck. He couldn't remember the last time he had been so livid. This Marco Quinn had killed her friend, and right in front of Tina. Then, used food as a weapon against her? All to keep him in sketches and the good graces of the designing world. The fucking fraud.

Lex had wanted to race over to this man's house, bust down his door and beat him within an inch of his miserable life. Trace had talked him down, taken Tina's sketch pad and loose drawings and promised Lex he would look into Marco's past first.

Lex knew Trace was right. Never go in blind if you can help it. Now that they knew who had put Tina in this situation, they had a chance to investigate him. That didn't mean he wasn't going to break Marco Quinn's jaw. That was just a matter of time.

TINA SAT STRAIGHT UP IN THE BED, COVERED IN A COLD SWEAT. IT took a moment to realize where she was and attempt to calm her racing heart.

She let out a loud gasp when her door cracked open. It was Lex. "Are you alright?"

Tina nodded. The memory of the nightmare rushed over her and though she fought against the emotions Marco brought out of her, hot tears ran down her cheeks.

Lex crossed the room to her, sat on the bed and pulled her into his arms. She reveled in his strength. He stroked her back and rocked her slowly. Tina took deep, shuddering breaths and just when she thought she didn't have a tear left to shed, another memory of Marco invaded her mind and they began again.

"Bad dream?"

Tina sniffed and nodded against his chest. To be honest, she had lived a bad dream for almost a year. A dream shouldn't hurt, but this one did. She couldn't focus on what brought her out here and what had transpired since. It was still way too fresh.

"Want to talk about it?"

She knew he meant well but in the past nearly several weeks they had been together, her dreams of that horror had been less and less. Hearing Marco just a few feet from her brought it all rushing back to her. She didn't want to really talk about it again and though she didn't want to let Lex down, he was already doing a lot for her.

"Hearing his voice again just brought back bad memories," she said. It was the truth, partially. She couldn't go down that road again. Not twice in one day.

"I understand," Lex replied. He shifted and helped her lay back against the pillows. "Can I get you anything? Maybe we could go for a swim?"

Tina shook her head no as the tiniest hint of fear gripped her. "I can't swim, remember?"

"We'll fix that. I'll teach you myself," Lex replied with a smile.

Tina returned the smile and lowered her head nodding hoping to cover her blush of embarrassment.

Lex had risen as if to give her privacy but she stopped him.

"Don't go." Tina hardly recognized her own voice. She sounded weak and needy, and maybe she was, but she didn't want to be alone just yet.

Lex removed his gun and set it on the nightstand. Kicking off his shoes, he sat on the back easing back against the headboard and opened his arms to her and with a brief hesitation she scooted over and into his embrace.

They lay together that way for a while. It was very comforting for her. He, with one arm around her shoulder, held her firmly while his other arm rested gently around her waist.

Tina felt very relaxed, safe and secure again. In her mind, she knew she was under his protection but being in the circle of his arms really drove it home.

His touch was gentle. He smelled good, too. Tina could feel his heartbeat against her cheek, drumming in time with each breath he took. Her own heart beat a little faster but not out of fear. She knew that she had been feeling more of an attraction to Lex over the past few days but she thought it might be due to him watching over her and her baby.

Certainly she cared about him. When he was gone, she thought about him and couldn't wait for him to get home. She delighted in seeing his smile when he accomplished something in the kitchen since it was obvious that he wasn't too familiar with that portion of the house. But he tried so hard and for her. It tugged at her heartstrings.

Today, he had come for her, held her close to him and comforted her. She felt an even stronger pull toward him. Tina had come to depend on him, a lot. She smiled to herself as the thought that he wouldn't disappoint her floated past her sub-conscience. Sleep finally came to her. A safe, dreamless sleep that would carry her until the morning.

Lex warred with his body.

He was trying to rise to the occasion as her husband and protector but other things were rising as well. She was, after all, a beautiful woman and he was definitely all man.

But she needed him right now so he would have to be satisfied with just holding her.

Tina had drifted off to sleep a while ago. He moved to ease a cramp in his arm and she snuggled closer to him. He groaned inwardly. She certainly wasn't going to make this easy, asleep or awake. Did she not have any idea how she affected him?

His eyes drifted down to the swell of her breasts. She had several nice nightgowns now but she still preferred his tee shirts and tank tops with shorts. Tonight she wore a tank top that cut way too low for public viewing. He made a mental note to assure that she never wore this outside their home.

His gaze lingered on her breasts again. They were so very full, larger than what they probably were due to the pregnancy. Lex could almost envision her feeding their son from her breasts and his insides tightened while his outsides hardened.

He lifted his hand from her waist to brush a stray lock off of her forehead. She stirred at his touch and turned her head up ever so slightly. Her lips parted as she let out a sleep filled sigh.

"God help me," he whispered.

Lex traced a finger down her cheek and hovered just over those lips he wanted to kiss before continuing his feather like touch journey down her body.

A slow circle over her bare shoulder before traveling down the slender arm that moved over his waist once before resting over his hand that held her waist.

Still lower Lex moved his hand until he came to the swell of her stomach. Faint flutters tickled his fingertips causing him to smile and he too joined her in a sweet dream filled sleep.

Tina stayed at home the next few days. If she had to be honest, she was grateful for the rest. Since Trace had taken her sketch book, she doodled on a steno pad, envelopes and even paper napkins from that great pizza place she craved.

She had to smile. Lex had been doting on her since the incident at Madison's home. Thankfully her nightmares hadn't returned.

Butterflies swarmed in her belly in remembrance of the night Lex had slept with her, holding her in his arms. He wasn't there in the morning when she woke and he had returned to his own room the next night. That had left her feeling very empty. Didn't he want to be with her?

Tina blushed remembering his hard, sexy body lying next to her. She couldn't help but notice how well she fit against his body. She also had woke in the middle of the night to find him snoring lightly, still holding her but his other hand was laying over her stomach.

Lex interrupted her thoughts by coming home with his arms full of bags.

"Oh, not more shopping," she said with a laugh.

"Oh yes, more shopping," replied a female voice behind Lex. It was Madison.

"Oh, Miss... I mean, Madison. I had no idea that you were coming today," Tina stammered, raking her fingers through her hair and smoothing her soft, cotton blouse. Lex would be on the receiving end of a serious tongue lashing for this.

But to her surprise, Madison was wearing a jogging suit, tennis shoes and had her hair pulled back in a pony-tail. Strange she had always pictured actresses always glammed up. It was nice to see they too had outside lives that involved sweat pants and tee shirts.

Tina would lay money that Madison would enjoy that pizza place down the way as much as she did.

Madison swept Tina into a hug and with a quick silent question by holding her hand near Tina's stomach, laid a gentle palm and sighed happily.

"Babies are so wonderful!" Madison exclaimed before directing Lex to drop the bags out in the living room and began digging through them.

Lex pulled Tina toward the door. "I have some things to take care of this afternoon. Madison will stay with you until Trace and I get back. Two guards are parked outside as well."

"Where are you going?"

Lex didn't answer. Instead, he gave Tina a quick kiss on her forehead and stepped toward the closet. She watched him take out his gun, load it and checking the safety, tuck it behind his back.

Fear raced through Tina. She would never get used to that damn thing. But if it kept him safe, she let it go. She locked the door behind Lex and joined Madison in the living room.

Tina picked a spot that seemed to be empty of bags and shook her head. "You really shouldn't have gone to all this trouble."

"What trouble? I don't know anyone with a baby on the way to shop for. It's me that should be thanking you."

Tina laughed. She showed Madison her room and the baby things that Lex and Judith had bought. Madison delighted at the cradle and deemed Lex a genius.

"So, as you can see, I really am good with baby things but I will take and appreciate your generosity," Tina said and meant it. She had never imagined being taken such good care of by anyone, let alone complete near strangers and a famous Hollywood actress.

"Well," Madison said as they made their way back out to the living room. "There is something you can do for me."

"I can't imagine what it is I can do for you, considering who you are, but if I can, I'll do it," Tina replied. "What is it?"

Madison dug into a bag Tina hadn't seen earlier and pulled out a large sketch pad along with several drawing pencils. Tina looked up at her confused.

Madison smiled and simply stated, "You can design my wedding gown."

CHAPTER NINE

LEX STARED ACROSS THE RESTAURANT AT MARCO QUINN. HE WAS tall, like Lex, but skinny and certainly didn't have any muscles to speak of, unless you counted the two men that accompanied him. Now there was some muscle. But Lex doubted that those two pinheads could think for themselves without their puppeteer pulling their strings. He dismissed them without a second thought and returned his focus to Marco.

Lex watched him laugh with the maître d before gliding along to his table, stopping to kiss cheeks of beautiful women here and there. Lex sneered in disgust. It wasn't just the designs that he claimed were his that were fake.

He wanted to rush across the room and pummel him until he limped, the simple bastard. But they had a plan, him and Trace. And he would stick with the plan until he didn't have to anymore. Then, payback.

He saw Trace give him the signal. Lex rose and started walking toward Marco. At that exact moment, Trace bumped into Marco and feigned apologies before walking toward Lex. They made a big show of it. Lex grabbing Trace, twisting his arm behind his back and demanding that he hand over the wallet he just stole.

Lex shifted a quick glance up to Marco who looked upset and started feeling around his coat and pockets, learning that his pocket had indeed, been picked.

Lex grabbed the wallet and shoved Trace away from him toward the door. Trace bolted out with Marco's thugs in hot pursuit.

Lex approached Marco and forced a half smile and nod. "Here you go buddy."

Marco took the wallet with one hand and stretched out his other to Lex. "Quinn. Marco Quinn."

Lex resisted the urge to grab him and bash his head against the bar top they stood next to. "Cameron Alexander." It wasn't really a lie, just a nice flip of his name to conceal his identity. He had used it before helping out a few undercover officers and a quick check showed the cover to still be in good working order.

They shook hands and Marco snapped to the bartender for drinks. "What's your pleasure?" Marco asked with a wide smile.

To kick your ass, Lex thought but answered with a simple request for a bottled beer.

Once their drinks arrived, Marco held up his dirty martini and offered a toast to Lex, sipped from the dainty, tall-stemmed glass then offered Lex a job.

"You don't really know me, Mr. Quinn. Are you sure that's such a good idea?"

"That's a very good point, Cameron. But I find that you not only have brawn," Marco said, shifting a gaze up and down Lex's form, "but brains as well."

"Again, you don't know me."

"I consider myself a good judge of character and tend to make good choices on the spot," Marco said, pride swelling his chest.

Lex smiled at his good fortune. And here he thought he'd have to hint around for work or a good reference for saving his wallet.

Lex tipped back the long neck beer bottle and took a look in the mirror that was over the back of the bar. He looked a little out of place, dressed in his finest leather jacket, black jeans, silver tipped black boots and black Ray Bans flipped up on his shaved head.

Not that this was a complete hoity-toity joint, but definitely not his style. He saw people in nice tops and dress pants, high-end khakis and polo's, designer jeans and the sports team of the week jerseys. Marco surely didn't fit in here for a wannabe designer but it worked in order to 'meet' Marco and try to gain his trust through employment.

Lex noticed Marco's two men returning looking sweaty and winded. Marco excused himself and went over to them. Watching them through the mirror, Lex saw the men get a serious tongue-lashing before he dismissed them to the outside.

"Please, I insist you join me for lunch. My treat since I have my wallet with money," Marco said, snorting a laugh.

"Well, I certainly can't turn down a great invitation like that," Lex said, oozing charm and appreciation at Marco.

They took a table in the middle of the room. Marco smiled and waved at people along the way again. Clearly he enjoyed being the center of attention. Lex was fairly sure that Marco wasn't going to enjoy the attention that he got from Lex later.

Lex ordered a steak while Marco chose a grilled chicken platter. He would gouge this pig for every dime, every time he could. Marco made small talk about the weather, ladies he knew and the fashion industry. There was Lex's opportunity.

"Fashion?"

"Yes. You may not recognize me but I'm a pretty famous fashion designer."

Lex gave his best perplexed look. "No, can't say as I do," Lex said and looked down at his attire. "I'm not exactly a fashion plate myself."

Marco let out his own laugh. "Well, I'm sure we could fix that."

Lex held up his hand to ward off Marco. "I'm good thanks."

Marco roared with laughter as their meal arrived.

After lunch, he walked out with Lex and gave Lex his business card. "As soon as I have you checked out, we'll set up your job duties," Marco said and waved for his car. His two shadows showed up too, eyeing Lex with disdain.

"Of course," Lex said with a nod and shook Marco's outstretched hand again. Marco climbed in the dark Lincoln Town car and drove away. Lex wiped the invisible germs from his hand on his jeans.

A moment later, a silver Hummer drove up to the curb. Lex got in the passenger's side and looked at Trace. "That man is so slimy, I already need a shower."

Trace snorted in disgust. "Do you know how hard it was not to beat him to a pulp today?"

"As a matter of fact, I do."

They gave a slow smile to each other and, after a quick fist bump, Trace accelerated down the road.

Tina stared at the blank sketch pad page. This was a total dream come true. Her dream. Carrie's dream, too, she reminded herself.

But her dream would go up in smoke if her creative charms didn't wake up soon.

Designing a wedding gown for A-list actress Madison Jordan was more than a dream. This would put her on the fashion map for sure. Not that she didn't try to talk Madison out of it.

"If you don't design my gown, I'll be getting married in a burlap sack."

Tina gave a mock gasp of horror. "I sincerely doubt that. You probably have famous designers lining up around the block to choose from. I'm a basic nobody."

"That's not true," Madison said quietly. "Your designs are already being worn by people without the proper credit. Once Trace and Lex do whatever it is they do," she said and waved at the air. "You design my gown, which by the way, is already fetching a seven digit payment for a photo spread agreement."

Madison held up her hand when Tina tried to argue the point more and, instead, told her what her childhood dreams for a wedding gown were.

Ideas rushed back and forth through Tina's mind as Madison

spoke but now that she was gone, her mind was a total blank. How did that happen?

It was then she realized that she hadn't thought about Marco for a whole hour. Quite a feat for her considering she hadn't been able to stop thinking about him since he made his surprise visit to Madison's a few days ago. That had been a real shock to her system. Thankfully, her baby was ok.

Tina rose and moved to stare at the ocean out of the window. Her hand automatically went to her stomach and gave it a slow massage. She was rewarded with several fluttering kicks that made her smile. After a few moments, she gave up on trying sketching and stretched out on the couch with a book of baby names instead.

She had noticed that the males in Lex's family had names starting with A, while the females started with J. She would keep that tradition going for Lex. It was the least she could do since he stepped up like he did.

Tina wrinkled her nose at several of the listed names when the baby gave a hard kick, startling her. "Well, aren't you a little soccer ace?"

A light bulb went off in her head and she smiled. Her son had a name now. She couldn't wait to tell Lex.

Smiling to herself, she closed her eyes and drifted off to sleep.

The scent of pizza drifted lazily to her sometime later. Her stomach woke up first and encouraged the rest of her into action and she opened her eyes. Shifting, she peeked over the couch at Lex. He was sitting at the kitchen table reading the newspaper and shoveling a large slice of pepperoni pizza in his mouth. The cheese string stretched from his mouth to the half-eaten slice as he pulled it up in the air in an effort to pull the cheese away.

"Ahem."

He stopped in mid-air and swung around to her. He had a very guilty look on his face.

The long string of cheese refused to break so she rose, walked over to him and pulled it apart for him. He coughed, swallowed what was in his mouth and grinned. "Thanks."

Tina smiled and wiggled her sauce covered fingers at him. "Napkin?"

Lex's eyes smoldered making Tina's stomach flutter even more than her son did earlier. He took her hand and raised it to his mouth. Eyes locked, their pulses beat in time, she watched as Lex parted his lips. He drew her fingers into his mouth, one by one, sucking each tip as he cleaned off the sauce left behind by the pizza and cheese.

He turned in his chair and pulled Tina between his thighs. His warm lips kissed the back of her hand then her palm before traveling to her wrist. Lex breathed in deeply, his lips pressing against the slow throb there and still his eyes never left hers.

Tina felt her own breath quicken in time with her heartbeat. It had been a long time since a man had touched her this way and made her feel this way.

Just made her feel.

His lips traveled up her bare arm, racing with the chill bumps that began when he first touched her. She leaned closer to him in order for him to reach more of her flesh; her shoulders, her neck, her lips.

Without realizing it, she had sat on his leg. He had groaned softly but she had thought it due to their deep kiss. Still she pressed closer, weaving her arms around his neck and pressing her breasts against his hard chest. He smelled so damn good.

Dragging her lips from his, their breaths ragged, she turned again to lean her back against his chest. Lex needed no urging, wrapping his arms around her waist while he returned to kissing her neck.

Tina pressed against his groin and raised her arms above her to touch his face before moving over his muscular arms. She raked her nails absently before reaching his hands and urging them up her body. And he complied.

∼

Lᴇx ɢʀᴏᴡʟᴇᴅ ʟᴏᴡ ɪɴ ʜɪs ᴛʜʀᴏᴀᴛ ɪɴ ᴘᴜʀᴇ ᴀɢᴏɴʏ. Gᴏᴅ ʜᴇ wanted this woman. His wife. His Valentina.

He was sure she had no idea just how incredibly sexy she was and how much he wanted her. When he had arrived home and had found her on the couch sleeping, he felt that familiar, slow throb as he began to harden.

Tina's hair fanned out around her on the cushions. She looked wild and uninhibited. Her mad-crazy, long lashes lay against her now full and rosy cheeks. And her lips, ah those lips, parted just a bit and in a slight pout. He had wanted her instantly.

Instead he gripped the pizza box tightly and turned back to the table and tried to busy himself by eating.

Yet now, here she was, offering herself to him; her body, her flesh, her lips.

Her breasts.

His hands moved under the softness of her low cut tank top to the hot silkiness of her flesh. Skimming her ribs and to his delight, finding her breasts free from the confines of a bra. They were a perfect fit for his large hands, surprisingly so since she had such a small frame. Nothing he was going to complain about though. Lex knew it was due to the pregnancy. And she had never looked more beautiful.

He cupped them, gently at first, then as she ground her ass against his full hard on, he increased his own pressure, moving them in circles as she was before he settled his fingers against the straining tips.

Tina gave a soft gasp and pressed against him again before pushing out against his hands with her chest, raking her nails up his arms to his hands encouraging him to not stop.

He gave a throaty chuckle and kissed her neck, trading back and forth between little nibbles and hot kisses. And still he pinch and pulled. He wanted more. He had to have more.

Lex smiled at the sound of her disappointment when he moved his hands out from under her shirt. He was sure that sound would turn to gasps of pleasure as soon as he tugged off her shirt when the phone rang.

No fucking way, he thought. His body screamed out its own disappointment. This wasn't a call he could ignore. The ringing came from his special cell and he was sure it was Quinn.

With a deep, tortuous sigh, he shifted in his chair to take the phone out and with a final kiss to Tina's shoulder, answered it.

"This is Cameron. Yes, Sir. I can be there within an hour." He gritted his teeth as he closed the lid.

He looked up at Tina. Her face was flushed and she crossed her arms to hide the tips of her breasts pressing hard against the material of her top. He pulled her back to him and laid his cheek against them, hugging her around the waist and sighing to himself.

"I'm sorry," he growled. "I don't think you know how damn sorry I am right now."

He felt her nod and was comforted by her returned embrace. Damn, he didn't want to go but he had to. If they were to ever be rid of that animal and her be safe, he had to go.

"I'll be late tonight," he said and with a heavy heart, eased her back and rose. He tilted her chin up so he could look into her eyes. They were still laden with passion. He leaned down and kissed her deep and hard until he forced himself to stop, before he couldn't, and strode out.

Tina collapsed in the kitchen chair. Damn that man was hot and sexy and irresistible. And damn that phone call's bad timing.

Lex had a raw sex appeal that she had never experienced before. Not that she had been with a lot of men. Obviously she was no virgin. Still, within the amount of time he had been kissing her, touching her, making her hot inside and wet below, she would have already been having sex. No man she had been with had really cared about foreplay.

But with Lex, it was different. He wanted to touch her, taste her and bring her immense pleasure and damn, did he ever.

She thought of Marco and their former physical relationship but only for a moment. He didn't make her feel inside the way Lex did. Marco was more about the physical moment. Why hadn't she seen his selfishness back then?

Because Marco was a deceiver by nature; in business, in life and in bed.

She wrapped her arms around her thickening waist as if hugging her son. *But he won't get you, my sweet baby. I'll die first.*

Her thoughts drifted back to her husband. There was no mistaking that he wanted her as much as she wanted him. The look in his eyes told her that.

Tina smiled. She knew it was time to let it all go. She had finally told him of her past, put her security in his hands and put her full trust in him, it was time she gave him her love. First her body, then her heart. That would fully consummate their relationship not only as friends, but as husband and wife.

Tonight, she would make love with Lex.

CHAPTER TEN

Lex cursed again as he drove the motorcycle up the drive to Marco Quinn's home. It looked fairly new. His blood boiled knowing this was purchased with royalties by designs stolen from his wife. A cold chill ran down his spine. What if Tina wasn't the only one Quinn had done this to? Besides her friend, Carrie, could there have been others?

He couldn't imagine what Quinn would have done to Tina had he found out she was pregnant. Didn't matter now. Tina was his wife and he would kill this sonofabitch before he put a single, manicured finger on her.

He rolled up near the door and gunned the engine. It brought the desired effect as two burly gorillas came running out. Lex shut off the engine and lifted a thick leg over the cycle and stood up. He was just as tall, if not taller than the two that sized him up even though they were covered in muscles.

More muscles did not mean an automatic victory and he was pretty sure they knew that. He also flashed the gun tucked behind his back when he turned around, feigning a long stretch.

When he turned back, they had taken a step or two back which caused Lex to smirk. "Hi, boys. Where's our boss?"

He purposefully stressed that he was one of them now, though he felt the bile rise up in the back of his throat over that thought.

Marco showed up a minute later with another guard in tow. One he hadn't seen before. Lex tried to size him up but he didn't seem like he would intimidate too easy. Lex tried to keep his focus on Marco but knew this other man was studying him. This didn't look good, Lex thought but kept his cool.

"Cameron, please, come in."

Lex did as asked and resisted the urge to cringe when Marco threw a friendly arm around his shoulder, chatting as they walked down a long hallway to the living room.

"So, it looks like you have a few things on your record."

Lex shrugged nonchalantly. He knew exactly what was there since he planted it. Just a few things to make a less than desirable person feel at ease with one of their own.

Considering what Marco had done, he was sure he was in with Quinn. Such a horrid pun but it was a laugh and would get him through the rest of this day until he could get home.

To Tina.

Marco poured Lex a shot of amber liquid along with one for himself. Handing the glass to Lex, Marco clinked his glass and downed his.

"Welcome to the family," Marco said with a wide, smarmy grin.

Lex smiled back just as widely and downed the drink. It burned going down and sat harsh in his stomach. Dealing with nasty little jerks like Marco Quinn usually left a foul taste in his mouth.

But the plan was in full motion now and that's all that mattered.

Continuing the play the part, he sat down on the white leather couch and swung his booted feet up on the coffee table. The man with Marco, Richard Miles is what he introduced himself as, gave Lex a less than pleasant look.

"Something stuck in your craw, Dick?"

Richard's eyebrows raised.

"I, uh, can call you Dick, can't I?"

"No, you cannot," he replied back through clenched teeth. Lex almost doubled over in laughter.

"My bad. Richie," he said and seeing an even more annoyed look on his face, turned away before anything else could be said.

Marco's cell phone rang. He pulled it out of his pocket and, checking the caller ID, winked at Lex and stepped out of the room as he answered it.

Lex tried to focus on Marco's conversation but found it muffled by his distance. He also tried to seem disinterested in case the meathead still in the room with him was watching. Lex shifted on the couch to appear to make himself more comfortable and looked at Richard. His assumption had been correct as Richard stared coldly at him.

He wondered if this was the same Richard that Tina had said forced her to watch Marco kill her friend. His blood boiled thinking that this bastard held her down with his knee to her head.

Lex gave him a thumbs-up as Marco returned, still on the phone but this time, Marco wasn't hiding his conversation. His tone and words stopped Lex's merriment dead.

"You find that design whore and bring her to me, dead or alive or it's your ass!" Marco shouted into the receiver before snapping it shut.

"Problems boss?" Lex asked, trying to sound half disinterested.

"Oh, nothing for you to worry about. Just another thief that managed to slip away with some of my property. No need to concern yourself with some worthless bitch," Marco said and turned to pour himself a drink.

Lex nearly flexed his hand into a fist but felt Richard watching him. Instead, he studied his fingernails and started to chew on one. Biting one off, he drew it up to his lips and with a quick breath, spit it out on the floor near Richard.

Richard cleared his throat and turned to Marco. "I have a few errands to run. I'll be back later."

Lex looked up to Richard and gave him a half-hearted salute before going back to his nails. His body tensed and his mind raced as he replayed Marco's conversation back over in his mind. That bastard was still looking for Tina. He was going to have to end this sooner rather than later. Once he had a chance to search the house, plant a few listening devices and call Trace, he would head home to Tina.

Hopefully, Marco would be stupid enough to give up some of the goods on his fraudulent activities along with what happened to Carrie. Once they could take him down and Tina would be safe.

Lex rose and looked around while Marco thumbed through some mail. "Where's the john? I gotta take a leak."

Marco motioned to the hallway and murmured a few directions and sent Lex on his way.

What a trusting fool, Lex thought and stepped out of the room.

Tina cleaned up the pizza and then the whole house. Once everything was sparkling, she took a long shower and dressed in one of her short, silk nightgowns. Thankfully it was lose around her stomach so she didn't feel fat but her breasts were almost too big for the top area. She smiled thinking that was ok.

Letting her hair air dry, she ran her fingers through the loose curls and with a pinch on each cheek for color, slipped out to the living room.

She lit a large candle on the coffee table, then one on the dining room table. The soft glow cast dancing shadows on the walls. Heading back to her room, she gave her wrists a quick spray of perfume, rubbing them near her ears and over the swell of her breasts.

Ok, it's now or never. She went into Lex's bedroom. She had been in here before, putting his laundry away, but she never really looked around. She didn't want to pry but now she couldn't help herself.

The room was very him; a king sized bed in a dark wood frame, black sheets and comforter and black curtains that were drawn into place. He wouldn't have to worry about the sun waking him up in the mornings, she thought and pulled back the curtain to look out. The house sat a little back from the road but from here, you could see headlights if anyone approached at night.

Tina tugged the curtains back into place and with a deep

breath, pulled back the bedding. She giggled nervously and chided herself. It's a little late to be virginal, she thought and climbed into bed.

The sheets were cool and surprisingly soft. The bed was so huge, too, but Lex was a big man and needed the room. She smiled and was sure there's room enough for both of them.

She laid her head on the pillow and took another deep breath, this time inhaling the fresh scent that was her husband. It was the scent of the ocean and leather. An odd combo, but that was Lex through and through.

Tina curled up and hugged the pillow to her. Just thinking about Lex, being in his bed and his smell all around her drove her crazy with need. Tina didn't think it was fair that she was tingling with sexual need and he was doing God knows what.

That's ok, she thought and gave a long stretch; he could make it up to her all night long. She smiled as drifted off to sleep.

LEX RETURNED TO THE LIVING ROOM TO FIND MARCO ON THE computer. He doubted he could get to that little gem right away but he would sooner or later.

Marco was smiling as he scrolled down with the mouse and laughed at whatever had his attention.

Lex slipped his hands into his pockets, finding the small, electronic device that would allow him to hear what was going on when he wasn't around. Sooner or later this dimwit would say something incriminating and this whole ordeal would be over with. He preferred sooner, of course.

Lex roamed the large room, his keen eyes looking for the best position for this last device and found it within moments.

"Mind if I fix myself another drink?" Lex asked, checking on Marco's attention span, but Marco merely waved him off without looking up.

Lex walked over to the tall table holding a silver platter, several short ball glasses and decanters of alcohol. He made a big show of delight in the choices of liquor available and pressed the sticky side of the device under the table top. The clicking of Marco's laptop shocked his heart briefly. Had Marco seen him plant the bug? The next few seconds would tell.

He downed another shot and returned to the couch, keeping his feet on the floor this time.

"Well now, Cameron. Perhaps you'd like to know what I have in mind for you."

Lex shrugged. "Would help."

Marco chuckled. "I like you," he said with a wide grin. "As you could see, the protection I have now lacks the skill and street smarts that you have."

And brains, Lex thought but kept silent.

"So I want you with me daily. I go out from time to time to eat but that's really to keep my name and picture in the public eye. Good for PR if you know what I mean."

"I do, indeed," Lex said. *And boy will you have a PR nightmare when I'm done with you.*

"Events, shows, that kind of thing," Marco had continued on before Lex realized it. "I'll make sure you have a copy of my schedule so you can be here on time..." Marco said, his voice trailing off.

Lex looked at him questioningly.

"Unless you want to move in. I have several spare rooms available. I'm sure it would save you the cost of that hovel you live in now."

No way was he going to move in here and leave Tina alone twenty four seven. Lex stood quickly and checked his watch.

"Oh shit. I forgot I have an appointment."

"For what?"

"Detailing my cycle," Lex said, thinking that sounded very stupid but he couldn't give too much away about his personal life without drawing suspicion.

"This dude is very good and in high demand. You know what that feels like, being a fashion wiz and all."

Marco merely grinned. Lex detested having to stroke his ego but he needed to say something.

"Yes, as a matter of fact I do. Many seek me out for my one-of-a-kind designs for all kinds of events. Why just the other day, I was at the home of Madison Jordan. She's getting married and asked me to design her wedding gown. That will fetch me a lot of money and cement my place in this industry."

Lex resisted the urge to punch him square in the face. Instead, he gave him the thumbs up and promised to call the next day for that schedule and assignments, then quickly got the hell out of there.

Going home, he checked several times to make sure he wasn't being followed. He doubted they were smart enough to keep up with him if he tried to give them the slip.

He parked the motorcycle in a garage half a block down from the beach house and jogged home. Quietly he opened the door, let himself in and secured it. He went through his usual routine of taking off his gun, the clip and making sure the safety was on. Once stored, he turned around to see two lit candles.

Tina had made his house into a home. And he liked it.

Storing the knife on top of the refrigerator, he tip-toed to her shut door and listened. Hearing silence, he assumed she was sleeping. As much as he wanted to wake her up in a very sweet way, he headed into the bathroom instead and took a long shower.

Drying off, he went into the bedroom for his shorts and stopped at the sight before him.

Tina was curled up, hugging a pillow and sleeping in his bed. Every part of his body sprang to life causing a sweet ache that he hadn't felt in a long time.

Her hair had fanned out over the other pillow, its wild curls beckoned to him to touch them first before moving onto the flesh of the woman.

She had turned at some point in her sleep and kicked the covers off. His eyes feasted on her painted toes before traveling up length of her legs, admiring toned calves and slim thighs. He nearly groaned out loud seeing her bare hip.

Damn! She's not wearing any panties.

Still, his eyes traveled up and fastened on her breasts. God, they were so beautiful. Large, firm and spilling out of the top of the short nightgown she wore. There was no mistaking the stiffened peaks as they pressed outward against the silky material.

Lex felt a cold sweat break out across his upper lip. He passed a hand over it and had to force his eyes to move away. Even more beautiful was the ivory column of her neck. He swore he could still see his bruising kiss from earlier. His groin tightened.

Finally, he looked to her face. Her gorgeous face, softened even more in sleep. Her lips had a gentle shine to them while her cheeks were rosy.

It all made sense to him then; the candles, her being in his bed and looking incredibly sexy. She was ready to make love with him.

He had been ready for a while, if he was honest. But somehow, the timing hadn't been right, even when they had been alone.

Lex smiled. The time was right now. She knew it. She felt it.

She was perfect.

With great caution, he lay down in the bed and pulled her to him, wrapping his arms around her waist and leaned down to press his lips to hers.

CHAPTER ELEVEN

LEX WATCHED HIS WIFE SLEEP AND SMILED. IT HAD BEEN JUST AS good as he thought it would be. But there would be more. He needed to feel her again but this time he would join their bodies with something other than his tongue.

He grinned wickedly at the thought and considered easing her legs apart right now. His body ached for it. For her. But he held back for now to give her time to recover. The anticipation would be worth it.

Her body was perfect. Why did she hide it under all those clothes? Well, some clothes were good. He didn't want some other man feasting their eyes on what was his.

His eyes raked her body again, memorizing each detail of her. It would be nice to have this picture burned in his memory next time he had an all-night stake out. Or would it drive him to total distraction? The thought made him smile.

Lex felt his groin tighten and he couldn't resist touching her any longer. Ever so lightly, he traced a path up her silky leg until he reached her hip, pausing to rest there a moment while he softly kissed her bare shoulder.

His fingertips blazed their way over her rounded stomach and up to the generous swell of her breasts. She turned toward him and with closed eyes, ran her hands up his arms and urged him closer. He needed no more encouragement. Once again, he made her his.

Lex kissed her neck, sliding his fingertips down her arm as he curved his body around hers.

This, was right. It felt right both with his body and his heart. And at some point in these crazy last few weeks, the realization hit him like a ton of bricks. He smiled.

He had fallen in love with his wife.

His arms wrapped around her body. Nuzzling near her ear, he managed to whisper before he fell asleep.

"I love you."

He didn't see the smile that came to her lips a moment later.

Tina stretched luxuriously, reveling in the soft sheets. Making love with Lex had been everything she hoped it would be, dreamed it would be.

And he loved her.

Turning over she felt a pang of disappointment that he wasn't there. Grabbing his tee shirt, she donned it and padded quietly out to the living room. The scent of the ocean drew her attention to the patio and she saw him.

Lex was leaning over the rail, staring out into the darkness of the night. She smiled and quietly stepped out to join him.

He smiled down at her and pulled her into his arms, kissing her deeply. Tina thought she would never get tired of the passion that was Lex. A moment later, he turned her in his arms so she could lean against his chest.

"You never cease to amaze me," he said quietly.

"How so?"

"You come barreling into my life by dashing in front of my motorcycle, then hop on the back of it taking the first of many wild rides with me," he said with a chuckle and nuzzled her neck.

Tina shivered but not due to the cool ocean air.

"Then agree to a quickie wedding all the while being an unknown famous designer running from a psychotic lunatic and to top it all off, you're pregnant," he said. "You are simply fearless."

She didn't know if she would agree with that statement. Yes, she ran, but it was to save the life of her child. If she'd had a moment to think about it all before she met Lex, she would have been a total mess begging for a strait jacket.

He turned her back to face him. Tina searched his face, drawing his eyes to her. Yeah, his words to her back in bed hadn't been said in the moment. It was real.

He opened his mouth to speak again but she cut him off.

"I love you, too."

Lex melted against her and swept her into a tight embrace before planting a kiss to cement that very statement.

A sharp kick from her stomach to him drew them apart and their gazes down to her stomach.

"Whoa, that boy needs to learn to share his mama with me."

Tina shyly smiled and patted her stomach. "Yes, Ace. You have to share me with daddy."

Lex beamed. "Daddy, that has a nice ring to it. I... Did you just call him Ace?"

Tina nodded. "I mean, if that's ok with you? I tried to stick with what seems to be a tradition in your family. Male names starting with A and well, I'm sure you would want a cool name for your son when you two go riding with the boys. You are welcome to change it if you prefer something else?"

Lex's silenced her with a kiss. "It's perfect."

Tina sighed in relief. "Whew. I wasn't sure how you would feel about that. Of course, you are going to have to work on the middle name. I did, after all, do all the hard work with the first name."

She squealed when Lex swung her up in his arms and whirled around on the patio. "I'll show you hard work," he growled in her ear.

She laughed out loud and clung to his neck as he carried her inside.

∼

"I found her," the man said into the phone, putting down his binoculars.

"About damn time. Where is that bitch at?" Marco's voice hissed into the phone. Finally, he would get that tramp back and designing and this time, there would be no escape.

"If I had to make a guess, rutting under your new employee in his beach shack."

Marco was silent. Cameron Alexander? What the hell? Remembering the words of the men he had searching for her when she first escaped came back to him. *We caught sight of her on a motorcycle leaving the area along with a partial plate.* Then Cameron's excuse of leaving earlier that evening needing to have his motorcycle detailed.

"Get back here now. I want you to run that partial plate that idiot gave us a few weeks ago against Cameron Alexander," Marco said, and slammed down the phone.

He downed the drink he had been toying with for the last hour and sighed deeply. It was too bad the new boy would have to die if he were indeed involved with Tina. Marco threw the crystal against the wall before screaming for someone to clean it up.

Someone would pay for this deceit. And they would pay dearly.

CHAPTER TWELVE

Lex made a bowl of fresh fruit, toast with strawberry jam and two glasses of juice and set it on the bed tray. Humming to himself, he carried it to his bedroom – correction, *their* bedroom, and stared down at his sleeping wife.

She was gorgeous even in sleep. He thought about waking her up some other way and his lips twitched with a wicked smile but he didn't want the toast to be too cold when she ate it. She was, after all, eating for two, and he would have his son just as satisfied as he left his mother last night.

His chest swelled with pride just thinking that this child she carried would be his son. Biology didn't matter to him, considering he was adopted himself. Though he always knew he would have a child or two one day, it would never have mattered if it was his or by way of adoption.

And she'd picked out a perfect name too. Ace. Yeah, it was a cool name. She was totally amazing, and totally his.

"Hey, sleepyhead. Time to wake up," he said and grinned at her groan. "I brought you breakfast," he said with a hint of temptation in his voice.

She popped right up eliciting laughter from him. When she

smiled at him, he thought his heart would burst right out of his chest.

Setting the tray over her lap and kissed her thoroughly. He sat on the edge of the bed and between the two of them, managed to eat all that was there by feeding each other or themselves. He downed his juice, set the tray aside and made plans to ravish her body when the phone connected to Marco Quinn rang.

Did this bastard have radar on when he was about to make love to his wife so he could interrupt? He frowned, but answered it anyway.

"Cameron, glad I caught you. I need to see you today to go over those schedules."

"No problemo, Boss. Give me an hour," Lex said with an easy tone and snapped the cell shut. Tina sighed.

"More bad timing, eh?" she asked with a smile.

"You have no idea," Lex said and gave his groin an obvious adjustment. She laughed.

"It's ok. I have some things to get done today, too."

"Oh? Lingerie shopping?" He leered at her.

"Not that I'll ever keep on lingerie long enough for you to appreciate it," she giggled. "No, I have a wedding gown to sketch and I think I've come up with the perfect design."

"You want to get married again in a dress that you designed?"

She looked up at him in surprise. "Didn't Madison tell you?"

"Tell me what?"

"She asked me to design the gown that she will be marrying Trace in."

Lex wasn't really that surprised, but he was humbled. He had such good friends.

Madison, despite her wealth, beauty and career as one of the most sought after actresses in Hollywood was really a down-to-earth woman. She was also crazy in love with his best friend, Trace, whom he had known nearly all his life. They would take a bullet for each other without question, without considering the consequences, no matter what. Lex would have to be careful more now that he had Tina and their unborn child to consider.

"She's a good woman," Lex nodded and helped Tina up from the bed. "And you are a damn talented designer. I have a feeling, Mrs. Cameron, that once this thing with Marco Quinn goes public and Madison's pictures of her wedding day are published, you will be well on your way to fulfilling yours and Carrie's dream."

She hugged him tightly, then was crying. He could have kicked himself for mentioning Carrie. Pulling back to look into her face, he only found a smile through tear filled eyes.

"Thank you, for remembering Carrie."

Lex dropped a kiss on her nose then tugged her hand. "You can thank me by scrubbing my back."

LEX ROLLED UP TO MARCO'S HOUSE AND ONCE AGAIN, FLEXED outside the door to show off his gun, reminding the meat puppets standing around that he could and would use it if needed.

He sauntered in and finding Marco and Richard in the living room, made himself at home by stretching out on the couch.

"How's it hanging, Richie?"

Lex smirked at Richard's frown then shifted his gaze to Marco.

"Cameron, glad you can make it. There are some plans I need to make and without you, I doubt I can make them."

"Well, here I am," he said with a devil-may-care attitude and wide smile.

"Yes, here you are," Marco said and played with something small between his fingertips.

Lex tried not to look at the tiny object. Years of training told him to let the little things go, even if they weren't so little down the road. But for the barest of moments, his training failed him and he looked.

Fuck. It was the listening device.

Before he could move, he was hit from behind and he fell sideways on the couch. Lex struggled to keep conscious but a second thump brought the darkness in an instant. His last thought was of Tina and her safety.

When he woke, he was tied to one of the wooden chairs in the dining room he saw when he was planting the listening bugs throughout the house. Realization brought out the ache in his head and he groaned involuntarily.

"Well now, look who is finally waking up. Alexander Cameron. Good play on your name, but not good enough," Marco sneered in his face. Lex mustered up enough strength to spit at Marco, catching him full on the cheek. Marco backhanded Lex before digging in his pocket for a handkerchief.

"You should have never come here, Mr. Cameron. You stuck your nose into business that doesn't concern you and now, it's going to cost you."

"I think that my wife *is* my business," Lex replied and congratulated himself on the shock that passed over Marco's face. He heard the clock chime twelve times and knew that Trace would be checking the bugs and recordings. He would find him in trouble and come save his ass. He hoped.

He was more worried about Tina than anything. If this crazy bastard knew who he was and what he had tried to do, he knew where to find Tina. His heart hammered in his chest. Please, God. Keep his wife and son safe.

"You married that whore?"

"Watch how you talk about my wife." He purposely didn't mention the fact that Tina was pregnant. Marco might have been arrogant enough to think that he could get away with claiming designs he didn't create, but he could count months and put two and two together.

Marco circled him, taunting him with little backhands. Lex subtly worked at the ropes binding his hands. They had started to loosen a bit but not enough to make a sudden movement for freedom.

"Who else knows you are here?" Richard demanded.

"John," Lex coughed. He had to stall these two jackasses and keep them more interested in him than finding Tina.

"John who?" Richard demanded with a hard backhand.

"Paul," Lex continued and hung his head low, hoping to avoid more headshots. He was already starting to hear a ringing that he shouldn't be.

"John Paul? Who is that exactly and who else!"

"George," Lex said and began to laugh.

"George?" Marco looked confused.

Lex raised his head to wink at Marco, merriment dancing in his eyes. "One more," Lex said and couldn't stop smirking.

"Who?"

"Ringo." He laughed harder, even as Richard balled up his fist and slammed it into his nose, catching a good portion of his eye.

"Oh no, that's going to leave a mark," Lex choked out and spat a stream of blood at Richard's feet.

Marco raged. He grabbed Lex by the throat and began to squeeze. If Lex hadn't been trying to breathe through it, he would have spit in his face again. Thankfully the phone rang and Marco released him to answer it. After a few minutes, he punched a button on the phone and turned to smile at Lex.

Lex thought that he had seen the face of evil before but it never scared him as much as Marco's did at this very moment.

Come on Trace. Don't let me down, buddy.

TINA LOCKED THE DOOR BEHIND LEX AND STRETCHED. THE MAN was insatiable and she didn't mind one bit. She snacked again and took a bottle of water, her new sketch pad and several pencils and sat on the couch to begin work on Madison's wedding gown.

Her eyes drifted several times to the tabloid magazine with Madison's picture on the front. Thankfully, she wasn't wearing one of her designs that Marco had stolen from her. She didn't think she could bear that but seeing her from head to toe as the magazine showed off the gowns from the latest award show, Tina had a better idea of what she wanted to sketch for her.

She worked for a few hours and smiled at the result. It was still a bit raw, but the basic design was down and well on its way to becoming a masterpiece if she could say so herself.

Tina rose, hearing keys at the door. She raced over there to open it for Lex. To her surprise, three men burst in instead and grabbed for her. In one, horrifying instant, she recognized them as having worked for Marco and with a strangled cry, she turned to run.

She only got a few steps before one grabbed her by the hair, dragging her back. Outraged, she managed to whirl and catch him with her fingernails across his cheek, deep vicious marks that stunned him enough to let go of her and howl in pain.

Tina snatched a water glass and tried to use it as a weapon against the angry man but he managed to grab it away from her and throw it past her. It broke into several pieces that she barely managed to sidestep. As he advanced closer, the glass cracked into smaller pieces.

A glass hurricane shade that had sat over a candle last night made her next target easy. She threw it at the same man but he ducked and it shattered against the far wall.

Tina backed further into the house, trying to keep all three in her sights. If she could get to the bedroom, she could block the door with the rocking chair and maybe changing table. Not that it would keep them out forever, but maybe hold them off long enough for her to call for help.

God, Lex! Where are you? I need you!

The men advanced faster and she dodged into the baby's room. She tried in vain to slam the door shut but it was too late.

The man she had scratched earlier bared his teeth in an angry rage before sending her flying over the bed with a vicious backhand. "That's for the scratch marks you bitch."

Tina crumpled to the floor, looking in vain for a weapon but there was nothing. She had to give up or they would just keep hurting her and she had to protect her baby.

She had no more time to think as another grabbed her by the hair and started to drag her out of the room. She screamed, trying to upright herself but only stumbled and was dragged along the carpet.

A searing pain shot through her as the shards of glass, scattered all over the carpet, cut into her legs and feet. Every inch of her hurt.

She didn't think she could take much more but the thought of her unborn son brought on a surge of adrenaline and she managed to roll away from the glass and struggle to her feet.

Tina hadn't got too far but enough to stop being cut by the sharp pieces of the shattered hurricane shade. She was pushed again, slamming against a wall. She slid down slowly before curling up to protect her stomach.

Expecting more, she waited but nothing happened. Instead, she heard them talking and realized one of them was on the phone.

"Yes Sir. I have the sketch pad. But there is something you should know."

Tina froze. *No, please. Don't tell him about the baby.* But even as she thought it, the man told her secret.

"She's pregnant. I'd say five or six months along. What do you want me to do?"

Tina heard the scream of rage through the phone. She cringed both inwardly, fear gripping her very soul while her entire body shook all over. Marco's next words cut her more deeply than the glass she attempted to pick out of her leg.

"I will *not* have some bastard whelp birthed by a whore. Throw her in the ocean. She can join that other thankless bitch, Carrie, for a late night, unscheduled swim."

The man snapped the phone shut and turned to Tina. The leering smile on his face frightened her more than the thought of being thrown in the ocean.

He winked to his cohorts. "Boss said to dump her with that other one. Didn't say we couldn't have a little fun first."

They advanced on her eliciting a scream of terror that echoed throughout the whole house.

A man clearing his voice surprised everyone. The three men and Tina whipped their heads in his direction.

Tina thought she would faint. He looked like her father-in-law, Adam, only a bit shorter, more stout and scruffy. He leaned causally against the doorframe and seemed to observe the scene before him.

"Old man, you need to move along. This is none of your business."

The man raised a scarred hand and rubbed at the thick, salt-n-pepper stubble on his chin, then scratched his head before he spoke. "I could swear this is my nephews' beach house," he began. He looked purposefully to Tina. "And if I'm not mistaken, that's his pregnant wife. So if anyone has no business here, that'd be you three punks."

Two of the men surged toward the newcomer. He might have been an older man, but he knew how to move. Tripping one, he grabbed the other in a headlock and swung him around to ram his head into the wall. Despite the other's recovery from being tripped, he was quickly dispatched with a well-placed elbow.

Wiping his hands, he turned back to the man closet to Tina.

"Son, my suggestion to you is to get out of this house before I throw you out."

"Bring it on, old man," the intruder snarled and leaped for him, but was rewarded by a boot to the face. Staggering, blood flowing from his nose and the scratches Tina left on him, he roared and tried to attack again but the older man was ready.

He dodged the rush and tripped him. When the man stumbled, Tina's savior took him by the collar of his shirt and seat of his pants and sent him flying through the sliding glass door. The sound of more glass shattering and cries of pain, this time, from her attacker being cut to ribbons rang in Tina's ears.

She was still shaking when the older man crouched down at her side. "You ok?"

Tina nodded briefly before hot tears streaked down her cheeks. "Who are you?"

"Jack Cameron. Alexander's uncle. And you must be Valentina."

Tina nodded. She was still trying to calm her racing heart. To her great relief, she didn't seem to be hurt anywhere near her stomach. She frowned at all the cuts and scratches on her legs.

"Big name for such a little lady," he commented and held out his hand to her. She took it and limped over to the couch.

"Wait here a minute," he said and pulled out his cell. She heard him talking to the police, then Judith. Closing the phone and pocketing it, he walked over to one of the intruders that was starting to stir, and gave him a boot in the face. Back down for the count he went. Jack headed in the kitchen returning to Tina with a bottle of beer and water.

"Never too early in the day to kick some ass, you know?"

Tina looked up at him in surprise. He gave her a wink and a smile before tipping back the cold brew. She finally smiled too before a new panic grip her.

"Lex is missing. You have to find him please."

"Don't stress, little Valentina. Trace sent me over here. He's heading to pick up that boy of yours."

Tina let out a sigh of relief but wouldn't release her fear until her husband was home, in her arms.

"It's just Tina, if you want."

Jack shook his head. "Nah. I kinda like Valentina. Suits you well enough."

"I thought males in your family had names that start with A," Tina asked out loud, then blushed.

"We do indeed. Anthony Jackson, at your service."

Tina smiled and bade him to sit with her. She laid a hand over her stomach. "Jack, meet your great nephew, Ace."

Jack returned her smiled. "Yeah, that's alright."

Tina knew she and her child were safe. All she needed now was her husband. God, let him be safe.

CHAPTER THIRTEEN

LEX FUMED LISTENING TO MARCO'S SIDE OF THE PHONE conversation. He had his thugs at Lex's house. He had Tina! Lex could feel his blood begin to boil over. For unknown reasons, Marco clicked on the speaker.

"Do you have her sketch pad? I'm sure that tramp has been working to take my limelight."

"Yes, Sir. I have the sketch pad. But there is something you should know."

Lex closed his eyes. He knew that Marco was about to find out about Tina's pregnancy. He had to get loose and get home. He couldn't lose her.

"She's pregnant. I'd say five or six months along. What do you want me to do?"

Lex opened his eyes to gage Marco's reaction and it was as he feared. Marco was livid. With a sweeping arm, he cleared his desk of all the items there, sending papers, pens and books flying across the room. He screamed with rage, more angry than he had been with Lex over the last hour. God help Tina until Lex could get to her.

But not even God could help Marco if anything happened to Tina.

He strained against the ropes harder. The ones around his feet and legs were loose enough he could do some damage with them but only if they got close enough.

"I will *not* have some bastard whelp birthed by a whore. Throw her in the ocean. She can join that other thankless bitch, Carrie, for a late night, unscheduled swim."

Marco's words stunned him. Lex couldn't stop himself from letting out his own cry of rage as Marco slammed his finger down on the speaker button. "You bastard! You killed that girl and now you would kill a woman who is pregnant with your own child?"

"Like I care? You think this is the only time I've gotten rid of some bimbo?" Marco roared with laughter. "I'll just be adding one more notch to my belt once Valentina bites the dust."

Lex felt sick to his stomach. What he had feared most about this worthless prick had been true. There *had* been others. But it would end here and now.

"Wow, just when I thought you were just a fraud of a designer," Lex said with a sad shake of his head.

"What's that supposed to mean?" Marco snapped at Lex.

Lex smiled inwardly. *I got you now.*

"I thought it was pretty clear but since you need me to explain it to you like a two year old, I will. You didn't design those dresses, Tina did. That makes you a FRAUD," Lex explained in a baby voice before stressing the word fraud in a loud, clear voice. He continued before Marco could say anything.

"Now that you are clear what a fraud is, you won't have any trouble understanding this when I say that it must be a tough blow to you now, knowing not only are you a fraud in the fashion industry, you are a fraud in life, including as a man."

Silence filled the air before Marco roared with rage and charged Lex.

Lex wiggled his feet and the ropes slipped down his legs and off his feet. He brought them up quickly and kicked Marco across the face before tripping him. Marco fell against the desk, smashing his face against the highly polished surface and slid to the floor.

Lex snapped the wood that his hands were tied to and managed to shake off the ropes there, pulling the remaining ropes from around his chest and turned around to see Richard leveling his gun on him.

"Time to die, Biker."

"Aw, Richie. You can't kill me."

"And why can't I?"

"You left the safety on," Lex said with a laugh.

Richard hesitated briefly and shifted his eyes down to the gun. Lex never moved toward him. He just crossed his arms and waited.

"The safety isn't on," Richard growled.

"Neither is mine."

Richard closed his eyes at the deep voice behind him and let the gun fall to his side.

Trace stepped from behind Richard and took his weapon, his own gun pointed at the back of Richard's head. He lowered it but only as far as the chest area and pulled out a walkie-talkie. "All clear."

Lex pounced on a moaning Marco. He raised his fist in the air, clenched and poised to come down. "You get that thug of yours back on the phone and call off the hit or I swear to God it will be the last thing you recall before I —" Lex began but was cut off by Trace.

"Stop, Lex. She's fine. The only incriminating thing said around here today is by Quinn. Let's leave it that way, shall we?"

Lex looked up to Trace. "Tina's ok? You sure?"

"Yep. I sent Jack over after I heard this morning's tapings. Too bad he found the bugs and destroyed them before he said anything about Tina's friend," Trace said as the front door burst open and police swarmed the scene.

Lex rose, stepping on Marco's hand, crushing his bones until he was sure they were broken. He would never lay a hand to pencil and sketch pad or against a woman again.

Marco howled in pain and curled up in the fetal position,

clutched his hand to his chest and cried. Lex looked at him in disgust before moving to Trace's side.

"But he did confess. I heard him. He killed Carrie and others before her."

"I know he did," Trace said quietly. "I heard him."

"So did we," a man said, stepping in and holding up a detective's badge. "Mr. Trace was wired when he came in here for you. He was outside this room when Mr. Quinn ran his mouth. We recorded everything."

The detective grimaced at the sobbing man on the floor. "We also believe we found the victim's body, Carrie Callaghan, a few weeks ago, washed up on a shore about five miles down the coast. She's just been listed as a Jane Doe."

Lex lowered his head. He knew that Tina saw the murder but to have to go through it all over again. The only saving grace was that Tina wouldn't wonder for the rest of her life what happened to Carrie's body.

"We have a strong case, Mr. Cameron. He'll never see the light of day again except from his cell window." Two officers gripped Marco by the arms and dragged him up, then out.

Lex gave a statement and shook the detective's hand then turned to Trace and lightly punched him in the stomach.

"What's that for?"

"What took you so long?" Lex asked playfully.

"I can't have you looking prettier than me at my wedding," Trace said with a huff and motioned to Lex's battered and bloody face, drawing laughter from Lex.

They embraced briefly. Lex felt a deep affection for Trace. He was like a brother in more ways than he could count.

"Hey, you best get home to that wife of yours, before my wife-to-be strings me up for keeping you from Tina."

Lex smiled and headed outside with Trace.

"Speaking of Madison, when can you two come over for dinner? She's anxious for more girl talk," Trace said dryly, making quotes in mid-air with his fingers when he said girl talk.

Lex grinned but before he could answer he stopped cold.

Whipping around, he held up his hand for Trace to be silent and listened hard. There it was again. Just the lightest of groans.

He crept silently to the corner of the house and motioned to Trace to circle around the police van. Once Trace was in place, they converged to a group of bushes and saw a body half hidden.

Lex's heart pounded harder than it ever had as they pulled the man by the feet out to see one of the police officers that had been taking Marco out to the waiting car.

Lex swore under his breath and turned to Trace but saw he was already on his cell. Lex knelt next to the young officer and patted his face several times. It took a few moments before he opened his eyes and groaned.

"Where's your partner? Where's Marco Quinn?" Lex's voice was demanding and anxious.

The young officer shook his head before speaking. "Partner pulled a gun on me before I was hit from behind. I'm sorry, Sir."

Trace snapped the phone shut drawing Lex's attention. "Jack isn't answering. We need to get over there."

Lex's fear began to heighten. That bastard had a plant on the police force. If Jack and Tina think he's there to help, they'll let him right in. And that will open the door for Marco.

Trace called for help, then raced with Lex to their motorcycles. *Please, let me be in time,* Lex thought.

Tina and Jack chatted while waiting for the police. She had to admire his skill in dispatching the three thugs that had attacked her. It was odd to her how Lex had followed in his uncle's footsteps and not his father's.

A siren approached. Jack peered out the window and saw the ambulance, followed closely by a police car.

"'Bout time," he grumbled. "Wait here, Valentina. I'll show them the way."

Tina relaxed a little. She was still a little shaky but fairly sure that would cease when Lex arrived. Everything that had happened to her over the past several weeks threatened to consume her and drag her into a emotional mess but she refused to let it. She was stronger than that. She had to be.

For Lex. For her son.

For herself.

The door opening caught her attention and she swung her legs down to the floor and stood.

"I'm fine, really. Just a few scratches," she began and turned to the man in the door.

Her breath caught in her throat and she swore her heart would slam out of her chest. Not even when the three men broke in and nearly killed her had she ever felt this kind of fear.

Marco stood in the doorway. He looked disheveled, bloody and angry; a murderous rage contorted his face. His eyes, however, were focused directly on her swollen stomach. She covered her unborn child with her hands, drawing his hate filled gaze up to her face.

"Time for you to die," he said, raising a gun with a shaking left hand while clutching his right one to his chest. Tina almost retched at the grotesque form his hand had become, bruised and broken.

"Marco, please. Don't do this. Think about your son," she pleaded. Tina didn't know if she should tell him the sex of the child, but perhaps if he thought he had a son, he would spare them long enough for her to give birth.

That brought a whole new round of worries. Marco raising her son? Marco raising any child? She could almost see him training the child to berate women, lie, cheat and steal. Maybe even, to kill. She swallowed the bile that rose in her throat.

"You think I care about some bastard child? Not to mention having you as his mother. Worthless, ungrateful slut that you are."

She bristled. "Ungrateful? What should I be grateful for?" Tina was angry. How dare he call her ungrateful after all that he had done?

"I took you in! I put a roof over your head and food in your mouth when you had nothing!" His voice echoed throughout the glass strewn room.

"Yes, you took us in but you also refused to let us leave. You stole *our* designs and murdered my best friend! And I should be grateful for that?"

Marco crossed the room so fast Tina didn't have time to get away. The butt of the gun connected with her cheek hard. Stars exploded in her head and she fell to her knees. Glass dug deeply into her legs again.

"All women are ungrateful and useless! And now because of you, I have to go into hiding for the rest of my life," he growled, shoved the gun in his waistband and leaned down to get a fistful of her hair. "But if you think I'm so unfair, I'll give you a chance to live."

He shoved her toward the door, quickly taking the gun back out and ground the barrel into her back. Tina stumbled out the shattered door, trying in vain to look around the side of the house for Jack, the police or even Lex.

They trudged through the sand before reaching the ocean's edge. The water lapped hungrily at her feet.

Tina looked up in fear to Marco's smiling face. Perhaps once, she did find his smile handsome, charming. This was anything but. It was the smile of smug satisfaction over what he knew she couldn't do.

"Sink, or swim."

CHAPTER FOURTEEN

Tina's mouth opened in horror. "I...can't swim."

He raised the gun. "Then I'll just shoot you."

Tina backed up into the water slowly. Each step was an agonizing step into terror. "Marco, please don't do this."

He motioned for her to keep going, smiling the whole time.

Tina swallowed hard and kept backing up. The water rose around her ankles, her knees, her thighs before the cool waves began lapping at her stomach.

"Keep going!" Marco's commanding voice jolted her into taking more steps. Soon the water was above her waist.

Marco's maniacal laughter rang in her ears, clashing harshly with the eerie silence of being so far away from the shore.

Tina opened her mouth to cry out for help but no sound came out. She had been scared before, but never to the point of losing her voice. This must be what true fear is like, she thought.

Marco was walking out into the water now, waving the gun in her direction and demanding she keep going. He looked crazed, screaming obscenities at her and her unborn child. Tears streamed down her face, dropping into the water as it eased its way up her chest and began to cover her shoulders.

Tina felt a gentle tug around her legs and was finally able to bring her voice forward. She screamed in terror as the current surrounding her began pulling her further out, trying in vain to keep her feet on the ocean's sandy bottom. She tilted her head back when the ocean's water splashed against her chin and cheeks.

A wave rolled past her and she bobbed below the water for what felt like a lifetime before she broke the surface, gasping and sputtering for air.

She was being pulled out farther and farther. She could no longer feel the bottom. Panic surged through her and every time she sank, she flailed her arms fast and furious to keep on top.

Exhaustion began to seep into her body. *I can't die this way. Not drowning. Please, no. My son.*

My son! A renewed sense of urgency filled her and she forced her memories of childhood to come to her. Tina had never learned to fully swim but the basics exploded in her mind. Doggie paddle.

Tina began to kick her feet back and forth while pushing down on the water in front of her. She took in deep breaths of the fresh ocean air and kept moving. She could do this!

"Why won't you die?" Marco's scream came from a distance.

Because I have someone to live for, she thought and kept paddling.

Another scream from Marco filled the air but Tina didn't look. She couldn't. All her concentration was focused on staying above the surface and breathing. But she was losing the battle. She kept sinking faster than she could paddle her arms.

Out of pure instinct, she took a deep breath then slipped under the water.

~

When Lex and Trace had arrived, his uncle had been battling the gun toting police officer. Trace managed to circle around the beach house and got the drop on him. Once secured, Lex and Trace entered the house and searched each room.

"She's not here!" Lex was half scared, half raging. His eyes roved over the living room, glaring at the amount of glass and blood droplets that stained the carpet.

"Maybe we can get the information we need from that guy out with Jack?" Trace suggested.

Lex agreed and was halfway to the door when he stopped cold. He heard her scream. He knew it was her. But now all he could hear was the pounding of the surf.

Oh god, he thought and tore out of the shattered patio door, Trace hot on his heels.

There was Marco, waving a gun toward the ocean, screaming at someone to die. Lex squinted and focused on a tiny dot that was bobbing well out into the ocean.

"Oh my god. He's chased her out into the ocean," Lex screamed and raced toward the water.

"What's wrong?" Trace asked confusion filled his voice as he struggled to keep up with Lex.

"She can't swim," Lex replied and ripped off his boots before dashing past the raving lunatic that was Marco. As he flew by, he caught Marco off guard with a well-placed fist causing the gun to drop into the water.

Lex was sure that Trace would deal with Marco. At least he hoped so. He couldn't hear anything but the slapping of the water as he cut through the waves with speed he didn't realize he had but to him, it was taking too long. She kept bobbing below the surface and drifting farther out.

Hang on sweetheart, I'm almost there, he thought, not wanting to stop to yell out to her. But when he was within seconds of reaching her, she disappeared under the water.

"No!" Lex dived below the water and pushed against the current as hard as he could. Where was she? *Please God, don't take her from me.*

Seconds later, though it felt like an eternity, his hand found her arm. He gripped down hard and kicked toward the light that he knew was the sun shining on the water.

Tina began coughing, spitting out water. Lex let out a breath of relief that she hadn't been under long enough to cause damage and pulled her to him. She let out a terrified scream. It took a few seconds before she realized it was him.

"I got you, baby. Hang on," he said.

Tina turned toward him and wrapped her arms tightly around his neck. Fear faded from him. She was safe. Their son was safe.

Lex towed Tina to shore then picked her up and carried her into the house. Trace had wrestled Marco to the ground and though he threatened to give him his own trip out to sea, Trace banded his wrists behind his back and drug him as far as the beach where he dropped him and waited for help.

Lex took Tina in the beach house and into their bedroom before helping her out of her wet clothes and into dry ones.

The EMT's had to wait until Lex checked each of their ID's before letting them back to the bedroom to assess her injuries. His mother had shown up as well then and shooed Lex out so she could take care of Tina.

Assured that she was safe, he returned to the beach where Trace stood with a few police officers and a wailing Marco.

Marco sneered at Lex and spat at his feet.

"I'd be careful if I were you," Trace said nonchalantly. "Lest I unleash this beast to give you a taste of your own medicine." Trace hooked his thumb toward Lex.

Lex lowered to squat before Marco. He swore he felt the heat of Marco's hate filled gaze but brushed it off. Instead, he smirked at the helpless man.

"I think you'll enjoy prison. You can make new friends and be the belle of their balls," Lex quipped and rose. "Oh, and I think they have an arts and crafts day. Then you can truly create your own designs instead of being the fraudulent bitch we both know you are."

Marco screeched with rage, struggling in vain to get out of the plastic bindings. Lex frowned down at him, turned and walked away.

～

TINA ASSURED JUDITH FOR THE HUNDREDTH TIME THAT SHE AND the baby were fine. The EMT's were dressing her scratches and cuts. She winced as shards of glass were removed but eventually they completed their bandaging and wanted to strap her down and cart her off to the hospital.

"Absolutely not. I won't be going anywhere until I see my husband," Tina said firmly and crossed her arms.

They all gave up and saw to her comfort instead. Jack was more of a comfort than she could imagine, distracting Judith from Tina so she could breathe.

Most of the police had left, carting off the three unconscious men that had broken in and terrorized her. Thank God Jack had showed up when he did. The ambulance that had been called for her, was now carting off a deranged and broken Marco. Now all she needed was...

The door burst open. "Lex!"

Tina wanted to get up but she didn't need to. Lex was at her side, sweeping her into his strong embrace, smothering her with tender kisses. In an instant, he set her in front of him and started scanning her body, frowning deeply at all the bandages on her legs and feet. Tina put a hand to his chin and tilted it up to look into her eyes.

"We're fine," she said and drew his hand up to her stomach.

Lex nodded and pulled her to him again. She reveled in his warmth and strength.

"Alexander," Jack said quietly.

Lex pulled back and embraced his uncle. "You saved my life," Lex said quietly.

"Don't you mean, he saved *my* life," Tina said with a smile.

Lex merely drew her up to him and brushed a kiss on her forehead. "You are my life now, Tina. So I meant what I said. He saved my life."

Jack grinned at Lex. "It's about time you settled down."

Lex looked shocked. "Look who's talking. You missed your opportunity with that enchanting songstress. What was her name?"

Jack frowned at him.

"Arabella Carson," Jack grunted.

Lex merely smirked at his uncle.

"As a matter of fact, I'm going to see her next week. That is, she works at Benji's new supper club and he asked me to stop by. I haven't been there yet so I can't tell you anything about it but if she's singing, it's sure to be a winner," Jack said.

Tina thought he choked back a hidden emotion and made a mental note to ask Lex about it later.

It was another few hours before everyone finally left. Tina promised Judith that she would go to the doctor in the next few days and covered a laugh when Judith made Lex double promise.

Lex swung Tina up in his arms and carried her to the bed. He pulled out a suitcase and started packing a few things, then after a few phone calls, escorted Tina to his car.

"We're going to stay with Trace and Maddie for a few days until this mess gets cleaned up," Lex said referencing the broken patio door, various holes and dents in the drywall and blood stains dotting the carpet.

Tina nodded, trying to block out the memory of what could have happened versus what did happen. She sent up a quick thanks and placed her hand in Lex's hand. Picking up her sketch pad, she glanced up at her husband. "I'm ready."

Lex leaned down and kissed her gently. "When we return, I have every intention of carrying you across the threshold. It is, after all, tradition." He grinned at her.

"Oh really, and just where to you plan to put me down?"

"The bed, of course," Lex said and tugged her by the hand out the door.

ONE WEEK LATER, TINA AND LEX STOOD SIDE BY SIDE AT A SMALL gravesite. They were flanked by Carrie's family, Trace and Madison and Lex's family.

She had been devastated to learn how Carrie's body had been so carelessly tossed into the ocean and that she had washed up on shore and remained a Jane Doe until Lex and Tina claimed her remains.

Lex had gone to great lengths to put together a small funeral, flying in Carrie's family and selecting the perfect place for Carrie to be laid to rest.

Tina exchanged information and said goodbye to Carrie's family. They were bringing a civil suit against Marco's estate as was Tina, but she didn't want any of the money. Despite the designs being hers and Carrie's, it was blood money, tainted by the evil greed of Marco Quinn. Instead, she would donate any court awards to a local battered women's shelter, in Carrie's memory.

Madison surprised Tina by opening a scholarship fund at a local college for art and design in Carrie's name. She didn't even know Carrie but had done it out of respect. Tina was touched.

As people began to leave, Tina found she wanted a private moment with her lost friend and urged Lex to go ahead with Trace and Madison.

Tina stood next to the ivory coffin that was being prepared to be lowered into the ground. She twirled a white rose between her fingertips.

"Carrie, God I don't know what happened this past year. Everything is such a blur. You don't know how sorry I am for what happened to you, to us," Tina said and paused to wipe away a tear that had streaked down her cool cheek.

The wind picked up a little sending her hair swirling around her face. Tina cleared her throat against the burning pain of emotion, of tears that wanted to flow endlessly at the loss of someone she knew and loved; someone so full of promise. Instead she tilted her head up to the warmth of the sun and smiled.

"I know you are looking down from Heaven, watching over me, over us," Tina said and laid a palm against her stomach. Her son kicked out at her in response. Tina chuckled.

"Our dream will come true, my friend. I'll never forget you," Tina said and placed a pure white rose on the pink spray of roses that covered the casket, pressed her lips to her fingertips and blew a kiss goodbye.

Tina walked quietly back to Lex and took his hand. They headed home in silence. The beach house was finally ready for their return and making good on his promise, Lex carried her over the threshold and straight to the bed.

They held each other quietly for a long time. Tina was exhausted physically and mentally and this was just what her inner doctor ordered.

"So," Lex said, breaking the silence with a smile. "What do you want to do next with your life?"

"You mean other than the obvious?" Tina giggled.

"I'm always up for the obvious," Lex said and wiggled his eyebrows at her.

Tina kissed him and snuggled back against him. "Actually, I do have something in mind."

"Oh?"

"Yeah. Swimming lessons."

Lex nodded without a hint of question. "I'll be happy to be your coach. I just have one rule."

"Oh really, and what might that be?"

"No swimsuits allowed."

Tina let out a loud laugh. "Swimming lessons aren't the same as skinny dipping."

"It was worth a try," he said with a shrug.

Tina drew him closer and kissed him fully before leaning to whisper in his ear. "I think rules are made to be broken. But in this case, I'll follow this one to the letter."

Lex grinned at her and tugged the sheet over their heads, covering their laughter as it echoed throughout the room.

WATCHING OVER HER

Her stalker wasn't the only one....
Watching Over Her
Tabitha Gibson

CHAPTER ONE

"WHAT ACCIDENTS?" JACK DEMANDED. HE WAS FURIOUS THAT Benji left that part out. Had he known, he wouldn't have dragged his feet getting here.

"Well," Benji began and tugged at his collar. "A spotlight above where she normally stands to practice broke off and shattered on the floor. She had just stepped off stage moments earlier."

Jack felt his blood pressure start to rise. "What else?"

Benji talked about a broken step that had just been replaced out back where she parks, a rock through the window and the microphone that nearly electrocuted her.

Jack downed the rest of the amber liquid, closed his eyes briefly as it burned a path down his throat and got up to pace. This was more than just a little issue that Benji had mentioned. He had been in the business of security and body guarding for too many years not to recognize the signs of a true psycho.

"She has to be told," Jack said, and held his hand up to Benji's protests. "She's already going to know something's up when she sees me."

Benji sighed and nodded. "Follow me," Benji said and headed for the stage. They ducked behind the curtain and started down a long hallway. There were several doors with stars on them, along with name plates.

Jack recognized Donny Miller as an orchestra leader. He doubted that all the members could fit in the room comfortably but it was nice to have a place to go to for privacy he supposed.

At the end of the hallway was the biggest star and several steps before they even got there, Jack saw her name in glittering script. He turned to give Benji an eye roll before he spoke.

"Classy, Benj, very classy."

A woman's scream came from behind that door and curdled Jack's blood. He knew it was hers and without considering anything other than getting to Arabella, Jack took a running leap at the door and gave a roar of rage as he crashed through the door, ending up lying on top of the door as it came off its hinges.

As Jack raised his head, his eyes focused on a pair of black stilettos, one tapping impatiently. Snugly in those stilettos were slim feet that led up well toned calves that were eventually covered by a sparkling black dress.

As he looked up higher, he roamed over those curves he knew so well before feasting his eyes on a very generous swell of her breasts spilling out of the tank style top of the sparkling material before he found the face of his angel.

Too bad, her eyes were filled with fire from the devil and she was aiming that hot gaze straight at him.

ARABELLA CARSON COULD NOT BELIEVE WHO HAD COME crashing back into her life. Literally.

Jack Cameron was the last man on this planet she had ever wanted to see again yet instantly her blood began to course hotly through her veins.

He looked like hell. Dirty jeans and a rumpled tee shirt greeted her from the floor. She wasn't surprised to see him wearing those same, silver-tipped leather boots either. His dark hair was now peppered lightly with more obvious marks of grey at the temples and too long for her taste.

She zeroed in on his face and found that besides a few extra lines and a few days growth of beard that matched his hair color, he hadn't changed a bit. He was still the sexiest man she had ever met.

Damn him.

She glared down at him for a very long time before lifting her chin to shoot daggers at Benji.

"Arabella, I'm so sorry. I had to call him," Benji said apologetically and helped Jack to stand. "Just give me five minutes to explain," he began but she cut him off.

"I'll give you one minute," she said, still angry. Memories of her past with Jack threatened to flood her entire being and drown her to the point that she could barely breathe. He always managed to do that to her.

"You have a stalker," Jack said, simple and to the point as always. "Fast enough for you?"

Arabella frowned at him. He had his nerve being snarky with her. After all these years, he thought he's still entitled to her unlimited time?

And did he just say she had a stalker?

"What? What did you say?"

"I said, you have a stalker," Jack said and handed her a piece of paper.

"Jesus, Jack, must you always be so blunt?" Benji asked with a groan and stooped to pick up the door. He set it to one side and looked back to Arabella, wringing his hands anxiously.

She scanned the letter twice and felt her heart race. What the hell was this? Turning it over and looking for more, she found none and looked up at Benji.

"Where did this come from?"

Benji explained everything from the letter to the falling light. Arabella thought they had just been accidents, never considered the fact that she was being targeted for some unknown reason.

"So why is *he* here?" Arabella asked, nodding to Jack. Surely

Benji didn't think that a bodyguard would be required for a simple nut job, did he?

"I just wanted Jack to check it out and maybe offer some advice," Benji said, trying desperately to reassure her, but it wasn't working.

"Advice my ass," Jack snorted. He looked directly at Arabella. "Until this crack pot is found and dealt with, I'll be staying and I'll be watching over you."

CHAPTER TWO

JACK DROPPED A FEW ICE CUBES IN HIS GLASS FROM BEHIND THE bar. He poured a healthy portion of Jack Daniels in the glass before topping it off with a splash of Coke. Taking a stir stick, he gave the liquid a twirl and frowned at the tiny, pink plastic stirrer. *Froo-Froo stick*, he thought and tossed it over his shoulder.

He stepped back from behind the bar and took a seat on a stool, took a long drink and let his eyes roam to Benji and Arabella.

They were arguing over by the stage. Jack would lay money on her any day of the week, but Benji had no say in the matter anymore. Jack didn't want to get paid. Making sure she was safe was payment enough.

Still, he was rather enjoying watching Benji squirm. That's what he got for keeping her in the dark. And for not telling Jack sooner what was going on. Had anything happened to her, he would have never forgiven Benji.

They headed toward Jack now. Well, she was stomping over and Benji was scurrying after her. Damn, she looked fine in that dress. He leaned his elbows back on the bar and waited. This should be good.

"You can leave now. I'll get a hold of the local police and let them look into the matter," she said and turned to Benji, giving him a look that would melt metal.

"Jack, I'm so sorry. I didn't mean to waste your time, dragging you here. I'd be happy to pay you for—" Benji started but Jack interrupted him.

"I'm not leaving."

Arabella swung around to glare at him. Her breasts heaved with each deep breath she took, her hands clenched open and closed.

He almost smirked. She always did that when she was mad. But, mad or not, he was here for the duration. Arabella turned and stalked away, toward the stage and behind it, disappearing from his view.

Jack shrugged and took another drink. Benji snatched the glass from him and took a drink himself. He looked sweaty.

"Jack, be reasonable."

"I am. Someone wants to hurt her or worse. I plan to make sure that doesn't happen."

"She's not very happy. With either one of us," Benji warned.

"She'll get over it," Jack said with another shrug and waved his empty glass at Benji.

"Oh no, you don't," Benji said and walked behind the bar. He dug around in a box and pulled up a black apron tossing it at Jack. "You'll drink me right out of a business if I let you. So while you are here, watching over Arabella, you will be working for me."

Jack stared from the apron to Benji incredulously. Surely he didn't think he was going to wash dishes.

"Your job will be a bar back. Stocking liquor and ice and glasses should keep your hands busy. It also will allow you access to both the back of the house and out here. No one can question why you are wandering around," Benji stated.

Jack thought it was a good plan and started to put the apron on but Benji stilled his hand.

"Maybe you'd consider clean clothes and a shower first?"

Benji had a pleading look in his eyes and Jack laughed. "Yeah ok," he said and turned to leave but stopped.

"By the way, why did she scream like that? I saw no one there," Jack asked as an afterthought. He had been ready to beat some ass.

"She saw a spider," Benji said and gave Jack a knowing nod.

Jack returned the nod. He remembered her one and only phobia and how it would nearly incapacitate her. He took one last look around and left.

ARABELLA WOULD HAVE SLAMMED HER DRESSING ROOM DOOR shut had it not been leaning against the wall.

Who the hell did he think he was? To think after all these years he could just ride back into her life and start ordering her around. She gave a quick glance at the clock. There wasn't time to deal with Jack right now. She was on in an a few hours but tomorrow, oh boy, would there be some things set straight.

Arabella picked up the sheet music and tried to concentrate. Not that she had to worry. She knew this song inside out. Still, she always gave a last minute run through. She hummed through the first few lines, then the chorus.

She smiled suddenly and took out a folder, thumbing through a few other sheet music papers before she found what she was looking for. Billie Holiday was one of her favorites and her rendition of *My Old Flame* was perfect. Her smile widened to a Cheshire cat grin and she started rehearsing for her song that night.

A few hours later, she met up with her piano man and handed him the sheet music. He looked confused but shrugged and headed for the piano.

Benji got up on stage and began to rev-up the crowd. Arabella smoothed her hair and touched up her lipstick before sliding the tube in a hidden pocket of her dress and took a deep breath.

"Ladies and gentlemen. Miss Arabella Carson."

The lights dimmed and the applause thundered through the room. Arabella walked out onto the stage and went through her routine.

She gave Benji a kiss on the cheek before he stepped off stage and strolled over to the piano, waving out to the audience. She spotted Jack. He looked like he had cleaned up a little, thank god.

Walking around the piano, she ran her hands over the piano man's shoulders and walked up to the microphone. Thank goodness she had talked Benji out of the more up to date looking microphones in favor of a vintage one that really stayed with the décor of the supper club and its theme.

She chatted with the audience for a minute, hoping their meals were good and bade them a good evening along with a wish that they enjoyed this song.

Arabella started to sing, low and soft at first. She let her eyes rove slowly over the audience while her fingertips caressed the microphone. Purposefully, she didn't look at Jack until she came to a certain line. She turned the full affect of her sensuality on him and him alone. And while she sung the words, she snarked them at him in her mind. Of course she could think of his name, but the rest was true: She'd never been the same.

She held the note for a long time, her voice echoing throughout the room. It was meant to punish him but in her heart, she was the one who felt the pain.

When she went to look for him again, he was gone. Had her song done the job? So many regrets surged through her but being a true professional she finished the song and stayed on stage to receive her applause.

After a few moments, she stepped off stage and raced back to her dressing room. Slamming the now repaired door, she collapsed onto her couch in tears. *Damn him.*

A soft tap at her door brought her to attention. She would not let him see her like this. She would not let him see how he still affected her.

"Just a moment," she called out and stood to check her make-up in the mirror before opening the door to see Benji.

"Oh, hey, Benji. Come in."

Benji stepped in carrying a long, thin white box. He set it on her table and gave her a hug. "You were fantastic!"

"Thanks," she replied and stared into the mirror again. She

didn't think so. She felt horrible. Never had she used her gift as a weapon to hurt someone, yet she had looked purposefully for a song with words that she could use as a knife, hoping he would feel the same stab of pain in his heart that she felt in hers.

"I just wanted to let you know that yes, Jack is staying but he will be working here. I signed him up as a bar back so he will be stocking the bar and keep things straight in the storeroom," Benji said, picking at a loose thread on his sleeve.

Arabella felt bad for him. He was caught in the middle and she had been callous with him when both of them had her best interest at heart. Still, she couldn't imagine that someone was really out to hurt her. She didn't think she had any enemies, did she?

She gave Benji a hug. "I'm sorry I was so harsh with you earlier, Benji. Just seeing Jack brought back way too many memories. It was certainly a shock to see him again after all these years."

Benji gave her cheek a soft peck. "I know, but I'd hire the devil himself if it kept you safe. Maybe he can wrap this up in a few days and be on his way," Benji said with a hopeful smile.

She nodded and turned toward the box. "So, flowers for me? That's so sweet of you, Benji."

"I didn't send you flowers," Benji said with a confused look. "No, wait, don't open that!" Benji said quickly, but Arabella had already taken the top off.

Her eyes widened and she dropped the box, backing away with her hands over her mouth. Tears filled her eyes and she covered them, turning away from the sight on the floor before her.

Benji jerked open the door and yelled for Jack and moved quickly over to Arabella's side, pulling her into his arms and shielding her from the box's contents.

Jack raced in the room with his gun out, holstering it once he determined that no one else was there and looked down at the box on the floor.

A dozen blood red roses lay in the box and on top, a dead bird, its neck bent at an awkward angle. A note stuffed between the long stems of the roses but it only contained two words, visible enough that it didn't need moved in order to read it.

You're next.

"Where the hell did these come from?" Jack demanded.

"I brought them back. They were on the bar when I got off stage, her name written on the top of the box," Benji said, regret filled his voice.

Arabella shivered, but turned hearing Jack's voice. Maybe Benji had done the right thing after all.

"What's up with the finch?"

Arabella cleared her throat, looking into Jack's eyes.

"It's not a finch. It's a song bird."

CHAPTER THREE

Jack tossed out the roses and dead bird. He would punch Benji in the face later for waiting so long to call him in. This was a real problem, not just some oddball that wanted an autograph.

Tomorrow, he would call his nephew to come and update the joke of a security system Benji had installed, and on Benji's dime. Arabella brought in the crowds which brought in the money. The least he could do was make sure she was safer than what she was.

As for tonight, he would drive her home and enjoy couch surfing. The thought made him smile. Not about sleeping on her couch but the fight that would come from his suggestion of that.

Arabella fought with fire and was damn gorgeous while she did it. Not that he looked forward to arguing with her, but when she was passionate about something she believed in, look out!

It was a few minutes before she came out of her dressing room. She had changed into jeans and an LA Lakers jersey. The corners of his mouth twitched a little. She still loved her Lakers. He'd have to remember to dig out his Boston Celtics jersey sometime.

Memories of her and him trash talking each other during those classic games warmed his insides. It was all in good fun of course. He grinned briefly recalling that the winner of the game determined who was on top later that night. Damn those were good times.

He studied her face while she talked with Benji. Though she was looking a little tired, he swore she hadn't aged a day.

Her skin was porcelain perfect, ivory and smooth. Her eyes, hazel in color, sparkled like crazy and those lashes, wow, just wow. A thin nose set above what he considered perfect lips. She always thought they were too small but every kiss they shared, he knew better. They stood out more when she used lipstick, so she always wore it but when she was fresh out of the shower, she was at her most beautiful.

"Jack?"

Jack shook his head to rid the thoughts of her naked body from his mind so he could concentrate on what she was saying to him.

"Sorry, what?"

"I said, thanks for coming. I'm heading home so I'll see you tomorrow."

"Yeah about that," he said, prepared for a fight. "I'm going to be staying with you for a few days until we set up proper security both at your apartment and here." Jack tossed a dirty look at Benji, who lowered his eyes.

"Alright."

He blinked. Did she just agree without arguing with him? The keys for her car dangling in front of him answered that question. He took them before she realized what she had really agreed to.

"Benj, I'm calling Alexander tomorrow. He should be out in the afternoon to deal with the club. Have a check ready." Jack left little room for Benji to argue. He would have slugged him right then and there if he had.

But Benji had nodded and bade them both a good night before going back out toward the dining room. There were still customers enjoying dinner and jazz music from the expensive sound system Jack had discovered while familiarizing himself with the building.

It irked him that he would spend a shit load of money on the music system but not security and his palms itched to hurt Benji but he knew in the back of his mind he was just being biased. It was

Arabella's life on the line now, not some stranger who paid him for bit security work, so he was more anxious than normal.

Hell, when was he ever anxious? He knew that he still loved her, but he'd always felt like he was in control. This crazy sonofabitch that set his sights on Arabella, hurting her or whatever, had him feeling not so in control and he didn't like it one bit. He needed to find out who this guy was and shut him down before anything happened to her.

Arabella led him out the back door and over to her car. She walked silently to the passenger side and waited. Jack unlocked and opened her door, closing it quietly after she was in. He walked over to the drivers' side and got in.

Thank god it was an automatic. He hated those stick shift boxes on wheels. He preferred his motorcycle to a car but if he had to drive one, it would be this kind. Of course, he would have loved to throw her on the back of his bike and ride off into the sunset but that wasn't feasible at this time.

She had a nice car, though. He grinned at her comment one time that Chevy's were totally American. "Lakers, cheeseburgers, apple pie and Chevrolet. Does it get any more American than that?" He had countered with Celtics, T-bones, cherry pie and Harley bikes, then smashed his piece of cherry pie on her nude body. They had their own private food fight before nibbling their way into a very hot lovemaking session.

Arabella's voice giving him directions snapped him back to the present and he turned onto the street before hitting the highway. He was glad to see that she didn't live too far from the club. And it was a nice, gated community. Not that some whack job couldn't get in but it made it a tad harder than an open community.

She directed him to the back of the complex where he slid the car to a stop in a numbered spot. He wanted to frown at how isolated she was from the road up front but he knew that she valued her privacy, so he kept mum. He was also glad to see a front entrance for her door. He had noted driving in that some front door entrances were behind buildings or on the side.

They got out of the car and walked up to her door in silence.

Checking the door to make sure it was still locked, he used the key and stepped in. "Stay here," he said and walked around the house, checking closet doors, the shower since her curtain was pulled and under the bed.

Satisfied, he went back out to the living room and checking the lock on the door, motioned for her to move about freely.

"I really do appreciate this Jack. I didn't know any of this was going on," she said quietly.

Jack was bothered by the defeated sound of her voice. She was more of a fighter than this. Maybe she was just tired and was dealing with quite a few shocks today including him showing up out of the blue.

"I'll make sure you stay safe, Bella."

He thought she flinched at him calling her Bella and sighed inwardly. He had to remember that she was Arabella now, she was a fiercely independent woman and they were no longer together. He couldn't just ride in and expect that she was still the same person, no matter how much of the past he never forgot.

"Sorry. Arabella," he mumbled. "I'll be staying on the couch just for a few days or longer if you prefer until we see if we can find this person and end this problem."

She smiled at him and his heart flipped in his chest. Still stunning as ever.

"I'm going to change. I'll be right back," she announced and went to her bedroom.

Jack closed his eyes against the images and swore under his breath. It was going to be a long night.

ARABELLA CLOSED THE DOOR BEHIND HER AND RELEASED HER long held breath. Not that she had much there. Jack always managed to take her breath away.

She quickly changed into her silk pajamas, a luxury item she allowed herself with her earnings and tucked her feet into her fuzzy slippers. Quite a contrast but she was all about her comfort and this was it. A quick trip to her private bathroom allowed her time to wash her face and think.

How could this possibly be happening? She didn't have any enemies that she knew of. This was just totally mind blowing, like the things that are acted out on television, not in real life. Not in *her* life.

She had been furious with Benji for bringing Jack back in her life, but after this evening's event, there is no one she trusted more.

And no one she loved more.

When he had walked out of her life, she didn't think she would ever climb out of the deep, black, emotional hole of pain. But just as his career was important to him, hers was to her. He said he understood, but his career would take him out of the state for long periods of time, several times a year. She didn't want to travel like that. They had basically given each other an ultimatum and the next day, he was gone.

Benji had told her that Jack had suffered the same heartbreak she had, but she found that hard to believe. As much as they loved each other, fit each other like a glove, he always had a hard time voicing that to her.

Now, seven years later, he was back in her life. Not because he was ready to settle down but because her life appeared to be in danger. She was a job to him.

That thought made her heart sink and the burn of tears sting her eyes.

Arabella bit her lip and stood up straight, squaring her shoulders and stared at her reflection in the mirror. She could live the façade that she didn't care anymore. He'd never know how much it both hurt and excited her to see him again. She just hoped her body wouldn't betray her.

With her newfound plan in place, she strode back out to the living room to find Jack asleep on her couch. She bit her lip again and willed her wanton thoughts to settle down.

Carefully, Arabella leaned over and draped the blanket lying over the back of her couch over his body. She reached her hand out to smooth a lock of hair that had fallen over his forehead back in place but stopped herself. *Strength,* she thought and turned away. Instead she hurried to the kitchen, grabbed a bottle of water from the refrigerator and dashed back to her bedroom.

She climbed into her bed and tugged the covers up to her neck. She closed her eyes several times but she kept seeing the dead song bird and the note saying she was next.

Giving up, the television lured her into an old movie that she and Jack had watched a dozen times. The memory of it made her smile and she squelched an urge to channel surf. When it was over, she fell into a deep and dreamless sleep.

The next morning, Arabella woke to the smell of coffee. She had almost forgotten that Jack was in her apartment.

She padded out to the kitchen and was met with a hot, steaming cup of the wonderful smell that woke her. She smiled sheepishly. "Morning."

"Good morning to you too. I just got off the phone with Alexander. He'll be at the club after lunch. He has to take Tina to the doctor."

"Who's Tina?" Arabella asked after a long sip, wincing a bit at the hot liquid but grateful for the caffeine.

"That's right, you don't know. He got married to Valentina Garrett."

Arabella stopped, her cup in mid-air on its way up for another sip. "The designer who had her designs stolen by that wretch, Marco Quinn, who paraded them as his own?"

Jack looked up at her. "You know him?"

"He's been in the club a few times. Sent me some drinks, which I dumped, but was polite to him," she said shrugging.

Jack frowned.

"What?" Arabella asked, confused. She hadn't known he was a fraud or that dangerous. Why did Jack look mad at her?

"What else did he say or want?"

"He wanted me to wear his designs on stage and announce that I was doing so, like I was his personal public relations Barbie doll," Arabella replied, her voice dripping with disdain.

She thought she saw Jack smirk for a minute but knew his mind was consumed with something else.

"What time do you have to be at the club today?"

"I like to get there after lunch as well so I have time to rehearse before dinner. Afterward I'll dress and go on stage to perform."

"Any chance you'll take a vacation?"

"Not a chance in hell," Arabella replied with a frown to Jack. "I'm not letting some lunatic run me off stage and out of a job. Not to mention poor Benji. We have some good acts, musical and singing wise, but I'm his biggest draw. He would take a hit in finances if I was gone for a long period of time."

This was exactly what she was worried Jack would try to do. Yes, her safety was important to her, but so was her freedom to live her life. If she had to fight some lunatic *and* Jack to make sure her life wasn't disrupted more than it already was, she would damn sure do it.

Arabella polished off the coffee in her cup and set it on the counter. "I'm going to go work out, then shower."

Jack raised his brows in question. "Work out?"

"Fear not, oh ye of pot belly. I have a fold up machine under my bed," she said with a grin and left without another word.

JACK LOOKED IN THE MIRROR OF THE HALF-BATHROOM NEAR THE front door. He turned sideways and lifted up his shirt, turning again to the other side and examined his stomach. He frowned.

"I don't have a pot belly," he huffed, then stiffened. A noise at the door drew his attention. Stepping silently to it, he jerked it open and grabbed the skinny man standing there inside.

The man dropped his basket. Fruits of several kinds rolled everywhere and he gave a terrified scream.

"Who the hell are you?" Jack demanded, nearly growling at the man while shoving his forearm across the man's neck.

The man rasped out something Jack couldn't understand but he wasn't letting go anytime soon. If this was the stalker, he didn't know if he'd make it to the police station or the morgue.

Jack pushed harder, reveling at the colors his face was turning before a slap on his arm caught his attention.

"Jack, what are you doing? Let go of Maurice!"

Jack turned to look at Arabella and mouthed the man's name in disbelief. She frowned deeply at him and slapped him again.

He loosened his hold and Maurice slumped to the floor. Arabella kneeled next to him. "Are you ok?"

It took several breaths before Maurice could answer without nodding. She helped him stand and slapped Jack a third time.

"What? I thought he was trying to break in," Jack said, half-apologetically.

"He can't break in if he has a key, right?"

Jack whipped his head around to look from Maurice to Arabella.

"Is this your…I mean, you and he?"

"Oh, for Gods sake, Jack. No. Maurice lives next door with his partner, Patrick. They have a key to my place and I to their place for emergencies and such," she explained and steered Maurice to the kitchen table before gathering up his basket and the fruit before setting it on the table.

"Oh, sorry—" Jack began before Maurice cut him off.

"Brute," Maurice huffed.

Jack felt an odd blush creep up his neck, but how was he to know she had freely given a key to anyone? He didn't like her being upset with him though. "I apologize, Maurice."

"As you should. Really, attacking people in broad daylight."

Jack stuck out his hand in greeting. "I'm Jack Cameron."

Maurice looked up at Arabella with raised eyebrows and an open mouth. Apparently, Arabella filled him in on their past. He wasn't mad though. She should have someone she could talk to and if this man had her key, someone she trusted.

Maurice grudgingly accepted his handshake. "Yes, I've heard about you. A pleasure," Maurice forced out.

This was not going well. Time to score brownie points.

"I'm sure this is a shock, Maurice, but Arabella is in some trouble and I'm here to watch over her."

Maurice turned quickly and looked at Arabella. She tossed Jack a baleful look. Score one for Jack.

She sat down and took Maurice's hand, patting it. "Nothing serious, hon. I promise."

"Nothing serious my ass," Jack snorted.

Maurice held his hand up for Arabella to be silent and looked meaningfully at Jack. "Please tell me all."

"Jack," Arabella began but Jack cut her off. He sat down across from Maurice and started telling him what was going on, including the dead song bird from last evening.

Maurice looked horrified. In fact, he was completely ignoring Arabella and asking Jack how he could help. Jack noticed that Arabella was angry. She stood, leaving the two men behind as she headed for her bedroom. A minute later, the shower began to run.

Jack just asked Maurice to be watchful of strangers in the complex and back by their building. He gave Maurice his card with a cell phone number on it and told him to call anytime if he noticed anything suspicious. Maurice promised he would and thanked Jack for watching over Arabella, then left.

Jack snagged an apple from the basket Maurice left on the table and munched on it, waiting for Arabella to emerge.

When she did, she was still mad. He could see it on her beautiful face. To her credit, she said nothing about the previous scene. She grabbed up her purse and looked expectantly at Jack.

He rose with half a smile and offered her his arm. She snorted and walked by him. His laughter filled the air and he followed her out.

CHAPTER FOUR

Arabella fumed but was confused. Since when had Jack apologized to anyone for anything? He had told Maurice about this stalker problem, too. Normally he was more private than this. Still, she was embarrassed by this whole situation and planned to tell Jack about it later.

Arriving at the club, they found Benji already there and he had lunch ready for them. She ate in silence, still upset with Jack. Benji chatted with Jack about ideas for security for the club. Jack's nephew was due to arrive anytime. She hoped he would bring his new wife.

"Arabella? Do you have any thoughts about these ideas?" Benji had asked, pulling her out of her reverie.

"Oh, sorry, Benji. No, not really. I just want to make sure my dressing room is kept as private as possible," she said, shifting a purposeful glance at Jack.

"Of course! Of course! Anything you need sweetheart," Benji cooed to her, ignoring Jack's frown.

There was a knock at the front door of the club prompting Jack to rise and go answer it. Benji hurried to clear away their dishes.

Jack's nephew, Alexander Cameron—or Lex, as he preferred— had arrived. Jack never called him Lex, though Arabella didn't know why. But Lex seemed to accept it well enough. Beside Lex was a petite, lovely woman.

Arabella stood to receive a warm hug from Lex. She smiled up at him.

"So good to see you again, despite the circumstances," Lex said with a smile.

"You too, Lex. And this must be Valentina? Jack just told me about you last night."

Arabella swore his chest puffed out with pride as he snaked an arm around his wife's rounded waist. "Oh! You're having a baby, too. Congratulations."

Lex introduced Arabella to his wife, calling her Tina and ushered them off so he could get to work on the security system.

Arabella linked her arm in Tina's and steered her to the dressing room so she could sit and be comfortable.

"I've never been here before," Tina commented while Arabella sat next to her.

"We've only been open a few months but we are doing really well. I'd love for you to come for dinner some night and let me sing for you," Arabella said, smiling at Tina. She glowed with her pregnancy.

Arabella had thought she might have a child someday but it wasn't possible due to an infection from her childhood. So instead, she doted on friend's children, volunteered at local hospitals in the pediatric wings and donated money as she could to women's and children's shelters.

"Well, Lex did promise to bring me here later this week," Tina replied with an easy smile.

Arabella started looking through her dresses for something to wear that evening. Through the dressing mirror, she saw Tina watching, her eyes examining the dresses.

Arabella went to sit by her, taking her hands. "I read about what happened to you. I know Marco Quinn, too. But you can rest assured that I never purchased a thing from him," Arabella said in a quiet voice.

Tina closed her eyes, lowered her head and sighed. "I'm sorry,"

Tina said, her voice filled with shame.

"Hey," Arabella said and urged her to look up. "You have nothing to be sorry for. Who knows how many of your designs have been sold to people throughout the states, the world even. You can only take comfort in the fact that you are that damn good that you will probably see your designs, even if your name isn't on the label."

Tina smiled. "Yeah, that's what Lex has said, several times. I can't help but look sometimes."

"Totally understandable," Arabella said with a nod.

"How did you know Marco?"

"He came to the club a few times for dinner, tried to buy me drinks and such. He managed to catch me at the bar one time and solicited his gowns, or, your gowns. There was just something about him that made me uneasy so I declined and made sure that he never had the chance to chat me up alone again," Arabella replied. She wondered if he was behind her recent stalking problem but he was in jail, so she dismissed it.

"I'm glad that he didn't go any farther than that with you," Tina said quietly then she brightened. "If I could, though, I'd love to design a gown for you. That is, if you would be alright with it."

"Are you kidding? I'd love that. Like I said, you are very talented and I would be honored to wear one of your designs."

Arabella laughed at Tina's blush and hugged her tightly.

That was how Lex and Jack found them, giggling with their heads together, whispering about fabrics and color.

"Should I be worried?" Jack asked, casually leaning against the door frame.

"Since my wife is a perfect angel, I think I'm the one that should be asking that question," Lex replied with a lopsided-smile.

Arabella watched the looks that passed between Lex and Tina and smiled to herself. They were totally in love with each other and it was a beautiful thing.

"Arabella, I need to fix quite a few problem areas with the security here. So you'll see me around here for a few days," Lex said.

"And while he is here, I'll be gone checking on a few things. But

I will be here each night for work and to take you home," Jack said, a look of promise in his eyes.

"For now, we are going to get going and I'll be here early tomorrow and throughout the day getting started," Lex replied again and held his hand out to Tina to help her up.

Lex leaned and gave Arabella a kiss on the cheek then escorted his wife out of Arabella's dressing room.

"She's lovely," Arabella said in the wake of their departure.

"She is indeed. And a scrapper, too. She'll keep that boy in line," Jack laughed.

"Speaking of keeping people in line, would you mind not discussing my private life with anyone you come across? I'd like to keep a shred of dignity," Arabella snarked. She didn't mean to sound so harsh but her mind was whirling with so many emotions.

"I was out of line in how I handled Maurice at the beginning, I'll admit that. But you trust him enough with a key to your place so I can do no less than trust him to keep an eye out and let me know if he sees something out of the ordinary."

Arabella frowned a little. "You mean, use him."

"He could have declined my card and number and that would have been fine, too," Jack said, reminding her that it was a choice.

"One thing you need to realize, Arabella, is that this lunatic will go through anyone he has to in order to obtain that which he desires. Namely you. Anyone else is just an obstacle that he'll have to remove; me, Benji or even Maurice, so it's better that people close to you know."

She hadn't stopped to think about it like that and it embarrassed her that she was being so selfish about the whole thing. She just wanted her life back to normal. Back when Jack wasn't here.

Back when her heart didn't hurt so much being so close to him.

But here he was, surprising her again with how much he had changed. She wasn't sure if she would get used to it or even if it was permanent. He wasn't exactly known for his good manners and grace. Still, it was his spur of the moment choices that drew her to him and his fierce love that kept her with him, made her fall in love with him as well.

It was their differences in opinion of what their future held that broke them apart. She had followed her dream and was well on her path to success. Had he done the same?

"So what have you been doing with your life these past several years, Jack?"

Her question caught him off guard. He had wanted to be in the security business as long as he could remember. He'd had a line on a very lucrative employer in Texas. When he had discussed it with Arabella, he was sure she would be ready to pack her bags and head there with him, but she said no. California was where she wanted to be.

They'd fought about it for days and when it came time for him to go, he left alone and broken hearted. He knew she was hurt too, but that had been a chance of a lifetime for him. He couldn't fault her for staying where she had her best chances at her dreams.

Years later, after he had done all he could for his employer, Jack turned in his resignation and headed to Mexico. He lived in and out of cantinas for months before a call from his nephew drug him out of his drunken stupor and back to the states. His sister-in-law had been diagnosed with cancer. He returned to give both her and his brother all the support he could.

From there, he took side jobs for Lex's friend, Trace. Nothing major, background checks and a few phone taps. But it got him back in the swing of life.

It was then he had heard that Benji finally opened that supper club and that Jack's ex was the main attraction. Jack had itched to go back to Mexico when Trace had sent him on a long road trip to check out a few suspicious deaths connected to the movie star, Madison Jordan. Perfect timing, too or he would have drowned himself in the first bottle of tequila he saw across the border.

"Oh, little bit of this, little bit of that," he shrugged.

"The Texas job not work out?"

She had remembered. Damn.

"Yeah, I was there for several years but there wasn't much more I could do so I just bummed around Mexico for a while."

"Why did you come back to the states?"

"Alexander called. Judith had cancer," he began and looked up at Arabella's gasp. "She's fine. But it was a bad scare for a while. All's good now. New grandson on the way, that woman is right as rain."

Arabella nodded. "I hadn't heard, Jack. I'm glad to hear she's doing well."

"I work for Trace on the side. Was on my way back from a job he sent me on when Benji called. Had to stop and help out Alexander first, though. I might have come faster had Benji been more forthcoming with information," he grunted and to his surprise, Arabella smiled.

"Benji likes to think he has everything under control at all times. It's endearing."

"It's annoying," Jack snorted and she laughed.

Damn he loved the sound of her laugh. It was infectious enough to make him smile at her description of Benji's action as irritated as he was with that man. He felt a twinge in his pants and shifted to discourage any obvious bumps that would distract him further or draw her eyes to a place she wasn't ready for.

He rose quickly and headed for the door. "I'm going to go check with Benji on, um, something. I'll be back soon."

A few hours later, he felt that he had cooled his adore enough to return to her dressing room. It was evening now and she had just finished dinner and was dressing for the evening show.

He opened the door to find her back bare, trying to pull the zipper up with no success. She turned with a soft gasp, holding the dress up at her breasts. The sparkling red gown had spaghetti straps hugging her silky, bare shoulders, red feathers around the top which was tight from top to her hips before flaring out around her thighs to the floor.

"Oh, Jack. Glad you're here. Can you zip me?"

Jack's mouth actually started to water. She turned around and presented him with her bare back. The first thing he noticed was that she had no bra on. Score!

He shook the instant visual and reached out with shaky hands and started to draw the zipper up. Stepping closer, he leaned forward and inhaled her very feminine scent.

Very slowly, inch by agonizing inch, he drew the zipper up to the top of the material while his brain screamed for him to stop covering her bare flesh from his hungry eyes.

Jack knew he should step away from her but he didn't. He had to touch her again, as he had before. It's not that he could ever forget the feel of her skin, but he still craved it, even after all these years.

He placed his fingertips lightly on her shoulders, traveling at a snail's pace to give him as much time as she would allow him to touch her before resting the full weight of his palm down as well.

Achingly slow, his palms skimmed down her bare arms, reveling in the softness of her skin, the smell of her perfume. When his hands had traveled down the length of her arms near her waist, he shifted them over and encircled her there pulling her back against his chest and groaned in her ear.

"Bella," he whispered and for the first time in what felt like forever, he tasted her flesh. His lips touched the curve of her neck, under her ear, lingering for only seconds. He thought he could devour her instantly but held back. He wanted this moment to burn eternally in his memory in case he never had this chance again.

She leaned back against him willingly and his heart gave a cheer. Her hands laid on his, caressing them in a gentle manner as she tilted her head sideways to allow him more access. Please don't let him wake up from this dream.

A knock sounded on the door and they both stiffened. Arabella almost appeared reluctant but stepped away from him and peered into her dressing room mirror.

"Come in," Jack said, his voice almost sounding strained.

Benji popped his head in, a wide grin across his mouth. He looked over to Arabella.

"It's showtime."

CHAPTER FIVE

JACK STOOD BEHIND THE BAR, WIPING DOWN GLASSES AND stocking ice. He felt like a grunt, but it kept him where he needed to be without drawing suspicion to what he was really doing at *Nightscape.*

Arabella had already sung once and was chatting up the crowd. He leaned back against the counter and watched her. She really knew how to work the crowd, a true showman. Or show-woman, whatever. She knew her stuff.

This evening, she appeared more relaxed than last night. She hadn't looked his way yet, but he kept hoping. Those gorgeous eyes looking his way made every fiber of his being hot as if he were on fire.

She started singing again and Jack was transfixed. The words were so sexy, so sensual they drew him to her mentally across the room. Her red dress flashed in the spotlight, like a Fever, the song she was crooning for him and him alone.

Her red, ruby lips just inches away from the microphone moved almost in slow motion, as the song was meant to be sung, and glistened.

And she was definitely hot. She gave him a fever like the song she now sang. Certainly in the morning, but definitely all night long.

Mmm, have mercy.

She was flawless on stage. He could feel her passion in the music. See her passion on stage with every subtle thrust of her hip as she swayed in time with the bass of the drum and cello. Her fingers snapped in rhythm with that of the band members that looked like they appreciated more than just the music.

He felt a flare of jealousy.

She looked his way as she breathed out the last few words of the song. His gazed locked with her as she crooned about the lovely way it was to burn.

Have mercy indeed.

The crowd erupted with wild applause, well-earned applause too. He was fairly sure that every male had a hard on, him included. She was on fire, he thought. Pun intended.

Benji practically leaped on stage to encourage more applauding and escort her back to her dressing room so Jack went to get more ice to restock the front bar. He held the cold bucket between his legs on the way back hoping for his own relief.

It was nearing ten in the evening now and Donny Miller came on stage with his orchestra to perform. The crowd thinned out a bit. It was a week night and people had to work in the morning. Thankfully, Arabella was off the next couple of days.

Donny filled in earlier in the evenings on those days. The weekends were shared by Arabella and several different singers who copied people like Dean Martin and Frank Sinatra. Jack was interested to meet those particular men so he could check them out. No one was innocent until he said so.

An hour later, he had things well stocked. Considering the crowd had really broken up and gone home, there were a few stragglers tapping in time with the music and eating a late supper.

Benji shuffled over to Jack, clapping him on the back, beaming. Arabella had really outdone herself this evening and Benji knew it.

"Where's Arabella?" Jack asked casually.

"Out here in the dining room having dinner," Benji said with a wave of his hand then hit the register to run its numbers.

Jack scanned the room but didn't see her. He frowned a little and felt his heart pick up the pace just a tad.

"I don't see her, Benji. Do you?"

Benji looked up and around the club. "Hmm. Normally she sits over in that corner. She likes to come out here and support Donny and the boys," Benji replied with a frown. "Jack, she doesn't miss his shows after she sings. Ever."

Jack threw down his towel and ran toward the back. His heart hammered with each stomp of his foot as he pounded the concrete backstage. He could see the star on her door and felt a panic grip him like an unforgiving vice. Faster! He had to get to her.

He heard Benji behind him shouting her name between gulps of breath. He wanted to tell Benji to shut the hell up in case there was someone there so he could surprise them but that was out of the question now.

Instead, he arrived at her door, resisted the urge to kick it in and tried the handle. It was unlocked so he opened it.

Quickly he scanned the room, seeing only Arabella, but not where he expected to see her. She was huddled on top of her dressing table, curled up and hugging her legs. Her face was buried under her arms and her entire body was shaking. What the hell was going on?

He saw them then and knew why she was on top of the table.

Three large, black and hairy tarantulas were crawling around on the floor, methodically trying to crawl up the slick, chrome legs without success thankfully.

Benji gave a scream behind Jack and grabbed a newspaper lying on the chair next to the door. Arabella didn't move at his voice, didn't react to Jack's calling of her name. He began to worry.

Jack stomped on each spider, grinding his heel hard to make sure each one was completely dead. He wiped the bottom of his boot on her throw rug and moved to her side.

"Arabella?" He barely whispered her name, touching her arm. She stiffened and turned her head to look at him.

Her eyes were wide with fear while streaks of mascara lined down her cheeks from the flood of tears. Her lips, still red from her make up but smeared now against her arm, trembled uncontrollably.

"They're gone now. You're safe, sweetheart," Jack said softly and opened his arms to her.

She shook her head no, or was it just a tremor that hijacked her entire being? Jack didn't know and it really didn't matter. He was getting her out of here.

Jack slipped one arm under her knees while the other supported her lower back and swung her up in his arms. She buried her face into the crook of his neck and he felt a whole new round of hot tears dropping onto his skin. His anger rose dangerously. This was getting out of hand. He told Benji that he'd call him tomorrow and walked out.

The trip home was long and eerily silent. She had barely moved out of her fetal position to put the seat belt on. Jack gripped the steering wheel so hard he nearly pulled it out of its socket.

Once home, he carried her inside and to her bed and not bothering to ask, crawled in next to her and held her for a very long time.

~

ARABELLA CAME TO HER SENSE SEVERAL HOURS LATER. SHE WAS at home and in bed with Jack.

In bed with Jack?

She sat up quickly, her eyes locking with Jack's, then darted around her room and the floor.

"You're safe, Arabella. Nothing is going to hurt you."

He sounded so sure but she wasn't. The memory of those tarantulas in her dressing room was too fresh. She drew her knees up to her chest again, closed her eyes and buried her face as she had earlier.

Jack drew her to him again, holding her tightly. "Hey now,

where's that fiery woman who fights me at every turn and can hold her own against the toughest of burly bikers?"

Arabella gave a short laugh against Jack's chest. He had a way of doing that even when she didn't want to smile. She knew he was trying to make her forget about what happened earlier but that wasn't likely to happen.

Arabella had a serious fear of spiders. That's how she had met Maurice and Patrick. Her patio door was open and she saw a spider crawling across her carpet. She gave a scream that would have woke the dead. They came over quickly and when she pointed it out, they understood and scooted it out the door. They had become fast friends ever since.

The ones in her dressing room weren't just your basic garden variety spider, however. She would have still screamed but stomped on them and after a few minutes to calm her racing heart, gone about her business. No, those tarantulas today were planted by someone. She didn't know if they were poisonous or not but they did their job.

She'd tried to scream. But when she'd opened her mouth, nothing came out. Her heart had raced so fast and beat so hard in her chest, she'd thought she would pass out, but the thought of falling to the floor where they could crawl on her was too much. She just climbed on the highest object she could find and prayed that Jack would come find her.

And he had.

Arabella sat up and wiped the tears that streaked her cheeks once again. "I bet I'm a sight with all this make up smeared," she said noticing the lipstick mark on her arm.

Jack caught her hand. "You're beautiful."

She smiled and mumbled something about taking a shower. But as she rose from the bed and stepped toward the bathroom, she stopped. Reaching out, she snapped on the bathroom light and stepped back quickly, peeking into the room first.

Jack didn't laugh at her as he got up, too, and walked into the bathroom to make sure it was all clear. He gave her the thumbs up and left her bedroom.

She groaned going into the bathroom and looked into the mirror. She looked horrible. She should kick him for saying she looked beautiful but somehow it made her feel good.

Half an hour later, she emerged freshly showered, face scrubbed and in a new pair of silk pajamas. To her surprise, Jack had a tray of fruit and a salad on the bed. He pointed for her to get in and eat which she did without question.

He had also pulled in the lazy boy chair from the living room.

"Didn't like the feng-shui of the living room?" She giggled at his confused look. She motioned to the chair.

"I'm sleeping in here with you tonight," he announced, stopping the progress of the fork with Italian dressing covered lettuce to her mouth.

"It was either your bed or this chair."

Her eyes drifted to the floor then back to his, a smile played around her lips.

"Not a chance," he grunted, put a hand to his back and stretched. She laughed.

He took her tray when she was done and hauled it out to the kitchen. She fluffed her pillow and snuggled down, pulling the comforter up to her chin.

Jack returned with a bottle of water, half drained and set it next to her bed. He made a big deal out of sitting on the chair and leaning it back. She smiled.

"Jack?"

"Yeah?"

"I'm really glad you're back," she admitted. She had been glad since day one but didn't want to admit it.

"Me too," he said.

"Are you," she began, twirling the fringe on the edge of her comforter. "Are you going to stay, this time?"

"Don't know," he replied. Tears stung at his honesty.

"But I know I won't be leaving until I find this crazy bastard and I'm 200% sure you are safe."

The comforting promise didn't ease her mind. She'd barely

made it through the last time he left her. She didn't know if she could handle it again.

Arabella clicked off the light before he could see the pain she felt. She had to force herself to not think about it and not let it affect her. It might be the only way she could survive.

"Good night, Jack."

"Good night, Arabella."

The next morning, Arabella was a different woman. Jack was merely watching over her and that was fine. She would not hide in her apartment or dressing room any longer. Even doing that much gave that freak a cheap thrill. If he wanted to get to her, he'd have to do it in the open. She was going to live and enjoy her life.

Jack frowned at her demand that he move the chair back out into the living room and he was to stay on the couch. He was even more unhappy that she insisted on running her errands today which including time at the spa.

He started to voice his concerns but she cut him off.

"I will not be a prisoner. If I am, he still wins."

She headed out with Jack hot on her high heels.

____

CHAPTER SIX

____

JACK STEWED ALL DAY AND HIS HEART ARGUED WITH HIS BRAIN.
He should just pack it up and leave. She had left herself out in the
open all damn day, which infuriated him. But his mind told him that
she was right. By hiding away from him, she was hiding away from
life.

He still didn't like it.

They arrived at the club after eight for dinner. It wasn't overly
busy but there was a good crowd. Slipping to a table in the back,
they ordered dinner and supported Donny as he performed.

Jack slipped away for a few minutes claiming nature's call but
headed to the back to check out her dressing room. Everything was
back in its place, the spider stained carpet had been replaced and
fresh roses were in a crystal vase on her table. Jack nosed through
the roses until he found the card and seeing they were from Benji,
he snorted. "Suck up."

Back out in the hallway, he checked for the cameras, frowning
that they still weren't in place yet, but the hardware to hold them up
and out of sight were.

On the way back out front, he stopped to check the lock on the
back door and stooped down low. Carefully, he placed a piece of

240

clear tape across the door and its frame. Benji had changed the locks so no one had a key but him and Jack now. Still, it could be opened easily enough from the inside and to test the theory that had been nagging him for a day, he brought tape with him. Satisfied, he returned to Arabella's side.

After they had eaten, a few of the patrons took notice that she was there and started whispering among each other. Soon they were being approached by people with compliments and asking for autographs.

Jack kept a watchful eye on each fan, an odd pride swelled within him. She really had found her dream.

He noticed that the music had stopped and glanced up to the stage. The band had disappeared and Donny had switched the sound system on before he turned to look into the audience. The look he shot Arabella wasn't a nice one and it stuck in his craw. Jealousy was such an ugly thing.

Benji hurried over to visit. He told Jack that Lex had been there for several hours and the updates should be completed by tomorrow.

"Lex said give him a call," Benji said and smiled at Arabella. "Your dressing room is completely cleaned with fresh roses delivered personally by and from me."

Arabella kissed Benji on the cheek. "You are such a dear man," she said and Jack was irked. It was Benji's fault she was in this mess, he thought moodily. Well, some of it was his fault.

"Jack, I need some sheet music out of my dressing room, then I'll be ready to leave," she said rising. He nodded and rose with her and escorted her to her room. As they passed Donny's room, they heard a cry of terror.

"Get her to her room and bolt the door," Jack said to Benji and turned to Donny's door, shouldering it hard to get in.

Donny was up on his couch, swinging a golf club wildly at something on the floor. Jack looked around and saw the tail of a snake slithering under the couch at the last second. Donny leapt off the couch and ran out the door before Jack could question him.

One of Benji's bartenders showed up right after Donny had left and Jack ordered him to get a large bucket with a lid. It took a few minutes but he managed to get the snake by the tail and drop it into the bucket, slamming the lid home.

"Fuckin' Wild Kingdom in this damn place," Jack muttered and snatched his phone out of his pocket to call his nephew.

"I know it's late but you said to call and I need to know when those damn cameras are going to be active. Things are just getting out of control," Jack snapped.

As he chatted with Lex, he stepped into the hallway and checked the back door, including the tape he set up earlier. It was still in place.

"You've got to make sure they are ready. I have some suspicions but I can't verify them without video," he growled into the phone.

Lex promised they would be up tomorrow by the afternoon and Jack grumbled his thanks and headed for Arabella's dressing room.

She had a worried look on her face but Jack assured her all was well, avoiding telling her about the snake.

They headed home in silence. She avoided looking in his direction, which bothered him. After what had happened this morning, she had been very businesslike with him all day and he missed her easy smile and silly jokes.

Once home, he checked out her apartment and once he was sure all was well, she bid him good night and shut her bedroom door behind her.

Jack checked the front door lock again and headed outside on the patio. He dropped into one of the cushioned chairs, kicked his booted feet back on the wooden rail and sighed.

"Woman problems?"

Jack didn't start to Maurice's voice. He had heard his steps on the gravel a few seconds earlier.

"Yep."

He oddly wished he had a cigar but he'd given them up a while ago when his sister-in-law had gotten sick. Cancer was a bitch.

Maurice sat down in the other chair and crossed his legs. He was silent for a while then turned to look at Jack.

"She never stopped loving you," Maurice said quietly. "I sat up with her many a night with a box of tissues between us, watching chick flicks. She was busy crying over you while I was busy crying over Sally Field."

Jack smiled. He lost count of how many times he had seen *Steel Magnolias* over the years they were together. He would never admit it to her, but he actually liked the movie. Mainly for Shirley MacLaine; she was a hoot. But he always made a big deal over having to sit through it, *again*, and that she owed him some caveman movie down the road.

"And I know you still love her," Maurice said, interrupting his thoughts.

"Yeah," Jack replied. "Never stopped."

"I didn't think so," Maurice said. "So what seems to be the problem?"

"There are a lot of years of heartache, Maurice. We need to talk about a lot of things."

"All you *need*, Jack, is love."

Jack looked sideways at Maurice who gave him a smile, rose and left Jack to his thoughts.

ARABELLA CLUTCHED AT THE SPARE PILLOW HARD. SHE TOLD herself she wouldn't cry, yet here she was, drowning her pillowcase once again.

She had tried the aloof thing with Jack and the only person she ended up hurting was herself. She had to face the facts: Jack just wasn't in love with her any more.

Oh, she was sure that he loved her. You don't go through that many years with someone and not have some feelings left even if the relationship was over. But that's not the kind of love she wanted, not the kind of love she needed. And definitely not the kind of love her body craved.

Every moment spent with him was sheer agony. Her heart cried for his love while her body yearned for his warmth. She cursed the light throb that started at her toes and centered itself in her most private recesses.

"Damnit!" She said out loud, threw back the blanket and sheet and trudged to the window, peering between the blind slats.

The knock on the door startled her. God, Jack. This wasn't a good time, she thought, but the sooner she answered it, the sooner she could get back to stewing about her problems.

Neglecting to grab her robe, she strode to the door and jerked it open, her breath catching in her throat.

He was wearing on his jeans, shamelessly unbuttoned but zipped. His hair was loose around his shoulders falling over very broad, very tanned shoulders.

"Is everything ok?"

"Yes, I just can't sleep."

"Oh," he said and openly roved her body with his eyes. It was more like a smooth, gentle caress and her body yearned for the real thing.

"Well, maybe I can get you an aspirin or some tea?"

"Tea? Since when did you learn how to make tea?" She chuckled to herself.

"I've learned a lot in the last few years, several things that just might surprise you." He smiled and reached out to stroke her cheek with the back of his hand.

Arabella couldn't stop the sharp intake of breath at his touch. This was insane. She was on fire and either she was going through the change or she needed one hot night with Jack. And since she was fighting age with every expensive night cream and massage she could, she was going to go with the night with Jack.

She didn't say anything when she lifted her hand up to his and held it against her cheek. His hands were strong and warm and if she remembered correctly, knew their way around her body.

She turned her head and kissed his palm, lifting her own hand to trail up his other arm and slip around his waist. She pulled him closer and turned to stare up into his eyes.

"I need you tonight, Jack."

Arabella watched his eyes widen for the briefest of moments

before smoldering from lust to love. It was a great one-two combo and managed to make her start to throb.

Jack drew her closer, feasting on her shoulder, sliding down the strap of her nightgown before ravishing her neck to growl softly in her ear. "My beautiful Bella. I have missed you so much."

He pressed his hips into hers and she smiled. *So I feel*, she thought and pressed back against his hips, laughing deep within her when he swung her up in his arms and moved quickly to the bed.

Jack stripped off his jeans quickly and kneeled at the end of the bed. Her breathing slowed. As much as she wanted a fast and hard night of sex, Jack apparently had other plans in mind. The anticipation of it nearly killed her.

He kissed her feet then massaged them gently. He spoke softly as he worked his way up her legs, telling her how beautiful she was and how desirable a woman he found her.

She arched her back when he placed feather like kisses on her knees, sure that she would find her own release right then and there, and encouraged him to come up to her and in her. He shook his head no, his hair tickling her thighs eliciting a little squeal of pleasure.

"Something wrong?" he asked with a grin.

"You are still a tease, Jack."

"It's only a tease if I leave you unsatisfied and I'm nowhere near done," he said and his grin widened.

A long while later, he rolled to one side, drawing her with him. He tilted her chin up and kissed her deeply. "Sleep now."

Arabella would sleep. Tomorrow was tomorrow and she would deal with the aftermath. Right now, she was holding on to the first bit of happiness she hadn't had in years, fleeting as it was.

CHAPTER SEVEN

Jack watched her as she slept. She was still hot as ever in bed and even more beautiful, if that was possible. It hadn't escaped his hearing that she had just said *tonight* but if that was all she was willing to give, he'd take it like a man dying of thirst, squeezing a drop of water from a damp sponge.

He didn't want to hurt her. Hell, just by being here it was hurting her, but he had to make sure she was safe above all else. Then she could tell him to go lay in the pit of Hades and he would.

Tonight had been a complete surprise. She had been so aloof lately. Not that he blamed her. He had come in and practically taken over her life, some crazy S.O.B. was out to kill her and she barely knew who to trust anymore.

With the camera's up and operational tomorrow, he would be able to end this mess sooner rather than later and get her life back to normal, whatever that was.

Now if that included him, even better, but he would leave that ball in her court. It was about time that she had some more choices in things.

Jack looked down at her again, sleeping peacefully in his arms. He wanted her again and shifted a little. She needed her sleep though. He would take what she was willing to give him when she was ready. He closed his eyes and joined her in a deep slumber.

The next morning he was up, showered and dressed before she woke. He made some coffee and brought it to her in bed, catching her naked body just before she tugged the sheet up and yawned.

"Good morning," he said from the doorway.

She blushed and sat up more against the pillows. He chuckled and padded over to sit next to her and handed her the cup.

"Now this is service," she remarked and took a sip.

"Oh I'm sure I could show you better forms of being serviced," Jack replied and gave her a lewd wink.

Arabella smiled and continued to drink the coffee.

Jack felt her pulling back already. His body warred between the need to take her again and agony of her denial. But he had made his decision last night and would stick with it.

"Jack," she began but he silenced her with a finger over her lips.

"No strings sweetheart. I think we both needed that last night. But today is a different day."

She looked confused but said nothing.

"Now you finish up that coffee and take your time showering and dressing. We are meeting Alexander for lunch then we will head to the club."

Jack leaned in, kissed her softly and smiled. "One for the road, no matter where it may lead," he said and left her to her thoughts.

Tina was with Lex at lunch. Jack teased her that she grew rounder by the day. She blushed furiously and Jack roared with laughter when Lex threatened to take him out back for cracks about his wife.

After lunch, Tina drew Arabella into a conversation and was showing her some sketches. Jack took the time to drag Lex up to the bar for a shot and conversation.

"I think this whole thing is an inside job," Jack said with a deep frown.

"Well, we'll find out soon enough. Is there anything else I can do for you?"

"Yeah, background on this one," Jack said and slipped Lex a piece of paper.

Lex's brow raised at the name on the paper but pocketed it and nodded.

Tina promised to see them this evening at the club and hugged Arabella. After they left, Jack escorted Arabella to the car.

At the club a short time later, Jack checked her dressing room and deemed it safe, left her to work on her show that evening. Lex showed up within the hour and finished installing the cameras. They were artfully hidden by faux sound absorbers. He patted himself on the back for the trickery. Jack rolled his eyes.

They went into Benji's office to set up the lap top and pull up the cameras to watch the halls, the stage, the kitchen and the parking lots both front and in back of the building.

Lex explained the recording time, storing the memory of the recordings to be able to pull up at a later date and how to switch the pictures back and forth between all the cameras.

"Even though you can't watch all the pictures at once, they are still always being recorded and stored. For as long as you need," Lex said.

Jack grasped his hand and pulled him in for a hug. "Thanks Alexander. I can't tell you how much this is going to help."

Lex smiled at Jack. "Anytime. I'm going to go work on this background and we will see you tonight at dinner."

After Lex left, Benji burst in with a huge smile plastered across his face.

"Uh oh. What have you done now?" Jack asked suspiciously.

"I've franchised!"

"Should I get you a towel?" Jack smirked.

"Very funny. Jack, don't you understand what I'm saying?"

"Yes, Benji. I know what you are saying. Where are you opening your second supper club?" Jack asked, assuming he meant perhaps San Diego or another major city in California. He was shocked at Benji's next words.

"Jack, I'm moving to New York. And I want you to be my

partner in this crazy adventure and take over the running of *Nightscape*." Benji was nearly bouncing with excitement.

"Excuse me? What did you just say?"

Benji laughed and explained that over the past few weeks he'd been in discussions with his banker and came up with a plan to open a second supper club in New York.

"Benji, you hate the snow."

"I know but it's the Big Apple! So of course I would be the one to go while you stay here and run this place. It's well on its way. And with Arabella in New York, I'm sure to be a smash there too," Benji said then found himself nose to nose with Jack.

"You aren't taking her to New York, Benji," Jack growled.

"Jack, if she wants the opportunity, I'm not going to tell her no," Benji replied quietly.

Jack stepped back and hung his head defeated. "I can't lose her again, Benji."

"Then don't. Take my offer. I can't think of anyone else I would trust my life's dream with than you," Benji said with his hand out stretched.

Jack stared at Benji and let his mind begin to wander.

ARABELLA WENT OVER THE MUSIC AGAIN BUT EVENTUALLY GAVE up. She couldn't concentrate to save her life. She knew the song well enough so she wasn't worried that she would flub it on stage. Still, as a professional, she should at least try to work on it.

Her mind kept drifting back to last night and the time she spent with Jack. It was incredible. He was incredible. Even after all these years, he still knew how to make her feel sexy and wanted and bring her to the heights of pleasure before his own. How could she ever bear to let him go again?

Tonight, she would sing for Jack and Jack alone, no matter how many people were in the audience. She thumbed through her music and found the perfect song. It wasn't set up as a torch song or even from that era, but with the right tweaking and dress, it would work.

Hours later, she was picking out her dress and nodded with satisfaction. She only used a little bit of make up with the exception of highlighting her eyes. She wanted to make sure they stood out and Jack knew they were focused solely on him.

She left her hair down in the back, pulling the sides up with a glittering clip. He had always said that he loved her hair down so she would accommodate his preference.

Benji came to get her, letting her know that Jack was out with Lex and Tina and two others had joined them as well.

"The place is packed!" Benji said with a delighted clap and grin. "I can't wait to see what New York thinks of our little venture."

Arabella looked at him confused. "New York?"

"Oh, baby, I forgot to tell you! I've worked a deal with my bank and am going to franchise to New York!"

She was stunned. Benji was leaving *Nightscape*? What would she do?

"But," she began, not knowing how to deal with this news. "What about this place?"

"Well, I've made an offer to someone to partner with me and run this place while I take care of the one in New York," he explained.

"But you don't like the snow," Arabella said with a half laugh. She loved Benji dearly and didn't want to lose him. Jack was sure to leave once this stalker thing was settled, but to lose Benji, too? It was too much to handle at one time.

"Arabella, the offer is for you, too, if you are interested," Benji said quietly. "This person knows that."

"Who is it?"

"I'm not at liberty to say at the moment, honey. But let me promise you that this club and you, if you stay here, will be in very capable hands. I have total faith and trust in this person."

Arabella frowned. "Maybe New York is just the change of scenery I need."

Benji kissed her on the cheek. "Let's just take this one day at a time, shall we?"

She smiled at him and nodded.

"You look gorgeous by the way. Jack is one very lucky and very foolish man," Benji said with a wink and escorted her out to the stage.

He gave his normal introduction and there was great applause before he offered her the front of the stage and stepped away.

Arabella thanked them all for coming and hoped they were having a good meal and fun time. There was plenty of agreeing noises before it became silent. She, too, was silent. For several, long agonizing seconds, she didn't know what to say.

Her eyes moved swiftly through the crowd and when she found him, she found her voice.

"I want to dedicate this song to a man," she began and swallowed the nervousness that threatened to overcome her. "To a man that I feel like I have loved my entire life. He is one of a kind."

The audience applauded her words then quieted as the music began. Arabella focused solely on Jack, locking her eyes with his for a moment before she spoke through the intro.

"This one's for you."

Arabella began to sing, pouring her entire heart and soul into the song. She felt her body yearn and tingle with each note, each word, each time she sung the chorus. And with each note and each word and every time she sung the chorus, she looked directly at Jack and placed her hand over her heart.

She hoped that she gave Olivia Newton John's song justice but you never could tell. It was all about how the song was sung: singing you honestly loved someone came from the heart and was harmonized by the emotion that came with that love.

The melody started to haunt her. She had to push herself harder to not only let him know what she was thinking and what was in her heart, but so that every single person in this building knew as well.

She had given up trying to hold him at bay and pretend as if this was just a business relationship. She had lived her dream and it was time to let that dream go and live her heart's dream.

That is, if he would have her.

She did, honestly, love him.

She held the last note for what felt like forever and as the music began to fade, she took the opportunity to speak one more time.

"I love you, Jack."

When the music ended, the crowd erupted in wild applause. They stood after a moment and continued their applause though Arabella could barely see them. Tears were filling her eyes as the emotion of the song overwhelmed her. She had to step away for a few minutes and motioned for the sound guy to start up any song while she composed herself, and walked off stage and back to her dressing room.

JACK STOOD FROZEN AT THE BAR. HE KNEW HE WOULD NEVER LET her go again and turned to Benji who was smiling at him with his hand held out again.

"You got a deal, Benji," Jack said and left to go find the woman he loved.

CHAPTER EIGHT

It took several moments for Arabella to calm down her racing heart. She had just poured her entire soul out to Jack like she never had before. What would he think of her? She hoped she still had a place in his life, even if it meant giving up her singing career. It would be worth it.

He was worth it.

A knock on the door drew her attention and she almost ran to answer it. She was disappointed it wasn't Jack.

"Lex, please come in."

"I brought my wife and our guests, I hope that's ok?"

Arabella nodded and turned away to make sure she didn't look like some crazy raccoon if her mascara had run from all her tears but she was fine, until she looked in the mirror at Lex's guests. She nearly fell over.

With a gasp, she turned around quickly and covered her mouth. "You're…you're Madison Jordan." Her voice was barely a whisper. *Holy shit!* Had she just sung and bawled her eyes out on stage in front of one of the biggest superstars in Hollywood?

"That's what they tell me," Madison said with a chuckle and elbowed a very tall and mean looking man next to her.

He frowned down at her and told her to find a new shtick, then leaned down and kissed her before slapping her rump right in front of them all.

Arabella's eyes widened.

Madison elbowed him harder then stepped forward to Arabella. "I'm so very pleased to meet you, Miss Carson."

Lex piped up then. "This is Jack's boss and my best friend, Lucien Trace and as you so aptly pointed out, Madison Jordan."

Arabella's hand shook in Madison's hand. Madison chuckled and led her to the couch, sitting down next to her. "Tina and I were just discussing my wedding," Madison began. "She showed me her design for you, it's simply lovely, but I must say, the gown for my wedding is going to blow the fashion industry away."

Arabella looked up at Tina in shock. Tina merely flushed and grasped at Lex's hand with hers, laying the other lightly on her rounding stomach.

"Well," Arabella began, trying to control the quiver in her voice. "Thank you so much for coming tonight. I'm sure Benji is over the moon at your appearance here," Arabella said, dryly causing Madison to laugh.

"I thought Trace was going to break his hand if he didn't let go of mine after kissing it three times."

Trace grunted and stuffed his hands into his dark slacks. Arabella thought that he looked like he would rather be wearing jeans. Just like Jack. She smiled to herself.

"I'm truly honored, Miss Jordan," Arabella began but Madison cut her off.

"Please, call me Madison. Especially if you are going to be a part of my wedding," Madison said and sat back with a grin.

"Only if you call me Arabella," she began and felt her jaw drop open. "I, uh, what?"

Madison laughed. "Tina asked us to join them for dinner tonight. She knows I've been trying to find a singer for my wedding and thought you might be just who I've been looking for, and she was right. That is, if you are interested?"

Arabella fell speechless. Her? Sing at the wedding of Madison

Jordan? Hell yes!

"It would be my honor to sing for you and," she glanced up at the dark eyed man who had scowled so much but had an easy smile on his lips at the moment. "Him," she finished, hooking a thumb in Trace's direction.

Madison burst out laughing. "Trace can be a bit intimidating," she began before she leaned in to whisper for Arabella's ears only. "He's really a softie for the ladies."

"I heard that," Trace grunted and to Arabella's surprise, winked at her. "If you want, I can give Jack the kick in the ass that he needs to wake up," Trace said with a grin, making Arabella smile.

"Thanks, I might take you up on that later. Right now, I want to share this fantastic news with him. Where is he?"

Lex and Trace exchanged glances with each other making Arabella's heart skip a beat. "Is something wrong?" she asked.

"He got a phone call from someone named Patrick. Some issue at your apartment. He said he would be back shortly," Lex said with a half-wave like it wasn't too important but Arabella knew better. She hoped Patrick and Maurice were alright.

Benji knocked and scurried in, stopping just short at Trace's frown. Arabella covered a giggle.

"Arabella, it's about time for your next set. Are you ready?"

She nodded and impulsively hugged Madison. "Thank you again, so very much."

Madison returned the embrace and stood with Trace, Tina and Lex. "We'll be out front cheering you on," she said and with thumbs up, left.

Arabella linked her arm through Benji's and smiled up at him. "It's showtime."

JACK CURSED. OF ALL THE BAD TIMING! SOME DAYS HE THOUGHT about giving his cell phone a swirly but snapped it shut and went to see Lex, explaining th,e situation before he took off out of the building.

As he cruised into the complex and back toward Arabella's apartment, he saw the flashing lights of both police and an ambulance. Oh man, this didn't look good. It took some convincing but when Patrick waved him over, he was finally able to see what was going on.

"What the hell happened?"

Maurice was refusing to be carted off on the stretcher, insisting an icepack was enough for the lump on his head.

"We heard noises in Arabella's apartment. I was trying to find your card and when I turned around, Maurice was gone. I raced over to find him slumped in her doorway so I called the police first, then you," Patrick said with a worried look on his face.

Jack shifted a glare to Maurice.

"What?" Maurice asked innocently.

"What the hell were you thinking? I told you this guy was dangerous."

Patrick leaned over and with his eyes on Maurice, whispered to Jack. "He's so brave."

Jack couldn't help but smile. He turned his attentions to the police to answer a few questions then was given the go ahead to look around and see if anything was missing.

After making sure everything was in its place, Jack continued to scold Maurice until his phone rang.

"Alexander, is Arabella alright?"

Lex assured Jack that all was well and that he would have that information Jack had asked for in the morning.

"Ok, well I'm on my way back. Looks like just a simple break in. Be there in a few."

Jack pocketed his phone and stood. "Let's go you two."

"Where are we going?" Patrick asked. Maurice started to protest that they were heading to the hospital but Jack assured him they weren't.

"I want to question you while your memory is fresh but I don't want to be away from Arabella too long. So we are heading to the club."

"But, I'm not dressed properly," Patrick said.

"You look fine," Jack said, anxious to get back to Arabella.

It wasn't too long before they were at the club and Jack had Maurice safely resting in Arabella's dressing room. Maurice hadn't been able to give Jack much information to go on about the intruder so he almost wanted to dismiss it as a simple break in. Almost.

Nothing was simple where Arabella was concerned; First this stalker and now, her song earlier tonight. God, he'd wanted to run onto the stage, take her in his arms and kiss her until the whole audience blushed.

So accepting Benji's offer as partner and manager of *Nightscape* while he went to New York felt right. He was tired of the travel. Tired of the lonely nights. He was just tired. He should have settled down a long time ago. He had lost too much time with Arabella already. He wasn't going to lose another minute by continuing down the path he was.

All this time, he'd thought his dream was to run security, but with enough free time to travel the open road. Well, he had done it. So where was his happy ending?

Right where she was all along. Jack could easily do security right here in the heart of California, take short trips on the Harley and be with the woman of his real dreams.

That is, if she would have him.

Tomorrow, he was going to buy a ring and propose. It was now or never.

Arabella had returned from the stage. He really wanted to sweep her into his arms right then and there, but with Maurice and Patrick there, he thought he should wait. He didn't want to put her on the spot, but he did brush his fingers over her cheek. The look in his eyes alone should let her know that he didn't forget about her song earlier. He whispered in her ear, "We'll talk later."

There was a lot of chattering going on after that as Madison and Trace came in as well. Maurice forgot all about the lump on his head and fawned over her.

The discussion came around to what had happened which drew deep concern from Arabella. Maurice assured her that he was fine.

Madison insisted that Arabella stay at her home for the night.

Jack thought it was a good idea since he had to replace the locks on the door. Arabella thanked Madison profusely but she waved it off.

"We'll be safe at Fort Knox tonight," she joked with a wide grin to Trace, who grunted.

Jack asked Trace to escort them while he finished up some business at the club with Benji.

An hour later, he was finishing stocking the bar when Benji stopped by. He had been in his office on the phone and had missed most of the evening's events.

"I told Arabella about my venture in New York," Benji said.

Jack was quiet. He was afraid what else he had told her, offered her and what her response might have been.

"Yes, I told her if she wanted a change, she was more than welcome to come with me. I had to Jack. She and I have worked long and hard on getting this place going and I didn't want her to think that she wasn't appreciated or that I had just used her to further my own career."

Jack nodded. "I suppose she will be heading out with you?"

"She didn't say. It was a lot to take in at one time," Benji said with a smile. "There's still time, Jack."

Jack shifted a crooked grin at Benji. "Find yourself a brand new act for the Big Apple, my friend, because I plan on proposing to her tomorrow."

"I've already been looking," Benji said and clapped Jack on the back. "It's about time you made an honest woman of her."

"Past time," Jack said as the truth slapped him hard in the face. "Way past time."

Jack left to head to Trace's and checked on Arabella immediately. She went to bed early so he found his sleeping beauty in one of the guest rooms. His body yearned to lay down right next to her and pull her into his arms but he couldn't just yet.

So he contented himself with pulling up a chair and stretching his legs out on the corner of the bed. As an afterthought, he slipped his hand into hers and closed his eyes.

Long into the night, Arabella shifted and laid her cheek against his palm. Jack cracked open one eye, smiled and drifted off to sleep.

CHAPTER NINE

ARABELLA WOKE UP LATE THE NEXT MORNING. JACK HAD thoughtfully went to her apartment and gotten her a change of clothes. She took full advantage of a very long, very hot shower before pulling her hair back and heading down the stairs.

She was stunned to have met Madison but the surprises kept on coming when she invited her to spend the night at her home and actually asked her to perform at Madison's wedding. This far and away surpassed her dreams. She could barely contain the smile that stayed plastered to her lips.

Arabella easily found the dining room but it was empty. Jack must be taking care of the lock on her door. She hoped he would look in on Maurice and Patrick. They were so dear to her and she hoped they were doing ok after the break-in last night. It chilled her to the bone to think about what more might have happened.

She walked quietly into the living room to the patio door, staring out into the brightness of the day.

"Good morning."

Arabella turned at the voice to see Jack's boss, Trace, sitting in a quiet corner. She flushed a little.

"Good morning," she stammered. She felt weird talking to Jack's boss. Despite his being best friends with Jack's nephew, she didn't really know Trace. Still, if Jack trusted him enough to work for him and leave her alone in his home, that was good enough for her.

She took a seat on the couch and tried to relax. Her mind was whirling from last night's events; the break-in, Benji moving to New York and his offer to her, the fact that she had poured out her heart to Jack and he hadn't said a word to her.

"Jack went to your apartment to see how the investigation was going as well as to change your locks," Trace said nonchalantly while reading the newspaper.

"I figured," was all Arabella could manage and she fidgeted.

Trace put down his paper and studied her to the point of making her uncomfortable. She was just about to tell him so when he spoke again.

"He does love you, Arabella."

She looked up quickly at him. Her heart beat faster hearing those words but she needed the confirmation from Jack. She didn't want to pressure him, though. God, this whole relationship, if that was what you could call it, was a mess.

Still, she knew that to be true, and she loved him too. But was it enough? They couldn't go back to the way they were, no matter how good it was. Something had to give. Someone had to give. Could she?

Trace's cell rang and after a moment of quiet conversation, he hung up.

"That was Jack. He said that you can return home now and that he had a few more things to take care of then he would meet you there."

Arabella nodded and murmured her thanks before rising. Trace touched her shoulder and turned her to him.

"Trust in Jack," was all he said and she impulsively hugged him. His embrace warmed her and gave her the strength she needed.

Within the hour, they were on their way when Arabella's own cell rang. It was Donny.

"Hello, Arabella. Benji wants to know if you will stop by the club. He wants to talk to you about some things."

"Of course. Thank you," she said and hung up. She loved Benji dearly but she couldn't go to New York just yet. She had to give it one more chance with Jack here, even if she gave up singing at *Nightscape*.

She asked Trace if he would drop her at the club. He hesitated.

"Benji will be there and I really need to talk to him about a few things."

Trace agreed but said he would be returning as soon as he could. And he had that look. Arabella smiled. Bodyguards were always so damn anxious.

After making sure she got inside the club ok, Trace took off and Arabella laughed. She'd say he and Jack were like two peas in a pod but she suspected Lex was just as bad with Tina.

She sat her purse on the bar and headed back to Benji's office. It was empty, so she headed for her dressing room to wait for him and go over her songs for the evening.

Arabella ran into Donny on her way to her room. He looked nervous and sweaty.

"Are you alright?"

Donny pull his arm from behind his back showing a gun in hand. She took a step back holding her hands up and pleaded for calm.

"Donny, it's just me. You don't have to worry," she began but he cut her off with a high-pitched, shrill sounding voice.

"Oh, it's just you? It's always just you!"

Arabella took another step back. She didn't like the look in Donny's eyes.

"Donny, let's calm down and talk about this," she said, mentally praying for Jack while kicking herself for not heeding Trace's hesitation.

Donny shifted the gun back and forth as if he was hearing something she wasn't. She feared it would go off at the rate he was waving it around, hitting her or Benji. Oh god, what had he done with Benji?

"Donny, where's Benji?" Arabella kept her voice as calm and

casual as she could. She didn't want to startle him with a scream. *God, I sound like Jack now,* she thought with an inward laugh.

Donny let loose with a nervous laugh and held his hands up as if he had no idea what she meant. "I swear, I thought I heard him say you called and ask him to go over to your apartment." He sounded as if he was telling the best joke in the world and covered a smile at her confused look.

"Oh come on, little songbird. Even you have to be familiar with your own fowl-ness," he said with a snort as he used his fingers to make quotation marks around the word, fowl-ness.

"Wild goose chase? Get it?" His laughter chilled her to the bone. From the fog of her fear, she got past his bad jokes and focused solely on what he had just called her.

Little songbird.

Arabella covered her mouth in horror as tears threatened to race down her cold cheeks. Even his gun didn't elicit the fear to her that his apparent insanity did.

It was Donny.

All along, it had been Donny who had been the stalker. Donny who had done all those horrible things to her. Donny who had attacked Maurice.

Donny who wanted to kill her.

She took another step back, then another, before he raised his gun again, freezing her into place.

So this was how she was to die. A lounge singer, shot to death by a madman in the back hallway of a supper club. How apropos. She supposed that there could be worse ways to die. Car wreck. Drowning. Venomous spider bite. She shuddered inwardly, trying to shake the insane thoughts from her mind. There was only one crazy person around here and it sure the hell wasn't going to be her.

"Why Donny? Why are you doing this?" Arabella had to stall him. Maybe Jack had seen what was happening on the hidden camera and was on his way to rescue her.

"Why? Please tell me you aren't this stupid," he said condescendingly.

"I guess I am," she admitted. She really didn't know, though it irked her that he thought she should know what went on inside his craze-filled mind.

Donny grabbed her arm and started steering her to the stage. He rambled on about how stupid she was and how anyone could see how hard he worked only to be upstaged by some skirt.

Skirt?

He roughly shoved her against the piano before grabbing her by her hair and pushing her head down against it.

"Can you hear it?" She didn't reply due to the terror that burned her throat. He shook her roughly and repeated his question, his pitch rising and filling with more insanity.

"Oh you are a stupid bitch, aren't you? Listen! It's your swan song! GET IT?" His maniacal laughter filled the club.

Arabella could no longer stop the hot tears as they ran down her cheeks, dropping onto the smooth surface of the piano. She didn't want to die. Who did? But she didn't want to die without seeing Jack one more time and telling him how much she loved him.

Trace said good bye to Maurice and Patrick and was heading back to the parking lot when he ran into Jack.

"Hey, where's Arabella?" Jack asked. He couldn't wait to see her and tell her his news. Wouldn't she be surprised to know that he was hanging up his travel gear and taking up management? Specifically *Nightscape*.

"She's at the club with Benji," Trace replied. Jack thought he looked uneasy.

"Oh, well, I'll head over there in a minute. I just need to call Alexander," Jack replied and motioned for Trace to come with him into Arabella's apartment.

To Jack's surprise, Lex drove up and called them over, shoving a file at Jack, a grave look on his face.

Jack frowned reading the information then handed it to Trace. "Donny has a record, spent time in a psyche ward and has a collection of snakes? What the hell was Benji thinking?"

"What the hell was I thinking about what?"

Jack and Trace both whirled, shock on their faces at seeing Benji there and not at the club with Arabella.

"Why the hell aren't you at the club?" Jack demanded. Immediately that sense of foreboding began to overwhelm him while his heart hammered harder than it ever had.

Benji looked at him confused before his eyes widened when Jack grabbed his shirt and shook him.

"Where is she?" Jack yelled. Benji began to stutter as he tried to answer Jack's question. Trace pulled Jack's hands off of Benji and with Lex's help, pinned him to the truck.

"Jack, calm the fuck down. Let him answer so we can figure out what's going on," Trace said quietly before he turned to Benji.

"Why aren't you at the club with Arabella?"

"I got the message that Jack needed to see me here. I thought he wanted to talk about our partnership," Benji said, his voice quaked with fear.

"Who told you that?" Jack whispered but in his heart, he already knew.

"Donny," Benji began but was left alone as all three men hurried into Lex's truck and it sped away.

Hang on sweetheart. I'm coming.

Arabella was startled when Donny slammed a coiled rope in front of her face on the piano. Her hesitation gave him time to wrap tape around her wrists behind her back. Her attempts to kick at him rewarded her only with an additional slam against the unforgiving hard wood of the piano.

"Donny, please stop this. I can help you," she started but he grabbed a fist full of her hair and whispered harshly in her ear.

"I don't need your kind of help. You, however, need all the help you can get!"

"What help do you think I need, Donny?" Arabella continued to try to stall him, praying with all her might that Jack would realize she needed him more than ever.

"Why, to fly, little songbird," he said, that crazed laughter of his ringing in her ears. He grabbed the rope and fashioned a version of a noose and stuck it around his neck before tilting his neck sideways and sticking his tongue out like an over dramatic hanging victim.

Arabella's eyes widened and she screamed. Catching Donny off guard, she whirled and landed a kick between his legs. As he doubled over, she shoved her shoulder into the side of his head and knocked him over then turned to run.

Donny howled in pain and anger as Arabella bounced off tables and tripped over chairs trying to make her way to the door. Running with her hands bound behind her back made it difficult enough, but the hammering of her heart and fear clawing her very being slowed her process.

She could hear him cursing her and chairs starting to be thrown across the room. She wouldn't make it to the front door so she turned and dashed as best she could for the backstage area. If she could get to her dressing room, maybe she could hold him off.

Arabella rounded the bar, slipping on the wet mats before making it to the back. She could see the star on her door at the end of the hallway. *Please God, please.* But as she passed his dressing room, a hand snaked out and pushed her to the ground.

Panic gripped her and she let out another scream before a cloth was stuffed into her mouth. She tried to kick out again but her feet and legs were trapped under his body.

Arabella didn't want to look at him. He would see the fear in her eyes and it would feed his madness. She in turn didn't want to see her death in his eyes. He kept shifting above her and though she tried to keep her eyes shut, she couldn't stop herself from opening them just a slit to see what he was doing. What she saw caused her eyes to open fully wide in shock.

Donny was putting the finishing touches on a noose, not just a loop with a knot but the old fashioned kind that they used in the movies. He grinned down at her.

"I was a boy scout in my former life. I know every knot in the book."

He actually looked proud. Arabella screamed through the dirty gag in her mouth and tried to throw him off of her by twisting and turning her body. Her efforts were in vain though. He stood and hauled her up over his shoulder keeping a tight grip on her legs so she couldn't kick him.

Arabella felt the breath whoosh from her body with each step from his bony shoulder digging into her stomach. It weakened her to the point where she could barely move as he rounded the corner going back to the stage. Through the burn of her tears, she saw the rope dragging behind them on the ground leaving a trail through the dust on the floor.

He dumped her on the ground suddenly, jarring her body even more. She knew she should try to get away again but she found it hard to move. Every part of her body hurt and she could barely breathe with the rag stuffed in her mouth.

Donny was singing to himself and shifting a little, she watched him fasten the end of the rope around one of the columns before stretching it up and trying to throw it over the light fixture hanging above with no luck.

Cursing he slipped away to find a ladder. Arabella began to inch away from the stage, each movement brought pain to her bound body and hot tears to her eyes. A moment later, he returned and dragged her back to the center of the stage.

"Why do you keep trying to run away, little songbird? You wanted the spotlight for yourself so I'm just trying to help you." His voice was eerily kind.

To prove his point, he flipped the switch on the wall to turn on a single spotlight and focused it on her. She shut her eyes against the glare of it. Instead, she watched Donny set up the ladder next to her and dragging the rope with him, climb to the top and slip it over the iron beam that held various spot lights of color.

Donny grinned down at her, waving at her with the ropes noose. He slipped it around his own neck and once again, gave her a face of someone that had been hung.

"You see, they'll find me with your body. Only you'll be up here and I'll be below, crying my eyes out over the loss of such a lovely lady," he said and paused before grinning once again. "Well in this case, crying my eyes out *under* you."

Donny roared with laughter over his own joke. He was completely insane. He swayed to his own humming again, flapping his arms like a bird.

Arabella couldn't watch anymore. She turned and began to roll under the piano. Each movement and inch she took hurt like hell.

Jack. I love you. Her mind tried to block from the pain her body had endured and the horrific scene that Donny had created. It was too much to bear anymore and she closed her eyes. Donny's scream filled her ears and she lapsed into unconsciousness.

CHAPTER TEN

Jack kicked open the front door of *Nightscape* and rushed in. Trace and Lex were right on his heels. His eyes worked to adjust to the dim light of the club from the brightness of outside as they scanned dining area before landing on the stage and the body swinging from the rope.

"Oh my god."

He moved to step forward but Trace grasped him in a bear hug and shoved him against the wall.

"Get off me," Jack rasped. The burn of emotions raced up from the pit of his stomach faster than his heart was beating.

"You don't want to see her like that, Jack," Trace said quietly and held onto Jack tight. Trace looked at Lex and motioned for him to go get the body down.

A moment later, Lex called from the stage. "It's not her. It's Donny."

Jack and Trace looked over to him in shock. What the hell? Where was Arabella?

"I'll go check backstage. You stay here," Trace ordered and Jack nodded numbly.

He thought he had been too late when he saw the body hanging.

A million thoughts raced through his mind but only one mattered. He loved Arabella more than his own life; more than his own needs of being out on the road; more than some stupid job of protecting someone else when he should have been protecting her all these years.

His hands shook as they clung to the chair in front of him, fighting the need to rush across the room and batter the dead body of Donny for what he had put Arabella through.

Where was she? Had he dumped her body somewhere then came back here to perform his last insane act by committing suicide?

Please, God, let her be alright.

Trace appeared back on stage and whispered something to Lex. Jack frowned and took a step forward. Trace held his hands up.

"She's not back there either, Jack. I told Lex to call the police so we can get their help in finding her and to get this mess cleaned up," Trace said and headed back toward Jack when he stopped.

Trace turned and crouched looking around, suddenly drawing in a sharp breath. "I've got her!"

Jack thundered across the room to get to where Trace was.

"Jack, you need to stay back," Trace said again, trying to arm bar him but Jack pushed at his arm roughly.

"Like hell," he growled and kneeled on the stage near the piano and crawled to her.

Arabella was in the fetal position, arms taped behind her back and a rag stuffed in her mouth. Jack swallowed the bile that rose in his throat and laid his hand on her bruised face. Her cheek was cold and she didn't move.

"No, God please no," he sobbed.

Jack had only shed tears once in his life. He'd never forgotten that day despite all the drinking he did, jobs he had taken and miles he had ridden on his Harley. The day he left Arabella and had clicked the door shut behind him, he had cried.

That right there should have clued him in that he should have stayed but they were both so damn stubborn. Maybe if he had stayed, she wouldn't be in this situation right now. She would be standing on stage, in all her glory singing a beautiful song to a large crowd. Or she might be chewing him out for not getting his hair cut or something ridiculous.

Jack reached out to take the rag out of her mouth.

"Jack, you shouldn't," Trace began but Jack shot him a look that said to shut the hell up. And he did.

Jack tugged the rag out of her mouth and tossed it angrily to the side and looked at her again. Tears poured from his eyes and he had never felt so old. How could he have let so many years go by without telling her what was in his heart.

"I love you, Arabella," Jack said quietly.

Without warning, Arabella took a deep, shuddering breath, startling Jack.

"Bella?" Jack cried out and went to pull her into his arms but Trace stayed his movements this time.

"Jack, don't touch her until the paramedics arrive. You don't want to further injure her."

Jack knew Trace was right so he hovered over her as much as he could from her position under the piano. He kept stroking her cheek and calling her name softly but she wouldn't open her eyes.

The sounds of sirens filled the air but Jack paid little attention. He didn't want to miss one second of her eyes opening so she knew he was there.

A few minutes later, light flooded the room as switches were turned on and flashing red and blue lights flickered against the mirrors. Trace had to force Jack to move so the paramedics could get to Arabella. Jack growled at Trace but Trace merely smiled.

"Been there, done that old man. We'll have a go at it later if you want. In the meantime, you need to answer some questions so you can go to the hospital with her when she leaves."

Jack hated to admit when the younger generation was right but in this case, if it got him to Arabella's side, he'd do it. So while Jack answered questions, his eyes kept straying back to her. He watched as they carefully cut the tape binding her hands and rolled her to her back.

He cringed as the neck brace was placed on her but he knew

that was just a precaution. Or at least, he hoped it was. She looked so damn fragile, but he knew better. He almost smiled knowing that she was a fighter and that fiery spirit is what kept her alive when he failed.

The thought that he didn't stop Donny from getting as far as he did tormented Jack. Maybe Arabella would forgive him, but he would never forgive himself.

He cut off the detective as they put Arabella on the gurney. He was leaving with her, he informed the detective, so unless they planned to tackle him and cuff him, he would answer any other questions later.

Arabella was taken out with Jack right behind her. He turned back one last time to see Donny still hanging there. Flashes from cameras by the investigators blinded the scene but Jack felt no remorse. He sneered at the madman and muttered harshly under his breath, "You got your spotlight now you bastard."

He turned and without another look, strode out of the club.

ARABELLA FOUGHT AGAINST OPENING HER EYES. SHE DIDN'T WANT to hurt again but the persistent voice wouldn't shut the hell up. So with great effort, she cracked open one eye, then the other.

Jack was hovering above her, concern filled his bloodshot eyes. His hair was in disarray and a good day of stubble had crept down his jaw line and over his chin. She grimaced.

"You look like hell," she whispered.

"You look beautiful," he whispered back and smiled widely.

"Liar," she laughed in a soft voice before she coughed and pain wracked her body.

Jack lifted her hand and sat on the corner of the bed, lightly stroking her skin. It felt good to have him here but where was here? She refocused her gaze and looked around before she groaned.

"Jack," she began and cleared her throat a little.

Jack raised a plastic cup with a bended straw sticking out of it to her lips which she sipped gratefully before continuing.

"You know I hate hospitals."

Jack grinned at her. "I'm just glad you are here to hate them."

"What's that supposed to mean?" Arabella felt confused for a moment before all the images of Donny and his insanity came flooding back into her mind. The beeping of a monitor began to race and her breathing quickened while she looked around the room in panic.

Jack raised her hand to his lips and shushed her fears. At the same moment, the door opened and she nearly screamed out loud, but a woman dressed in paisley scrubs with a stethoscope around her neck stepped in. She looked from Arabella to Jack and back again.

"Your monitor is going a little crazy, hun. How about some pain meds?" She approached Arabella but Jack stopped her when Arabella squeezed his hand and shook her head no.

"Not now," Jack said dismissively to the nurse, keeping his focus on Arabella. She calmed down a little and so did the monitor.

Neither saw the nurse leave but knew she was gone by the soft click of the door. Arabella sighed in relief. She did hurt but she didn't want to be drugged right now. She had to know what happened to Donny.

"Did you get him?"

Jack nodded. "You don't have to worry about him anymore."

Arabella thought he looked grim. Had Donny escaped? No, he couldn't have. Jack wouldn't say she had no worries if he was still out there.

"Where is he?"

Jack bit his lower lip uncharacteristically. That was never a good sign. He moved to stand but she held his hand tightly and stared up at him.

"Jack, where is he?"

Jack looked right into her eyes and gave her a blank expression. "He's dead."

Arabella's monitor began to race again. She hoped that nurse wouldn't race back in here. She doubted the woman would leave a second time without shooting something into this dreaded IV.

Jack stroked her hand again before raising his hand to brush the tears that had escaped her eyes without her knowing. Donny had been a friend at one point but proven mentally ill and needed help. She couldn't believe he was dead. Had it been at Jack's hand?

"How?"

"I was hoping you could tell me," Jack replied.

Arabella was confused again. Jack didn't do it? Maybe Lex or Trace? She closed her eyes and though the thought of trying to recall what had happened with him in the club that day.

Flashes invaded her memories; Donny cursing her and calling her little song bird; the rope; the ladder and him climbing up it with the rope; his mocking of a person being hung.

"Oh god," Arabella whispered and the monitor raced faster.

"Calm down sweetheart. We don't have to do this now."

"He said something about me being in the spotlight and he got a ladder and took the rope up on the lighting grid. He put the rope around his neck and was making a joke about hanging and flapping his arms like he was flying."

The words raced from her. She couldn't get them out fast enough feeling that if she didn't, the horrid memory would fade out of her mind forever but she knew better.

"The last thing I remember was him screaming at me from the top of the ladder and the rope was still around his neck," her voice trailed off and her hands flew to her mouth in shock.

"He fell and hung himself, didn't he?" She was terrified to hear Jack's reply but she had to know.

Jack rose and went to stare out the window.

"Didn't he?!" Her voice was loud and strained.

Jack turned back and simply nodded his head yes.

Arabella let out a strangled sob and reached for Jack. He was there in an instant, helping her to sit up and holding her gently. It hurt like hell but being held by him was the best medicine she could think of.

She felt so much pain for Donny. He deserved better than life gave him, but made the wrong choices to go down the wrong paths. She hoped he would find the peace in death that he hadn't in life.

Her door opened again and the nurse looked nervously at Jack who nodded. Arabella leaned back against the pillows and frowned but Jack held his hand up to her.

"You need to rest more now and I'd rather you not have the nightmares now, while you are trying to recover, that you will probably have the rest of your life."

The nurse slipped the drug into the IV and left quietly once again. Jack took her hand again and smiled at her.

Arabella felt her whole body warming and relaxing though she kept forcing her eyes back open and tried to shake her head from the drug induced sleep she knew was coming.

Her last bit of strength was used to grip Jack's hand tighter and though her lips never moved, her fading thoughts were to tell Jack she loved him.

～

Jack watched her sleep for a long time. The ugly bruises that marred her face, arms and body would fade with time, but what about what Donny had done to her mentally?

He wished that bastard wasn't dead so he could kill him himself. Not that Jack was a killer. He preferred a straight up fight to a quick kill with a gun or knife. Let them feel the pain and limp for a while was his motto.

But Donny had gone too far with his Bella. With the woman that he loved. Donny would have killed her had he not accidentally killed himself. Or had Jack arrived sooner, he would have done it to save her. No matter what the cost.

Jack reached out and brushed a stray lock of hair from her forehead so he could lean forward and press his lips there.

She had a long road ahead of her and Jack meant to make sure that she fully recovered. After that, it would be up to her. He hoped that she would allow him to be a part of her life, for the rest of their lives.

Jack slipped out quietly and addressed the group waiting in the small, private waiting room. He and Arabella were fortunate to have such good friends.

Trace and Madison sat with Patrick and Maurice, Lex paced with his pregnant wife, Tina, while Benji wrung his hands and stared out the window. A detective waited with them, having been summoned by the hospital that Arabella had finally woke up. It had been a long twenty-four hours.

Jack explained that Arabella had recalled some of what Donny had done to her. His fists visibly clenched and unclenched while he explained that Donny had put the rope around his neck that he meant to hang Arabella with and had slipped off the ladder and accidentally hung himself.

It was quiet then. What do you say to something like that?

After a few minutes, the detective excused himself to leave but said he would still have to interview Arabella in the coming days.

Once again, it was quiet. Jack's thoughts weren't with them in the room. They were back with Arabella in her hospital bed. He cringed at the thought that she was even there. Jack had to face facts: He was no spring chicken anymore and though he was just past his golden age, he wasn't *that* old, but it was time that he settled down both personally and professionally.

"Trace?"

Trace looked at Jack and Jack felt and odd sadness. Trace was a good man and he would always appreciate the chance he gave him but…

"I quit."

Trace roared with laughter. "Good thing. I hate to fire people."

Madison cleared her throat and glanced at Trace sideways. "No, you don't."

"Shush woman," Trace huffed and covered her laughter with a kiss.

Jack smiled and looked at Lex.

Lex held his hands up as if to ward Jack off. "Don't look at me. The economy's in the crapper. I'm not hiring." Lex grunted with Tina elbowed him hard in the stomach.

Jack chuckled. "I'm not looking for a job, I'm looking to give you a job. Or at least, my business."

Jack walked over to Benji. He felt badly for his friend. Benji took full blame for what had happened to Arabella and had hardly spoken a word since he arrived at the hospital. He also looked worse than Jack did.

"Benji, we still have a deal, right?"

Benji shifted a tired gaze to Jack and nodded, but put a hand on Jack's arm when he turned to leave.

"The deal includes letting her go if she wants to, Jack. Agreed?"

Jack took a deep breath and nodded. Jack swore to himself that he would do what was best for Arabella and if that meant her going to New York and leaving this nightmare behind, then he'd let her go.

He would just have to convince her not to.

CHAPTER ELEVEN

It was a few weeks before Arabella walked back into her apartment. She had been out of the hospital for nearly two weeks but Madison had insisted that she stay with them and recuperate. Not that Arabella minded. Who wouldn't love to stay in a mansion like that?

She didn't see much of Jack though. He stopped by daily but sometimes would only see her for a few minutes before giving some excuse about work and running off. Despite being surrounded by staff and friends, she felt very alone.

Benji had opened the club back up two weeks after the incident with Donny. He'd had to keep it closed for a short while due to it being a crime scene, but when it was released, he just couldn't bear to open it again. Not until Arabella gave him a tongue lashing to rival a drill sergeant and after a peck on each cheek, he ran out to get things in motion.

Arabella herself was due back on stage at the end of the week. It would be her first time back in *Nightscape* since that day.

She was nervous. Not about going back into *Nightscape*. She had made up her mind to not let Donny have that kind of power over her for the rest of her life.

No, she was nervous about what people would say about her and whisper to each other while she was on stage singing. Of course she knew that none of this was her fault but people couldn't help but to talk.

This is a simple case of stage fright, Madison had told her. *Getting back on stage and singing that first song is all it's going to take.*

Easy for her to say. But Madison had spent a lot of time with her these past few weeks and they had shared a lot with each other. Secrets and phobias, dreams and broken heart moments; Madison was more down to earth than the media gave her credit for.

Arabella collapsed on the couch and closed her eyes. Donny's crazed stare and maniacal laughter filled her mind. She frowned to herself and was grateful for the knock at the door.

She peered out the peephole that Jack had installed and smiled seeing Maurice, opening the door for him instantly. They embraced and adjourned to the couch.

Arabella laughed at his stories from the past month that she had apparently missed. He was such a dear friend and she was so glad that he had been alright after hearing that Donny had attacked him, too.

That also explained where Jack had gone after she had sung her soul out to him. She had been hurt that he hadn't really acknowledged her that night but having heard the story about the attack on Maurice, she understood.

Still, it didn't explain why Jack wasn't really acknowledging her now. It was almost like he was avoiding her, but why? Now that all this stalker business was behind them, he should have tons more time for her.

For their relationship.

Maybe now that there was no more threat, he would be going back to where he was before and was tying up some loose ends before he left.

Her stomach hurt at that thought. Having Jack ride out of her life was had been hard enough but for him to do it a second time? She wasn't sure she could bear it again. Perhaps she should talk to

Benji and take that job in New York at his new club. At least she wouldn't have to watch Jack walk out on her again.

"Sweetie? Are you with me?"

Maurice's voice brought her out of her reverie.

"I'm sorry, Maurice. What did you say?"

Maurice smiled at her and took her hands in his.

"It's Jack, isn't it?"

"How'd you guess?" Arabella asked with a blush and a smile.

"Well, who wouldn't be distracted by a hunk on a Harley. That is, if you like that kinda thing," Maurice said with a sniff, then looked sideways at Arabella.

Arabella laughed loud and hugged Maurice tightly. "What would I do without you, my friend?"

"You'd lead a totally boring life and have no fashion sense," Maurice replied, returning the hug.

JACK STARED IN THE MIRROR BEHIND THE BAR AND STROKED HIS fingers through his hair a third time. He must really love Arabella to cut off his hair and shave off his beard. He did have it styled into a goatee though. He couldn't let his chin be totally bald, the top of his head was already racing in that direction.

"How's it hangin', gorgeous?"

Jack turned and frowned at Trace. His nephew stood next to Trace, covering his laughter with a very fake cough. Still, he gave in and grinned at them.

"Speaking of gorgeous, where are your better halves?"

"Back with Arabella, of course," Lex said dryly.

Jack nodded. Tonight was her big night. It was his big night, too. He was officially a businessman now. And maybe, by the end of the evening, he would be even more.

A slap on Jack's back brought him back to reality. He turned to smile at Benji and shake his hand.

"You ready for this, Jack?"

Jack took a deep breath and shook his head no, but answered yes out loud. He took a look around the club and whistled low.

"I don't think I've ever seen it so packed," Jack said and frowned. "There's a line out the door and so many damn paparazzi. I know Arabella is good but what the hell is all this about?"

Trace grunted. "Madison casually mentioned she was coming here this evening to a few friends, who accidentally let it slip to the media beasts and add water, instant circus."

Benji smiled widely. "Isn't it fantastic?" All three gave him a disapproving look so with a shrug, Benji hurried off to greet more people.

"Well, you two best find your lovely ladies and take your seats. It's showtime."

Jack began to weave his way through the crowd to Benji and whispered something in his ear before heading up to the stage.

Arabella gasped at the dress presented to her by Tina. "It's exquisite," she breathed, almost afraid to touch it.

Tina beamed at her and laid a hand against her very swollen stomach. "It's my best design ever, until you get a look at Madison's wedding gown," she replied. "If I do say so myself."

"And you should brag," Madison said with a nod. "Confidence is key in the fashion industry."

Arabella already stripped down to her slip and was stepping carefully into the gown. With help from her two friends, she had it up and zipped into place. When she turned and looked into the mirror, she was breathless.

"Oh Tina, I'm stunned."

"Don't you mean stunning?" Madison said with a smile. "Jack won't be able to take his eyes off of you."

Arabella's smile faded a little. She wasn't sure what Jack would say or do for that matter. After this evening, she would decide whether to stay here at *Nightscape* or head to New York and start a new life.

A knock on the door interrupted their chat as Trace and Lex appeared with Benji right behind them. The men smiled approvingly at Arabella and the foursome stepped out leaving Benji alone with Arabella.

He shook his head with a wide smile at her. "You are totally gorgeous. I'm really going to miss you," he said and gave her forehead a kiss.

"Benji, I can't thank you enough for the opportunity you have given me here. Maybe New York could stand the both of us?"

Benji patted her hand gently. "Let's talk about that tomorrow. Right now, there are a few people out there waiting to see you again. I believe you call them an audience?"

Arabella smiled and linked her arm through his.

"It's showtime."

Benji lead her down the long hall and around the corner to the side of the stage. Arabella was stunned to see the front door standing wide open and people crowding to get in. Wow, Benji had taken her gripe at him to heart and had done some serious PR.

The lights began to dim but Benji was still standing with her. She nudged him.

"You better get on stage for my introduction," she whispered. He shook his head and smiled at her.

"My new partner and manager of *Nightscape* will be taking over those duties as of tonight," Benji replied.

Arabella was confused. New partner?

The crowd began to quiet and a very familiar voice spoke into the microphone. Not that he would have ever needed it. His voice could be heard in any room over any noise with no electronic help needed. That voice that moved over her like a velvet glove.

Jack?

"Ladies and gentlemen. Welcome to *Nightscape*."

Her heart began to hammer hard in her chest in time with the loud applause from the crowd. Jack was Benji's partner? New manager? What the hell was going on?

"My name is Jack Cameron and I will be your new and

permanent host here, but fear not. He's here for one last hurrah. Come on up here, Benji."

The crowd went wild as Benji left her side to join Jack on stage. He told a few jokes then announced that he would be heading to the *Big Apple* for a brand new supper club and of course, they were all welcome to come see him there.

Laughter erupted along with applause but Arabella barely heard it. She was still trying to comprehend the news that Jack wasn't leaving. He wasn't leaving *Nightscape*.

He wasn't leaving her.

Tears welled in her eyes but she willed them to stay back. She would cry later after she performed, hugged Benji and kissed Jack. All in that order.

"And now, the one you all have been waiting for. Please welcome back, Arabella Carson!"

Arabella took a deep breath and stepped on stage.

JACK TURNED AND HELD OUT HIS HAND FOR ARABELLA. HIS JAW dropped at how beautiful she looked. He made a mental note to thank Tina later.

The white gown she wore was astonishing and sparkled and clung tightly in all the right places. Her long, dark hair, though pinned up on the sides, couldn't wrangle all the curls in place. Her beautiful face was flawless.

She smiled widely, he noticed, but never once looked out to the crowd. She looked only at him as she approached. His heart skipped a beat when she stopped in front of him, her gaze roaming up and down his form. He might have felt self-conscience at his new look, but the smoldering look in her eyes made him feel something totally different but familiar.

That telltale bulge had returned and this time, it was totally in sync with Jack's mind and heart. Yeah, this was going to be alright.

And just when he thought he had a handle on everything,

Arabella threw herself into his arms and planted a very long, very hot kiss on his lips. Oh yeah, it was all good.

The crowd whistled and cheered as Jack returned the kiss, wrapping his arms tightly around her silk clad body. An afterthought that the air needed turned up ran briefly through his mind and he grinned as he pulled away. She spoke on the microphone but kept a tight grip on his hand.

"Well, Mr. Cameron. Aren't you full of surprises?"

"You have no idea," Jack replied back in his own microphone.

Arabella brushed against him in a tantalizing way and grinned out to the crowd. "Why Mr. Cameron! Is that a box in your pocket or are you just happy to see me?"

The crowd roared with approval and laughter. Jack looked in shock at Arabella. She was very saucy this evening and a jaunty wink at Jack made him crack his own smile. *Oh, two can play at this game.*

"Why, Miss Carson, it's both," Jack said and kneeled in front of her.

The look on her face changed from playful to shock. Jack smirked inwardly and reached into his pocket and produced a small box to the soft gasps of the audience and it was suddenly pin-drop quiet. Jack pulled the microphone back up to speak.

"Arabella Carson. You are, and have always been my world, my heart, my soul. I might have taken the long ride around this crazy adventure we call life, but I always felt that it would bring me back to you."

Arabella's eyes began to well up with tears. Jack reached up and took one of her hands in his and kissed it gently before releasing it and continuing.

"I'm hanging up my riding boots and taking up the new title of businessman. But what I really would love, is you at my side for the rest of our lives."

Jack slowly opened the box. A cluster of tiny diamonds surrounding a single solitaire ,wrapped in gold, sparkled inside.

"Arabella Carson. Will you marry me?"

Tears flowed freely down her cheeks. He was sure she would

give him hell later for making her cry and ruin her makeup but it'd be worth it if she just said…

"Yes!"

A loud sound of thunder filled the club as the hundred plus gathering applauded, cheered and a few tears of their own filled the room.

Jack slipped the ring on her finger, rose and drew her into his arms before kissing her again. A kiss filled with hope and promise of their future together, never apart again.

It took her a few minutes to compose herself. She refused to let Jack's hand go even as she was thanking the crowd for coming and their support of her and Benji over the past year and of Jack taking over.

"But this first song goes out to my fiancé," she began and giggled. "Fiancé." She grinned and the audience laughed.

When she turned back to Jack, she had a very serene and soft look on her face. Jack thought he would melt right there.

"This one's for you, Jack."

He turned to leave but she wouldn't let him. He felt a slow blush creep over his face as she whispered something to the band behind her and they started the music and she began to sing.

He recognized the song at once. Each lyric described their life together perfectly and he lost all of his earlier embarrassment of being onstage and sung to and focused solely on her. Celine Dion said it first, but just as Jack mentioned earlier, they did take the long way. But they both knew, in their hearts, they'd get there someday. And that's what she sung to him.

Amen. The very long way. But they did overcome everything and were together again. He sighed happily and smiled as she continued her song, looking only at him, her hand still firmly in his.

Arabella continued her song, telling him that he was still the one she loved and dreamt of. The only one.

He grinned widely thinking of the dreams he'd had of her since he'd been back. He couldn't wait to share them with her later.

When she finished the song, the crowd clapped enthusiastically.

She kissed him just as enthusiastically and whispered in his ear. "I love you, Jack."

Jack turned to her and whispered back. "I can't imagine my life without you ever again, my Bella. My love."

Jack gave her a wink then turned to the crowd. "Let's hear it for Arabella Carson!" And they did, so Jack called for another song and stepped off stage to let the spotlight shine only on her. There would be plenty of time later to reaffirm their love properly. He grinned.

Six months later, Arabella thanked the man in the custom made suit and worked her way back over to Jack. She looked like she would burst from excitement.

"We meet next week to discuss the record he wants to produce!"

Jack smiled at his wife. She thought she had done it all by performing on stage in *Nightscape* and several guest nights at Benji's new club in New York but there was more to come.

Jack knew there would be a record producer here at Madison and Trace's wedding. Madison had warned him that there would be several important people at the wedding from movie producers and directors to people in the music and fashion industry as well as several high profile actors, actresses and the paparazzi.

He shifted a gaze over to Madison as she and Tina, who had given birth four months earlier to his great nephew, Ace, were nearly blinded by the flashing of bulbs from the dozens of cameras allowed into her wedding ceremony and reception. Tina had designed Madison's dress and it sent tongues wagging.

The story of Tina's captivity and her designs stolen by Marco Quinn had already made the headlines so it wasn't too surprising that the press were hungry to see a "Valentina Garrett" original and did they ever. It helped to have a friend who just happened to be one of the top actresses in the industry, but to have her wearing a gown on the most important day of her life? It had been a dream come true for Tina and Jack couldn't have been happier for her.

Jack hugged his wife tightly and dropped a kiss on her forehead.

She twirled once and whispered to Jack. "I have to head over for pictures with Madison now but later, I'll give you the details."

"Later, I'll be too busy reminding you about the details of our own wedding night," Jack growled low in her ear and discreetly swatted her on her rear end.

Arabella blushed madly and hurried over to Madison. All three of them looked fantastic, arm in arm as the paparazzi had a field day.

"Those women will be the death of us all yet," Trace grunted, appearing next to Jack. Lex had arrived with the baby tucked into a blanket, shielded from the invasive picture taking and slept soundly in his father's arms.

"Yep," Lex replied and yawned loudly, stopping as he felt Ace shifting in his sleep.

"Yeah," Jack agreed. "But what a wonderful and wild ride it will be."

Trace clapped his hand on Jack's back and winked at Lex.

"That's damn right," Trace agreed to Lex's quiet nod.

"Yeah, it's damn alright," Jack said and smiled. "Alright."

AFTERWORD

Thank you for selecting **Bodyguards, Inc.**

I hope you enjoyed reading this series as much as I enjoyed writing them.

Please visit me at my website, www.tabithagibson.com for more information... and a few free reads too.

Tabitha Gibson

Hello!

My name is Tabitha Gibson. I've been writing since I was a teen, mainly fantasy & fan fiction. Reading romance for many years, I thought I would give it a try. You'll find me writing mainly Romantic Suspense. I enjoy being able to explore my imagination by writing Paranormal & my humorous side in Romantic Comedies as well. I also write for children under the pen name Shea Gibson. More on that down the road... Hopefully.

I keep busy outside the writing world working a regular job, but I have super hero power: I am a domestic goddess! I also married the love of my life, Arthur. We live in the 'burbs of Columbus, Ohio raising our beautiful daughter, Marie.

I am an ocean loving, tea drinking, 80's music listening, action film watching, cheering for the wrestling heel, chase your dreams kinda girl. Whatever you might be, I hope it's with an kind heart and an open mind. Have a beautiful day!